Spydar

...dar used to wear a suit, work in ....., and get paid to lead teams of staff working for international nature conservation. Today he possesses no suit that fits, has no office nor staff, and he doesn't get paid ... although he still volunteers in support of nature.

For the last few years, Bruce has thrown himself into writing. Perhaps it's a last-ditch attempt to harness his creativity, before his brain turns to mush. On many an afternoon he can be spotted gazing out of an upstairs window of his house near Cambridge, searching for inspiration.

Bruce has at times been described as reserved, shy and introverted, and, at other times, caring, considerate, intelligent and witty ... and not only by himself. Bruce is not to everyone's taste, but perhaps his humour and sense of mischief will appeal to you.

If you've chosen to read *Refining My Dining*, you will encounter a character called BJ. He is also the principal character in Bruce's *Shy Backpacker* series. BJ shares many of the same character traits as Bruce in his younger days, and his adventures are inspired by some of the author's own experiences.

The *Shy Backpacker* series was Bruce's first dabble with fiction, and *Refining My Dining* takes on a different dimension, as a standalone spin-off, in which the world is seen through the eyes of Megan Turner, a character based on a person that Bruce met years ago in Australia.

Bruce believes it's never too late to try something different. It's also never too late to say goodbye to other people's expectations, and start being yourself. So, why not launch into *Refining My Dining*, and discover a taste for something new?

To all those who dare to dream

Refining My Dining

The changing tastes of Megan Turner

Bruce Spydar

Dear Sheila
Thanks so much for your continuing support
B.

Refining My Dining Copyright © 2022 by Bruce Spydar.

All Rights Reserved.

No part of this book may be reproduced in any form or by any electronic or mechanical means, including information storage and retrieval systems, without permission in writing from the author. The only exception is by a reviewer, who may quote short excerpts in a review.

Cover designed by Bruce Spydar

Although parts of the story derive from real-life characters and experiences, this book is a work of fiction. Except for some historical facts, the names, characters, places, and incidents are either products of the author's imagination or are used fictitiously. Any resemblance to actual persons, living or dead, events, or locales is entirely coincidental.

ISBN: 9798405523804

Contents

Prologue 1
Chapter 1: Ingredients 4
Chapter 2: Opportunity knocks 10
Chapter 3: Advent 17
Chapter 4: Turkey sandwich 24
Chapter 5: The menu 30
Chapter 6: New Year's resolution 34
Chapter 7: Cleaning the decks 41
Chapter 8: Gin and frolics 44
Chapter 9: Naughty but nice 59
Chapter 10: Nothing to write home about 69
Chapter 11: Getting acquainted 72
Chapter 12: Slap and tickle 75
Chapter 13: Sweet potato 83
Chapter 14: Ding-dong! 85
Chapter 15: Questionable intent 92
Chapter 16: The bus from Tennant Creek 105
Chapter 17: Walk of shame 115
Chapter 18: Ducking and diving 120
Chapter 19: Besties 125
Chapter 20: A new vibe 131
Chapter 21: Three's a crowd 135
Chapter 22: Stay or go? 139
Chapter 23: Casual or slutty? 141
Chapter 24: Batting for my bestie 145
Chapter 25: Casually accessible? 158
Chapter 26: Champagne Charlie 160
Chapter 27: Just friends 165
Chapter 28: So ... did we? 166
Chapter 29: Winds of change 170
Chapter 30: Buzz 174
Chapter 31: Now we're cooking! 180

Chapter 32: Appetizer 190
Chapter 33: Dish of the day 195
Chapter 34: Sweet! 202
Chapter 35: Unfinished business 218
Chapter 36: A new morning.. 222
Epilogue: A new Megan 228

Prologue

Saturday 29 August 1992

Hi! My name's Megan Turner and I'm from Newcastle. My accent may be milder than many from the north east, but I'm still a bona fide Geordie.

Now, you might think it an odd way to begin a story but, a year ago, I didn't eat seafood ... well, except for the occasional prawn and, of course, fish and chips.

OK, so why am I telling you this? Well, the point is that, until this year, I'd never tasted much in the way of fish and shellfish, and I'd also never really thought to do so. I was brought up on beans-on-toast, jacket potatoes, meat pies, pasties ... you know, cheap, filling, simple food. But nowadays, having recently travelled to Australia, I'm addicted to seafood, especially shellfish ... and I can't seem to get enough. Langoustines, crayfish, mussels, scallops ... I never knew what I was missing. It adds such a different dimension and variety to a diet, and it's also meant to be healthy.

Travelling to the other side of the world gave me a fresh perspective on life. I discovered exciting new places, fascinating people, and tried different and exotic food. The trip certainly precipitated a change to my dietary tastes but, in addition, it catalysed a change to what I sought in other aspects of life and relationships. I was no longer content with the staleness of familiarity ... I needed change.

Last summer, aged 21, I was fresh out of university. A degree in history from York made my parents very proud; I'd been the first person in my family to have studied for a degree. However, the three years had come full circle, and I was back living in the same house with Mammy and Beth, and still dating my school-sweetheart, James. In itself that was OK, I suppose, but I was also unemployed.

I started doing a bit of temping work but, with no career path ahead of me, I lacked any sense of direction. A degree was meant to lead somewhere, wasn't it? In my case, I seemed to have missed the boat.

After a few months applying for different jobs, I finally secured a graduate placement with a London-based legal firm. It wasn't necessarily the ideal next step, but training to be a solicitor seemed like a fairly sound career choice. It appeared reasonably interesting, and ought to pave the way into earning some decent money. The biggest downside was that, at least during my training, I would be based in London, and away from my roots in Newcastle. Perhaps most significantly, it would put distance between me and James. However, there was nothing else on the table, and it seemed like an opportunity I had to take. The decision became a no-brainer when I heard that my best friend Suzi had also landed a job in London, starting around the same time. We could make a fresh start together.

Our contracts didn't begin for a few months and, with some free time on our hands, Suzi and I decided to buy some backpacks and spend a couple of months travelling in Australia, followed by a few weeks in New Zealand and South East Asia. Neither of us had travelled much before, and we'd never been beyond the boundaries of Europe. So, in jetting off Down Under, we were both keen to explore a bit more of the world, and also rather eager to find some winter sunshine. While I imagined I'd gain new insight into these different countries, I hadn't expected my backpacking experience to become such an eye-opener about myself.

Anyway, we are now in late August, and I'm living just off Baker Street in central London. The last few days have been spent in induction meetings with the new firm, preparing me for the beginning of my formal legal training. The week was quite exhausting, but I'm really looking forward to the challenge ahead. To celebrate starting this new chapter of my life, I decided to invite a friend to dinner. He's a guy that Suzi and I met on our travels ... and there's a bit of a story.

At this point, BJ is just a friend, but there's definitely a connection between us. Beneath our breezy companionship there's a spark that could ignite; an ember that so nearly caught fire before. I'm planning to cook seafood tonight, and let's just see how the evening progresses.

Chapter 1: Ingredients

Saturday 29 August 1992 - Baker Street, London

2:30pm. I'm in Portman Square, starting to walk up Baker Street, having just emerged from Marks and Spencer with shopping for tonight's dinner.

"Oh knackers! I forgot to buy the double cream."
Oh, sorry ... I don't normally swear aloud, but I need double cream for the trifle. Oh well, I've got lots of crème fraiche in the fridge ... I suppose that'll have to do. Oh my god, would you hear me? I've only been down here a couple of weeks, and I'm eating crème fraiche all the time; it'll be avocados and smoked salmon next. What would Mammy think of me going all up-market?

Oh, I suppose I should explain. Well, I'm from the north east, and you don't find much crème fraiche in Newcastle; I think it might be more of a southern taste.

I've found a few things in London quite different from up north, but the language is the main one. I'm so glad that my accent isn't stronger ... if it was, I'm not sure that anyone down here would understand me. It used to be more prominent, but I taught myself to restrain my mother tongue during my three years at York University. I had to mix with people from all around the world, and most of them learn 'The Queen's English,' not Geordie, Scouse or Glaswegian; well, that is, unless they're American or Australian ... but anyway, outside the north east, nobody understands a Geordie. Oh, and do forgive my 'Oh knackers' ... I'm not very eloquent, and I do swear a bit ... well, rather a lot actually; Mammy's always telling me to wash my mouth out.

Anyhow, I've just been shopping in the Marks and Sparks up near Marble Arch, and I forgot to buy double cream. I'm just on my way back to the flat after buying ingredients for tonight's dinner. I've invited BJ around: he's a guy that I met in Australia. It's quite a long story, but I'll be telling you more about him as we go along.

I guess that you've started my story because you want to read a romance, am I right? Well, I hope you won't be disappointed, but it rather depends on how things turn out for me tonight. You see, at the moment, I'm young, free and single, and back in the market. It's been a while now since I split from James, the bloke I dated since my early teens. Well, we split up at the beginning of April actually, just after I returned from my trip Down Under. And before you ask, I haven't had sex since January. It was January 8th by the way ... not that anyone's actually counting.

It's so convenient living only a short walk from the shops. I haven't quite got the hang of the bus routes and timetables here yet, and there are so many of them that go along Oxford Street. It's handy, but it doesn't make for the best air quality: sometimes the diesel fumes are really choking. I know that Newcastle isn't exactly the cleanest of cities, but there appears to be more pollution around here, and the air also seems to taste different. I don't know, maybe it's just a greater concentration of buses and taxis, but there's also probably less wind here to disperse it.

Anyhow, so far, I've found that I can usually catch a bus along Oxford Street that will take me part of the way to where I want to go, but very few go the whole distance. I guess that sums up men too, doesn't it? Most girls find several blokes who appear great for a short ride, but very few are sound investments for a long journey ... oh, not that I have experienced many of them, I might add. Well, what kind of girl d'you think I am? OK, just hold your reply; I guess you don't know me yet.

So anyway, these three shopping bags are for tonight's dinner. I'm cooking posh food this evening. Well, maybe not really posh, but perhaps a bit more refined than Mammy's home cooking, and certainly more upmarket than the meals I used to cook at uni. I'm accustomed to buying much cheaper ingredients, but now I'm in London ... well, the prices here are so much higher than up north. Even the Safeway that I found on Edgware Road seems to be between ten- and twenty-percent more expensive than in Newcastle.

Anyhow, no worries ... tonight I'm cooking a special dinner to celebrate finally being settled in the new flat. Oh, by the way, I picked up saying 'no worries' in Australia. It's a great phrase, don't you think?

The flat where I'm now living is just across from Marylebone Road. I don't own it ... Strewth! I'm not sure I'd ever have enough money to buy a place around here, and it'd also be a long time before I could afford renting. *Strewth ... did you notice a bit more Aussie lingo there?* Anyway, I've really fallen on my feet with this flat, but none of it was planned. If circumstances had worked out as intended, I'd be sharing a place with Suzi, my bestie from uni, and travel buddy in Australia. I'm sure that we'd have rented something way out in the sticks but, as things turned out, Suzi decided to remain in Newcastle following her dad's heart attack.

So, here I am now, living by myself in a mansion flat in Glentworth Street, just over there ... and the flat's amazing. It's owned by Peter and Gill Wallace, a couple who have gone off to Singapore for nine- to twelve-months. Peter is a partner in Everwoods law firm, which is where I'm beginning my legal training. On arranging his secondment, Peter wanted a quick deal and a reliable tenant ... although house-sitter might be a more accurate description. I just happened to be in the right place at the right time.

It was also lucky because Peter knows Phil Burnside, who you'll learn more about soon. Phil is married to Laura, Mammy's brother's ex-wife, and it had been Phil who persuaded me that I should apply to Everwoods (among others) for my legal training. Phil also works for Everwoods, but in Perth.

It was when I came down here in July to meet with Peter and Gill about the flat, that I last saw BJ, or Bruce as others know him. I bumped into him at Kings Cross Station; he'd also been in London looking for places to rent. BJ's starting his accountancy training with one of the big firms in the next few weeks ... with Coopers, if I remember correctly. He's from Cambridge, but went to uni in

Oxford ... and, yeah, he's a bright cookie. He's state school educated, incredibly down to earth, and he has his mind in the gutter just as much as I do. Perhaps that's why I love him so much. Oh, did I just say love? Well, I love him as a friend, definitely ... and, yeah, perhaps there's a bit more than that.

It's funny, up until after I left uni I thought solicitors and accountants were boring people, doing incredibly boring jobs. Until recently, I'd never even considered this type of career move. But, having spent a few months temping last year, doing boring admin work for very little money, I had to find something a bit more rewarding and with longer-term security. And OK, maybe I'm a bit boring too ... but BJ certainly isn't; he studied zoology, and he's fascinating to talk to. At least, he is when you can prize him out of his shell; he's not the most talkative of people, until you get to know him.

I'm really looking forward to catching up tonight; we've got so much to talk about. Last time I saw him, we only had half an hour over a coffee, and we've not talked much over the phone since. BJ says he's found a flat-share in Maida Vale, which is an area I know next to nothing about. All I know is that it's two stops north of Paddington on the Bakerloo Line.

I should also tell you that BJ made quite an impression when we spent a few days together in Australia. He was a breath of fresh air. BJ was somebody who listened to me, and who seemed interested in me as a person. The hours we spent talking really helped to catalyse my thoughts about where my life was heading. Anyway, he's a fantastic bloke ... well, you'll soon see for yourself.

♦ ♦ ♦

3:00pm. At the flat. I set the shopping down in the kitchen, which connects onto an open-plan lounge-diner.

As I was saying, this flat is pretty awesome; it's as big as our whole house in Newcastle ... well, I should say Mammy's house, as I guess I'm no longer living there.

The location here is fabulous; it's just a short bus or tube ride, or a half-hour walk, down to the training centre in Holborn. And we're only a stone's throw from Oxford Street shops, and right next to Regent's Park for a lovely place to walk.

I understand that many of these mansion-flat blocks were built soon after the Second World War, as London rebuilt after the bombing. This block looks that sort of age, but this flat looks as if it was re-decorated less than a year ago.

I'm not so sure that the furnishing is quite to my taste; the bright red sofas in the lounge are a bit livelier than I'd choose for myself, but they're certainly cheery, and comfy for slobbing around on ... which is becoming one of my favourite pastimes.

The flat's got three bedrooms, two doubles and a single, with one ensuite as well as the main bathroom ... more than adequate for a single girl. One of the doubles is out of bounds, as Peter and Gill say they might be back from Singapore for the odd long weekend. I can't complain about that though, because they both seem really nice, and I'm getting this place dead cheap. However, it's just as well it isn't costing a lot because, over the next year, although Everwoods are paying my conversion-course fees, I won't start earning much yet. They are also paying me a living allowance or stipend, but I can't go wild ... well, not with the money anyway.

Perhaps you might see a bit of my wilder side tonight, who knows? Having said that, I think it's unlikely; BJ and I are just mates and, as I said, there's a bit of a story which I'll elaborate later. Anyway, I need to get my skates on to get this place tidy and, after that, I need to work out how to cook dinner.

While I make a start, you can go back to the end of last year, and I'll give you more of a taste of where I come from.

Chapter 2: Opportunity knocks

Thursday 7 November 1991 – Newcastle, UK

Late evening. I'm at home, in our 3-bedroom semi in the Grainger Park area of Newcastle. The day's post had brought welcome news.

I'm waiting for Mammy to return home from work; I'm eager to share my news. It's difficult to predict when she'll be back, as her working hours vary significantly depending on what problems she has to deal with. Mam's a catering manager at the County Hotel, and has been working there for several years. She helped me get a bit of temping work there after uni, and also over previous summer holidays. I'm still doing a bit of work there, and also some similar admin-type work at the Polytechnic. The last few months have been quite hard and demotivating; I thought that with a degree, I'd find something a bit more inspiring. However, I suppose temping is still better than being on benefits. Anyway, perhaps my luck is turning; I got a letter from Everwoods in the post today ... it's what I want to discuss with Mam.

I'm passing the time watching Poirot on the TV. There's not much else to watch this evening but, anyway, I quite enjoy the odd bit of murder mystery, and David Suchet plays the character so well, don't you think?

Beth's in her room, probably doing some homework; it seems like she's actually beginning to worry about her mock exams. Beth's my baby sister. Well, I say baby ... Beth turned 18 in November, but I still can't think of her as an adult. She's doing her A-levels this coming summer and, with any luck, she'll be studying Chemistry at Nottingham University this time next year. Up until recently, I don't think she was really taking the study seriously; Beth's always been someone who seems to get by with little effort, but I think she's had a few shocks with her recent grades.

I've not told Beth yet about my letter; I've been dying to tell someone all day, but I felt that Mammy should be the first to know, as it affects us all. You see, the letter I received this morning is a job offer. Everwoods have offered me the chance to train as a solicitor with their graduate intake next September. In recent weeks I've been applying for so many jobs, but this is the first real breakthrough that I've had. As I mentioned, I've been temping since coming back to Newcastle after uni, but I need to find something longer term; something that provides me with a career pathway ... and this opportunity could do that.

After leaving York, I always thought I'd find work around Tyneside, stay close to family, and indeed to James. I'd also visualised that, perhaps one day, James and I would even settle down, get married, and start a family. This opportunity changes all that ... it's in London.

Nobody around here has been terribly positive about me looking for work down south. For some, like Mammy, they thought me being in York was too far south, let alone in London. My family and friends still have this north-south divide mentality; this concept that I'd be selling out, seeking money at the expense of family values and society. Firstly, I think that it's rather a blinkered view of the world; and secondly, it's all very well taking that stance when you've got a safe job and money in the bank ... but I haven't.

So, what's my choice? Should I wait, holding out for an opportunity that may never turn up, or should I snap up something positive, the likes of which rarely seems to appear in the north east?

James has been particularly negative about me looking at jobs in London, but I know it's only because he doesn't want me to leave Newcastle. He says I should continue temping indefinitely, or settle for something low paid, but anything that would keep me living around here. I know he means well, and I know money isn't everything, but if I don't use my brain, what's the point of having one?

In fact, Suzi's the only person who seems positive about me looking at jobs in London, and that's partly because she's been doing the same thing. Suzi's been applying to accountancy firms, while I've been more focused on the legal profession. I think she's also had some success over the last few days, and has received two or three job offers.

I hear keys in the front door and, moments later, Mammy pops her head into the lounge.

"Hey Mammy!"

"Hi darling!"

"Fancy a cuppa? Shall I put the kettle on?"

"Oh, thanks pet."

"Of course."

"I'll just go check in on Beth, then I'll be right down."

Before moving on ... a quick aside. Us Geordies are stereotyped as commonly using the word 'pet' as a term of affection ... and you might have noticed Mammy just using it. She frequently does but, thankfully, it's something I never picked up. However, instead of 'pet', I've been told that I have the habit of using the word 'babe'. I never notice myself doing it, but I suppose that most people don't perceive their own quirks.

I abandon Hercule Poirot and make my way to the kitchen, fill the kettle, and get a couple of mugs from the shelf. I take the box of *Typhoo* from the cupboard, and put a teabag into each mug. It's funny, Mam's quite particular about her tea ... she likes Earl Grey and Assam, but won't buy any brands that she doesn't know. Mammy never pays a little more for the likes of *Twinings*, and also insists that we never share a tea bag. At uni, I always used to share them with Suzi; it doesn't affect the taste, but it does save the pennies.

As the kettle boils, Mam appears at the kitchen door, closely followed by Beth. There's quite a family resemblance: Beth's inherited Mam's blond hair, brown eyes, shapely curves and big bust. That girl's going to be a heart-breaker for many a young man ... well, actually, I think Beth's already left a substantial trail of male devastation in her wake. I only hope that she's being sensible, what with AIDS and other STDs to worry about, not to mention the prospect of getting pregnant and becoming a young mum on benefits.

And it's not that I don't want kids myself: I probably do one day, but only once I've seen something of life, and only when I can afford to. I think it's unfair on any kid, unless you can give them a good start in life. It's weird these days bumping into some of my old schoolfriends, seeing them trying to raise kids, struggling to make ends meet, with no job, no husband, and seemingly no future ... it certainly makes me think.

It's difficult to believe Beth's now 18, she's grown up so fast ... but I guess we both did. After Dad walked out on Mammy soon after Beth was born, we had to look after each other, and support Mam the best we could. I can't remember exactly when they separated; I was only four or five at the time, and maybe I'll never know the exact reasons why. And, of course, there are usually two sides to every story; Mammy always said that he'd had an affair, but Dad maintained there was more to it, without ever elaborating.

Luckily, the split didn't leave either with horrendous financial difficulties, and I was glad that Dad didn't move too far away. In fact his house is just across the river, a stone's throw away from the new Metro Centre, and also quite close to where Suzi's family lives. Dad hasn't remarried, but he has been near a couple of times. The latest woman he's shacked up with is a blond bimbo called Jennifer, who's about ten years younger. Well, that sounds a bit mean of me, doesn't it? To be fair, I actually quite like her, and she's always been great with me and Beth.

"Is there enough hot water for a third one?" asks Beth.

"Yeah, there should be," I reply. "D'you wanna share mine, or d'you want your own bag?"

"Duh!!! ... My own bag of course; I'm not a peasant."

"Maybe next year, sis, when you have to buy everything yourself."

"Yeah, right."

I begin to pour the water, then leave them for a minute to infuse before adding the milk.

"Anything interesting at work today, Mammy?" I ask.

"Nah ... the usual. Quite a quiet day actually, no evening functions."

"Well, I've got some news," I declare.

"Oh, that's wonderful," Mammy replies. "Did he finally pop the question? I've always liked that boy."

"Sorry?!?! Oh my god, you think James proposed? Really???" I'm gobsmacked.

"Well, didn't he? You could do a lot worse than that young man."

"Meggy could also do a lot better," says Beth, grinning.

"Hey, that's enough Beth," scolds Mam. "James is a responsible young man."

"Responsible maybe ... boring, most definitely," adds Beth.

"Have you two quite finished?" I'm now becoming irritated, although I know Beth is only teasing ... she always teases me about how dull he is.

"Sorry," they both reply.

"Look, that's not my news. Here!" I show them the letter. "I've just been offered the job with Everwoods. I've finally landed something half decent."

"Is that one of those London firms?" asks Beth.

"Yep," I reply.

"Cool ... so you can finally start earning proper money. You'll soon be shopping in Knightsbridge, and mixing with the glitterati?"

"Well ..."

"Yeah Meggy, you can leave this dump behind and start living. You can finally ditch James and begin dating merchant bankers with their penthouse suites and BMWs."

"Beth!!! Stop that!" Mam interjects. "James is a fine boy, and how dare you talk about this place as a dump?"

♦ ♦ ♦

OK, so this gives you a tiny flavour of homelife in Newcastle. In the one corner is Mammy, and she's down-to-earth, northern, and respects her working-class roots ... and she also gets on well with my boyfriend. In the other corner is Beth; she's still an idealist, has big aspirations, and won't let anyone stand in her way. And regarding James, Beth says he's not fit to zip-up the back of my dress, let alone unzip it ... yeah, she has a distinctly low opinion of him.

Beth and Mammy continue their sniping, which is quite normal these days, before Beth disappears again upstairs, and I'm left alone with Mam in the kitchen.

"Have you decided whether you'll take it?" Mam asks.

"Not yet, but I'll need to make up my mind over the next couple of days."

"London would be a big change."

"I know, Mammy ... it'd be a huge change." I can sense she might try to dissuade me from accepting.

"But it does sound like a great opportunity, I suppose."

"It is, Mammy, and I've not had any luck with anything else."

"Well, don't rush to make the decision. You never know, there might be another opportunity tomorrow, with something that's a bit closer to home."

"Oh Mammy, it's not like London's on another planet; it's only a few hours by train. And, well, it's not likely much else will turn up, at least not around here. It's possible one of the other London firms will also offer me a job ... but it'd still be London."

"And what about James?"

"What d'you mean?"

"Well Megan, you probably need to make your mind up about him. He's waited for you to go through university ... don't you think it's time you might settle down?"

"Settle? What d'you mean? Settle for what?"

"Well pet, you know ... get married, find your own place, start a family ..."

"Oh Mammy, how can I even be thinking about it? We've got no money to afford anywhere and, if I don't find work, we're hardly ever likely to."

"But James must be earning good money by now?"

"Well, it's steady, but it's hardly much more than his outgoings. He's not put much away in savings; he spent everything he had on his damned car. And anyway, I don't want to be dependent on him. What if we split up?"

"Well, you're far more likely to break up if you decide to move to London. How on earth is that going to work?"

"Oh, I don't know, Mammy. We made it through the last few years OK, didn't we?"

"Yes, but that was only because he knew you were coming back."

"Well, I don't know then ... but maybe there's a bit more to life than James."

Chapter 3: Advent

Saturday 29 August 1992 - Baker Street, London

3:00pm. At the flat. I've just re-emerged from the bathroom, having made myself more comfortable (I guess you didn't need to know that).

So, you've just met Mammy and Beth, and you've probably worked out that I must've accepted the Everwoods job offer ... you didn't need to be Hercule Poirot to guess that. Anyhow, let me tell you about the run up to Christmas, and also a bit more about both James and Suzi.

First, I'll introduce you to Suzi.

So, as you know, Suzi's my best mate. She lives south of the Tyne, in Gateshead. We became friends in our first term at York University, and we shared a house for our final two years. Suzi studied biology, while my subject was history.

After leaving York, Suzi and I both had a hard time finding long-term employment. Both of us regretted that we'd not made more use of the job-fairs and 'milk round' of career opportunities while still at uni. We were like so many others who drifted along, like tiny shrimp on the ocean currents, seemingly safe amongst the crowd, but vulnerable and exposed when left alone. When we weren't studying, perhaps we'd just enjoyed the social life too much to worry about what came next; but then after uni, it was a real shock to the system. Anyway, as you know, I eventually secured a legal trainee position with Everwoods, whereas Suzi's preferred route was accountancy, and she landed a training contract with one of the big international firms, also in London.

We both received job offers within a few days of each other, and it was fantastic to have something to look forward to together. Being best friends and both relocating to London, we immediately jumped at the idea of finding a rental flat together, and the timing of the move suited us both. We were part of our respective firms' main autumn graduate intake, which allowed us plenty of time to find somewhere to live, but also left time to do something else beforehand. So, after a week or two of dithering and contemplating the cost, we decided to do a bit of travelling. Neither of us had much in the way of savings, but we'd both soon be earning, so we could always use a bit of credit.

Neither Suzi nor I had been outside of Europe before, so we looked a bit further afield. We considered USA and Mexico, but decided instead to fly out to Australia for the New Year, with the view to travelling around Australia, New Zealand and Thailand. We fancied some winter sun, and who knew whether we'd ever get a similar opportunity?

♦ ♦ ♦

Up until going to university, I'd always had some kind of pathway mapped out. Being the first in the family to get a degree was quite an achievement, and I remember how proud Mam and Dad were, standing beside me for photos at my graduation ceremony. Neither of them had the same opportunities when they were young. When they left school, they had little choice but to start earning ... but aspirations were also different in those days. There were no government grants back then, and there wasn't any money within the family. James didn't really have the opportunity either but, even if he'd had the chance to go to uni, he most definitely lacked the motivation. I should tell you a bit more about him.

So, James is not necessarily the brightest star in the sky. No, perhaps that's a bit mean ... I'm just saying he's not academically oriented. Anyhow, while he may never have been a top-grade student, he's a real whizz with his hands ... you know, he's great at anything practical. Ever since we were teenagers and became friends, and then later after we started dating, he was always tinkering around fixing things. When I was at sixth-form doing my

A-levels, James secured an apprenticeship with a local construction firm, and he now spends most of his life on building sites. He can build walls, fix roofs, install fridges, take engines apart, fix kettles; you name it, he can do it. And, to be fair, in the early days of us dating, his hands were also pretty skilled in the bedroom department ... when he could be bothered.

OK, so our sex life has never been brilliant, and it's part of the reason Beth teases me that James is dull. In contrast, Beth's only just legal, but she seems to have got up to all kinds of stuff with her recent parade of boyfriends. I wouldn't necessarily say that James and I were dull; but it's all relative, isn't it? And, if there were deficiencies in our sex life, they weren't all his fault. Whenever he stayed overnight at our house, it was all a bit squashed trying to sleep together in my single bed, and James usually ended up on the floor. It wasn't much better at his parents' house either and, in both places, we could always sense our parents or siblings eavesdropping. We simply didn't get to do it a lot and, when we did, we could hardly ever feel relaxed.

I suppose I should be grateful that Mammy allowed James to stay over; well, at least, she did after I'd started university and was back for the holidays. Before that, and before I was eighteen, she wouldn't have it, and Mammy's only just giving way to Beth on the same issue. Although she's not really a church-goer, Mammy does subscribe to Christian values; well, perhaps they're Victorian rather than Christian but, either way, she doesn't believe in sex before marriage. However, once I'd gone up to uni, and when Mam saw that James still wanted to be with me despite us spending months apart, she started to warm to him as a person, and also relaxed her house rules.

While Mammy eventually warmed to James, Dad was a different matter. I think he never got beyond the first impressions, and James's teenage years were spent as a chain-smoking, spiky-haired punk, dressed in torn denim and scruffy leather. His hairstyle and dress sense have mellowed a bit since, but it can be difficult to shake off the past. Dad always told me I could do better, and that I should find someone with a bit more ambition. The uncomfortable thing I've come to realise is that he was probably right. It wasn't necessarily the ambition as such; it was more that our interests had become increasingly divergent, and our paths were just heading in different directions.

James had been OK with me going to university, despite knowing that we'd be apart for much of those three years. He knew that I had my heart set on it and, as York wasn't too far away, we could still see each other on some weekends during term time. I'd return home about once a month to see Mammy and Beth, and James too; and on other weekends he'd drive over to York. It was also an excuse for him to take his beloved Peugeot 205 GTI out for a spin ... and, oh boy, did he love that car. He spent all his savings on it, washed it every weekend, and tried to keep it spotless ... in fact, it was so precious to him that he never allowed us to get frisky on the back seat.

Before starting uni, I'd held thoughts that we might settle down together afterwards, and I know he did too. We talked about it sometimes, but it always seemed a few years into the future. And, during those three years while I was at York, we both seemed quite content. I never so much as looked at another guy, despite occasionally getting the odd suitor. I considered myself attached, and believed that I'd found the love of my life, so I was blind towards anyone else. We had survived through those years reasonably happily.

When I arrived back from uni, in some ways it was like I'd never been away. I soon picked up a bit of temping work, and then settled into a routine whereby James and I would see each other every couple of days, alternately spending the night in our house, or over at his.

When I told James that I'd started applying to London law firms, he became really unsupportive. To begin with, I suppose he didn't expect anything to come of it and, before I started to get interviews, perhaps neither did I. James wanted me to take a supermarket job or something like that; he never understood that I could use, and indeed wanted to use my brain.

Having returned from York, I also became frustrated by the reversion to old habits, old interests, and to old conversation. Life had regressed to old-and-stale ... there was nothing fresh and exciting. Whenever James and I would go out, either just the two of us or sometimes with his mates, the conversation was always about such trivial matters. We talked about football, or the latest TV soaps, or which girls his mates Danny and Mark were currently shagging. OK, so I'm not someone who doesn't enjoy a bit of gossip, but such mundane subjects were hardly inspiring.

During term time with my uni friends, I used to be involved in the most broad-ranging and sometimes, dare I say it, even intellectual conversations. The loss of such mental stimulation really hit me hard.

Years before, when James and I had been at school, we'd hung out together every day. He'd been quite good looking ... darkhaired, well-muscled and acne-free. He was also a bit of a Jack-the-lad, and respected by most kids, even in the years above. We were frequently getting caught smoking in the playground, and we often ended up in detention together after class. Back then, there were more people whom we both hung around with, and shared more common ground; whereas after returning from York, we had different work environments and separate circles of friends.

It seems sad to say it but, being back in Newcastle and spending more time with James again, made me realise how much I valued socialising with others. It probably brought me closer to Beth, but I was also glad that Suzi wasn't far away; we phoned each other almost every day, even if we only met up every couple of weeks.

Leaving Newcastle to work in London was not an easy decision. I was torn, but I figured that if London didn't turn out well, I could still return home. I also knew that, with any luck, I'd be qualified sufficiently within a couple of years to have greater choice. I'd be on decent money, and also have the skills and knowledge that would make a move back north reasonably straightforward.

I knew that Mammy would eventually support whatever choice I made, despite being sad at the thought of me being further from home. She would have a double adjustment to make, as Beth would also be away at uni. However, with James, I was far less sure that our relationship would survive me relocating to London. While I never intended the move to break us up, perhaps it was inevitable and would've happened regardless. As James and I had been growing up, we'd also been growing apart.

My decision to fly out to Australia with Suzi didn't sit too well with James either. His world didn't extend much beyond Tyneside, and he couldn't understand me wanting to explore further afield. I guess it shouldn't have been a surprise, but I had really upset the applecart, and we began to argue a lot. James saw me as selfish, spending thousands of pounds to fly off to the far side of the world, when I might instead be saving for a life together.

In the couple of months leading up to Christmas our relationship had become strained, and at times was quite tense. I think he could sense me slipping away from him, even before I realised it for myself.

♦ ♦ ♦

The build up to Christmas was certainly different, but there was still an element of normality. Similar to the previous few years, Christmas dinner was a small affair, with just Mammy, Beth, and Mam's brother, uncle Jack.

I helped Mammy to cook the turkey and trimmings for the four of us, although in reality there was sufficient food for ten. And, of course, Mammy insisted on serving Christmas pudding; she does so every year, despite nobody really wanting it once they're stuffed full of turkey. But Mam always insists on it; she says her mother always did so, and Mammy's not one for breaking with tradition. It was a good thing that Jack had a pretty good appetite.

I was glad that uncle Jack was there again; he's great value and always entertains us with dirty jokes, much to Mammy's annoyance. I think it's now been about five Christmases he's spent with us; he first started coming the year after he divorced Laura. Jack has remained single since then, but he'd be a good catch for someone who shares his sense of fun. Thankfully, since their divorce, Jack and Laura remained on pretty good terms. I say thankfully, not only because Laura's also great fun, but it was Laura who'd offered Suzi and me a place to stay when we arrived in Perth, at the beginning of our trip to Australia.

After a fairly quiet Christmas Day, the plan was for Beth and I to go over to Dad on Boxing Day, before returning home on the 27th. That's when James would come over and spend the night, and then I'd fly out to Australia with Suzi the next day.

Chapter 4: Turkey sandwich

Friday 27 December 1991 - Newcastle, UK

Late evening, in my bedroom at home. With Christmas behind me, I'm now looking forward to spending New Year in Perth. James is currently in the bathroom brushing his teeth, while I'm changing into pyjamas getting ready for bed.

Christmas turned out to be quite fun and relaxing, perhaps more so than I'd expected. I enjoyed cooking Christmas lunch with Mammy and Beth, and then listening to tales from Mam and uncle Jack about when they were young ... most of which, of course, Beth and I had heard many times before. And yesterday, being around at Dad's was also quite a laugh. Jennifer is definitely growing on me. She's got such a potty mouth; she fits in so well with me and Beth, although at times Dad does try to rein her in.

Today however, the atmosphere has been a little more strained; James has been around for the last few hours, and I've been in quite a foul mood. In part, it's the tension that's been building in our relationship since I accepted the Everwoods job, but it's also my time of the month. I've been taking the pill for a few months now, and the doctor did say it might help reduce my PMT. Wrong! It doesn't appear to make any difference; I still turn into a foul-tempered hormonal badass for a few days every month.

Despite my mood, one thing has been really fun today ... meeting Beth's new boyfriend, Stu. Ruggedly handsome, rippling muscles, well-dressed and polite; it seems like Beth's bagged herself quite a hottie, and I've been teasing her about him all day.

Stu's gone home now, much to Beth's annoyance. He's only been her boyfriend a few weeks, and Mammy won't allow him to stay overnight yet. Beth turned eighteen in November and, since then, has argued with Mam almost daily about it. I guess I'm not surprised; Mammy was always protective of me, and it took her years before she agreed to let James sleep over. These days she doesn't mind, and just accepts that we're adults, despite our behaviour frequently indicating otherwise.

♦ ♦ ♦

It's funny, when James and I first started sleeping together, it was so exciting, and sneaking around was all part of the fun. These days there's no challenge, nor any great excitement ... it's like we're a married couple, including all the arguments. A few minutes ago, James and I had another difficult talk about our future; it seems like we keep having the same inconclusive discussions. However, as it's our last night together for a while, we agreed we'd try not to fight.

"Hey M, what time d'you say you've gotta leave tomorrow?" James asks as he returns to my room. He always calls me M, whereas with Beth it's Meggy, and with Mammy it's either Meg or Megan, depending on whether she's annoyed with me.

"Suzi's dad is driving over at around 9:00am, and taking us both to the station. Then we catch the 9:45 train down to Kings Cross, followed by the District Line to Heathrow for an evening flight."

"I'm gonna really miss you."

"Yeah, I know babe ... but I won't be away too long."

"I guess so ... but three or four months seems like forever. We've never been apart so long before ... at least, not without seeing each other at weekends and phoning. And then you'll be in London."

"I know babe, but if we're meant to be together, then this isn't going to break us, is it?" *I don't think I sound too convincing, and I'm not so sure I believe it either.* "And, in any case, if we're spending more time apart, we can always have make-up sex each time I get back."

James laughs.

"Perhaps we should start now," he suggests, slipping out of his jeans, getting ready to join me in bed. "Are you OK tonight?"

"Well babe, just what were you thinking of?"

I know exactly what he has in mind as, whenever we have sex these days, there is so little variation. And I don't blame James entirely, it's just as much my fault. But variety can be quite challenging, with two adults trying to squeeze into a single bed next to the wall. It's not so easy to perform much by way of horizontal acrobatics ... especially so, with such thin walls and with Mammy sleeping in the next room.

James removes his t-shirt and, now attired only in his boxers, climbs under the duvet at the foot end of the bed. As usual, I'm wearing knickers and an old t-shirt. He crawls up my body under the covers, and arrives in front of my face presenting his boxers to me in his teeth.

"I don't think we'll be needing these," he says.

James then slips back under the duvet, and progresses down my body. He ignores my tits, which perhaps is just as well because 'my girls' are a bit oversensitive today. *Is 'my girls' an odd thing to call them? Perhaps it's strange to call them anything, what d'you think?*

Anyhow, James heads straight down to my knickers, which are nothing exotic, just a black lacy number from Next. I don't possess much sexy lingerie anyway, but these panties are old ones that I'm not taking with me on my travels. James then struggles, within the spatial constraints of the bed, to ease my knickers over my thighs, and down my legs to remove them. Moments later he re-surfaces again in front of my face, this time with the black frilly lace between his teeth.

"I don't think we'll be needing these either," he says.

"And why might that be, babe?"

As I speak, I can feel the answer. James's erection is already pressing against my folds, and he's now beginning to stroke it up and down. He's never been a great one for chit-chat before or during sex and, unfortunately, he's also no devotee of foreplay. Even this bit of rubbing is more than I normally get, but I do still enjoy the feeling of penetration ... which is just as well, because he soon pushes his not insubstantial cock inside, and begins to thrust.

Sex at home has never been relaxing. Aside from the spatial restrictions, my bed creaks like the floorboards in a Hitchcock horror movie. It's probably the main reason we always do missionary; when I'm on top, I get way too conscious about the noise. If I was to moan or scream, or if I tied James to the bed and started riding him like a bucking bronco ... well, I'd never hear the end of it, particularly from Beth.

To me, the creaking of the bed is deafening. We've even tried oiling the joints of the metal frame, but it doesn't help. I'm sure that Mam and Beth always know when we're humping; they can probably tell when we start, what stage we're at, and even how long it will last. Frequently, I imagine them standing just outside the door, ready to burst in at any moment ... I bet that they're eavesdropping out there right now. Such thoughts are certainly off-putting, and often prevent me from enjoying the moment. I'm sure it's distracting for James too, although we don't often talk about it.

The situation is no better when we try it at James's house, because the spatial parameters and furniture are also much the same. The main difference is that the eavesdroppers are James's parents, rather than Mam and Beth. Even at uni, during the weekends when James came down to York, I was always mindful that others might be listening in ... we just never seemed to be totally alone.

So, all in all, I have to say that sex with James has never been that orgasmic dreamworld experience you sometimes hear about. I guess none of that was his fault, but I really yearn for a place of my own now. I want to be someplace where, at least occasionally, I can let myself go, and let a bit of the animal out. And what animal is that precisely? I don't really know ... perhaps I see myself as a panther, but maybe I'm more of a monkey or even a cheeky puppy. Don't ask ... a psychologist would have a field day. Anyway, I digress. Let's get back to the sex ... which I know is what you're interested in. Am I right?

OK, well, after the initial entrance and a couple of minutes of rhythmic plunging, I feel James shoot his load before he collapses on top of me. It was quite enjoyable, but far from earth-shattering. And, as per usual, I fail to reach a climax.

Anyhow, this is just how it normally is, but with the nature of the sleeping arrangements, we always have to be so quiet. In the early days, James did manage to treat me to an occasional orgasm, but I've almost forgotten what that was like. In those days, I also had to learn to bite on the pillow or duvet whenever I let go.

Lately, orgasms have become such a rarity, and I'm not so sure that James has even noticed. These days he never asks "how was it for you?" I know that might seem like a cliché, but at least I would know if he still cared.

I also don't think he's noticed that I've been more distant during sex recently. I know it's bad but, in the last few weeks, when we've been doing it, I've imagined being with somebody else. Are you shocked? Well, I was shocked at first myself. But don't you ever do that? Perhaps with a film star, or a footballer? No? Well, I guess you must get greater fulfilment from your sex life than I do. I feel a bit guilty about it though. I mean, when James was pounding into me just then, I was in another world, with someone else appearing in my mind. Should I tell you who it was? Have a guess.

Well, OK, my particular crush for the last few weeks has been Ryan Giggs of Manchester United. D'you know who I mean? He's a new guy, and he's a real hottie. I think I might have to give up supporting Newcastle, and cheer for Man U from now on. That boy could certainly run up my left wing anytime, if you know what I mean ... and I know you do.

Don't get me wrong, I do still quite enjoy doing it with James, but when you start to feel that the best bit is when it's over ... well, there's something not quite right. Our sex just isn't fresh anymore; it's like a crisp and juicy apple that, after a few days, becomes soggy and flavourless.

And while we're on the subject of flavour … one way of illustrating how I see our relationship is to compare James to food. James is like fish and chips; he's uncomplicated, comforting, and is great for warming you up on a cold day. But he's also unsophisticated, perhaps even boring, and most certainly fails to deliver on all your dietary requirements. Or maybe, since it's Christmas, I should liken him to a turkey sandwich: simple, predictable, safe, filling and definitely better than Brussels sprouts … but also lacking in excitement, and never truly satisfying.

Chapter 5: The menu

Saturday 29 August 1992 - Baker Street, London

3:15pm. At the flat. I'm in the kitchen, starting to visualise and plan the evening.

So, that was a glimpse of last Christmas, and also a snapshot of James. Looking back now with the benefit of hindsight, perhaps I'd started to sense it might be our last Christmas together, even before I'd landed the Everwoods job. James and I had already begun to drift apart, and I knew that the next few months could only make it worse. At first, I found it quite hard to accept that our lives were diverging. Up until then, and indeed it remains true today, James had been the only love of my life, and the possibility of us not being together was difficult to contemplate.

◆ ◆ ◆

OK, so tonight's dinner is not like cooking the Christmas turkey with Mammy. The requirement here is for speed and accuracy, whereas most of Mammy's cooking is old fashioned English-style food ... you know, the type of stuff that takes a decade to cook. The meal I'm attempting tonight won't actually take long, but it's all about the preparation.

Before going to uni, I'd hardly tried much cooking; beans on toast or a bacon butty was about my limit. I did quite a bit at York when sharing the house with Suzi, although not so much with our other housemates, and nothing too complicated. Back then, it was mainly quick meals like stir fries and spag bol ... you know, stuff that's fast and cheap, with cheap being the primary consideration when trying to live on a student grant.

Well, tonight's meal certainly isn't cheap. Blimey! I had no idea how expensive the Marble Arch M&S would be ... it was a bit of a shock at the checkout. Still, at least they had a three-for-two offer on the wine.

So, what am I cooking for BJ?

Well, I'm about to tell you. But before we get to that, I should just explain that BJ is short for Bruce John; it has nothing to do with blowjobs, although there's actually a little story that I'll tell you about later. No, when Suzi and I first met him in Darwin, he explained that he thought the nickname was because his mam had fancied one of the surgeons from the *M*A*S*H* TV series, or perhaps because of the CJ character in *The Fall and Rise of Reginald Perrin*. Oh, I used to love Reggie Perrin; did you see it? Leonard Rossiter just cracks me up, and the mother-in-law being a hippopotamus ... it's priceless.

Anyway, where was I? Oh yes, I was going to tell you the menu for tonight.

So here goes ... drum-roll please ...

OK, for the first course ... we have pan-fried scallops with chorizo on a bed of sweet potatoes, topped off with a garnish of fresh parsley. That's pretty special, isn't it? And pretty bloody expensive too; I can't believe the price of scallops.

And then ... another drum-roll please ... we have ... oh wait, perhaps I should first say what's just come into my head. Sorry about the flow, but you know me now, and you know how my mind jumps around.

Well, a little while ago, you may remember that I likened James to fish and chips, and also to a turkey sandwich. D'you remember? Yes, of course you do, you're paying attention.

Anyway, with BJ ... well, I would liken him to scallops and chorizo; which is partly why I'm doing it tonight. There's the understated, delicate flavour of the scallop, which is paired with the contrastingly spicy taste of the chorizo. And BJ really is so full of contrasts, but you only get to see them once you've prized open his shell. He's shy, sensitive, self-deprecating and caring ... and on the other side he's sharp, witty, and has his mind in the gutter. He's really tuned in to my wavelength.

Now, another drum-roll please ...

Yes, for the main course we have seafood linguine with warm smoked salmon, prawns and mussels, together with a side salad. I hope BJ likes this one, but I bet it won't be as good as the one we shared in Auckland. Oh, I met up with BJ in Auckland too, not just in Australia ... didn't I tell you? I'll come to that later.

So, two courses of seafood ... are you impressed? I'd never have believed it just a few months ago; I never used to eat seafood, let alone cook it. I guess it was partly the cost; and you don't see too many working-class northerners eating crayfish and scallops. But also, before going to Australia, I never really wanted to try it either; I mean, I thought that eating shrimps might be like eating grasshoppers, and shellfish akin to eating snails and slugs. And, it's quite possible they are; you tell me, because I have no intention of ever tasting insects or slugs ... that's a step too far. However, soon after arriving in Perth I began to be converted to seafood.

So, last but not least ... the dessert ... and another drum-roll please ... and no, don't expect more than three courses, I'm not bloody Delia Smith. Yes, lastly, we have a Choco-Baileys trifle ... ho-hum, I think I'm gonna get a bit tipsy tonight.

Oh, and I suppose that brings me nicely to tonight's drink ... and yes, a final drum-roll please ...

Well, as part of the three-for-two deal at M&S, I picked up a bottle of Champers ... well, Prosecco actually. I'll put it in the fridge just in case, but I don't think that's for tonight.

What we do have, however, is any remains of this bottle of Baileys once I've got the trifle made. But, before that, we're going to have a special reminder from my travels. M&S were selling Chardonnay from Clare Valley, South Australia and, although I don't know much about wine, I do remember having Clare Valley Chardonnay on New Year's Day. Suzi and I were on Coogee Beach, taking in some sun, sea, sand and sssss ... no, I know where your mind's going ... not sex, but seafood; we were just enjoying a fantastic lunch on the beach with Phil and Laura. Anyway, I picked this Chardonnay, and also a bottle of Marlborough Sauvignon Blanc, as I recall that BJ and I shared a similar bottle in Auckland when we ate that seafood linguine. I remember it was excellent.

Anyhow, I think we've got sufficient to drink.

So, while I start preparing for tonight, I should probably tell you a little about my travels, beginning with Perth.

Chapter 6: New Year's resolution

Wednesday 1 January 1992 – Perth, Australia

2:00pm. Coogee Beach, South Perth. Suzi and I are with Laura and Phil, enjoying a wonderful beach barbecue.

Well, I have no complaints about starting the New Year like this. I'm lying on my towel, stretched out under a huge parasol on a soft sandy beach, and I'm looking out at the waves rolling in from the Indian Ocean. Shades of turquoise and blue extend out to the horizon, where the darker hues of the sea meet the paler tones of the clear sky. My best mate Suzi is sitting next to me, and we are here with auntie Laura and her new husband Phil, who works for Everwoods here in Perth. Laura and Phil have been wonderfully hospitable to us since we arrived.

Suzi and I are also observing some eye-candy in the form of Phil's son Shane, and Shane's best mate Zak. They are splashing about with their surfboards, trying to catch a wave. Their tanned bodies are making Suzi and I feel a bit self-conscious; we're still ghostly white, having just arrived from a British winter.

It's funny, I think this is the first time I've ever seen Suzi in a swimsuit and, I have to say, she looks pretty hot. Neither of us swam when we were in York and, although we shared a house and saw each other half-naked going to and from the bathroom, I don't think I ever appreciated just how curvy she is. Mind you, I don't think I look too shabby either. Both of us are around 5ft 6 to 5ft 8, with beyond-shoulder-length dark brown hair, and we can both show a decent cleavage; but Suzi definitely has more where it counts around the hips and bum. Yeah, if I was into girls, I'd definitely be into Suzi.

Anyway, we've just been enjoying a wonderful barbie on the beach, including some fantastic shrimp-and-crayfish skewers, and some rather spicy chicken. I was a bit reluctant to try the shrimp and crayfish, but all I can say is "WOW! What have I been missing?" The crayfish, in particular, was heavenly: so succulent, and with a dash of sweet-chilli to bring out the flavour ... OMG, I've really found a new taste sensation. And besides this wonderful food, Suzi and I are now just relaxing with our second or third glass of South Australian Chardonnay. Today, life seems pretty perfect.

Perhaps the only thing that could possibly be better is that the temperature is upwards of 30 Celsius, and Suzi and I have both brought black swimsuits with us ... not such a wise colour choice. We're also both a bit irritable today as it's our bloody time of the month, literally. It's definitely worse for Suzi, as she's a heavier bleeder but, for both of us, the combination of Tampax and panty-pads is rather inadequate to allow much swimming ... well, at least, not in Phil and Laura's pool.

It's been better today on the beach, and we've both been for a dip in the ocean. The water's fabulous, and the sensation of breaking waves washing around you is so soothing. The surf is also rather helpful in hiding any minor leakage ... I know you didn't want to hear this stuff, but sometimes it does interfere with one's enjoyment. Thankfully, neither of us suffers excessively with PMT but, as we have our cycles and hormonal mood-swings broadly in-sync, we're not a great pair to meet at this time of the month.

Suzi and I have been period-synchronized ever since we began sharing the house in York. In those days, I wasn't on the pill; I only started when I returned to Newcastle last summer, and it didn't affect my cycle. I began taking the pill because I thought that removing the need for condoms might improve my sex-life with James. With hindsight, it might've actually made things worse, as the greater sensitivity allowed him to finish sooner. Anyhow, while we travel, Suzi and I being in-sync could be a good thing, as we're less likely to want to do conflicting things each day.

♦ ♦ ♦

Having arrived in Perth two days ago, we're still getting used to the time difference, but Phil and Laura have been really welcoming, and their home is lovely. They own a wonderfully spacious five-bedroom bungalow, situated close to the beachfront in the suburb of Coogee, just to the south of Perth. They also have a swimming pool but, due to the aforementioned timing, Suzi and I have yet to take a dip.

Laura and Phil met each other in 1989, when Phil was over working in London. They hit it off quickly, and got married in 1990 before moving out to Perth. I remember their wedding, and thinking back then that Shane looked quite cute. I also remember that James was far from impressed, as he thought Shane was trying to hit on me ... and, who knows, maybe he was.

A couple of years on, and now seeing Shane in his natural environment attired only in tight-fitting Speedos ... mmm-hmm, he really does look well proportioned ...

"Wouldn't you say so Suzi? What d'you think of Shane ... marks out of ten?"

"Yeah, I admit he's quite pleasing to the eye," replies Suzi, as usual the queen of understatement.

"So ... would you?"

"Hmm-possibly," Suzi smiles, "... I certainly might consider a closer inspection."

"Are you talking about my stepson?" asks Laura, overhearing us. "Yeah, Shane ... that boy's full of spunk."

Suzi spits out her wine.

"Ha-ha girls ... no, that's not what I meant," Laura laughs. "Spunk means something quite different out here. Yeah, it means he's attractive, or perhaps brave or courageous ... not what you might've been thinking."

"Oh yeah??? And what would that be?" asks Phil, a knowing smile spreading across his face.

"Well Phil, I'm surprised you don't know … it translates as semen in the Mother Tongue; in proper English, I mean."

"Oh yeah, ha-ha. Well, I guess that Shane's now reached that sort of age," says Phil, grinning.

"No matter," continues Laura. "Anyway, you can look elsewhere; Shane's head-over-heals for this girl at uni in Adelaide. We've only met her once, but she seems really nice."

"Uh-huh … and how about Zak?" I ask, "Is he single?"

"Hey Megan, you're already spoken for," replies Suzi. She's right of course, because I have James, but Suzi hasn't been dating anyone seriously for about a year. The last guy was Matt; they were together for much of the time at uni.

"A bit of window shopping wouldn't hurt," I reply. "And anyway, I'm asking for a friend."

"I don't know about Zak," continues Laura. "We don't see much of him, and Shane doesn't talk about him either."

"Perhaps I should go and find out," I say, smiling as I rise to my feet. "Suzi, d'you fancy another dip in the sea?"

"No, you're alright, I wouldn't want to cramp your style. I'll just read the Lonely Planet for a bit, and think more about our itinerary."

♦ ♦ ♦

Of the two of us, Suzi's always the sensible one, the person who thinks things through, and the one who makes sure that everything's organised. Before we came, she'd spent hours poring over the Lonely Planet guide, working out which route we should take, how to get from A to B, and which backpacker hostels we might try. In contrast, I was happy just to know that we'd be met by Phil and Laura on arrival in Perth, and was content to take it from there. I've never been a very organised or detailed person, and I see that might have its disadvantages when I return home to begin training as a solicitor … I'll cross that particular bridge later.

While I go for a splash around with Shane and Zak, Suzi discusses our itinerary with Laura and Phil, and when I return, our plans have progressed.

"Phil says we should forget about buses in Western Australia," says Suzi, as I arrive to pick up my towel.

"Ah-ha?"

"Yes, he says that the bus network isn't coherent, and we'd be better off flying to Broome or Darwin, before buying our Greyhound passes up there. Apparently, we can fly to Broome for less than it would cost by bus, and it's only about 4 hours, as compared to two days."

"OK, that sounds good," I respond.

"They've also offered to take us on a trip up to see the Pinnacles."

"Yeah, if you'd like to," Phil adds. "We could drive up there tomorrow or Friday, and stay overnight in Cervantes. You should certainly try to see the Pinnacles if you can; it's probably the most impressive landscape in Western Australia."

"That'd be great, thank you," I say, as I dry myself off with the towel.

"No worries, it'd be a pleasure to take you there."

There's a short pause as our eyes focus back towards Shane and Zak.

"Well Megan, did you find your answer?" asks Suzi.

"Oh yeah."

"And?"

"No, Zak's off limits too; he's also hooked up."

"Well, so are you," says Suzi, looking at me with disapproval. "Or have you forgotten about James?"

"No Suzi, I've not forgotten … but …"

"But what?"

"Well …"

"Well, what? Is something up between the two of you? Did something happen over Christmas?"

"No, well, not exactly ... I just feel ... well, maybe that we're going in different directions."

"What d'you mean? Are you serious? But you two have been together for years."

"I know ... a long, long time ... since we were thirteen or so. But that's just it; I've always felt attached to him. All this time, I've never strayed; I've never so much as looked at another bloke ... well, not properly, I mean. I know I joke around a bit, and that my mind wanders, but ..."

"But what?"

"Well, when you see eye-candy like Shane and Zak, don't tell me that your mind doesn't start to stray?"

"I guess ..."

"Look Suzi, you may have your shades on, but I could see you eyeing up their six-packs ... and you don't see too many like those on the shores of the Tyne."

"Uh-huh ... well, that's because I'm young, free and single. My god, I've been single for nearly a year now."

"Wow, is it that long? I still don't understand why you and Matt split up."

"No, nor do I really, but something wasn't working. Anyway Megan, don't change the subject ... this is about you and James." Suzi's always adept at turning the focus back towards me. And although we're best mates, she's quite guarded about her own love life. I guess that's not such a surprise, as most of the time we've known each other, neither of us has been on the market.

"Well, perhaps it's the same with James ... something isn't working these days, and I just get the feeling we aren't destined to be together. I'll be in London soon for at least a year, and more likely two or three. And you know, as I've said before, having returned home after uni, it's clear that we seem to enjoy different things these days. Perhaps we both need a fresh start."

I pause for a moment, considering whether to continue, but think 'what-the-heck'. "And another thing Suzi, we just aren't excited by each other these days. In fact, I'm starting to forget why I first fell for him. When we have sex it's like ... well, it's like ... oh, I don't know what ... but it just doesn't hit the spot. And doesn't every girl deserve an orgasm from time to time? Lately, I've even started dreaming of Ryan Giggs when we do it."

"Wow Megan! Ryan Giggs huh?" Suzi laughs. "Well, that's a new one ... and you never mentioned you were into football. Well-I-never! ... Ryan Giggs. Girl, I'll hand it to you; he's quite a hottie. Although, saying that ... have you seen that French guy playing for Leeds?"

"Ooooohhh-aaahhh-Cantonaaaa ... oh yeah, I'd definitely let him squeeze my onions."

Suzi laughs ... "Is that the best French stereotype you could think of? An onion seller, really?"

"Well, can you do any better?" I look at Suzi, who's now struggling to think. "It's quite hard, isn't it?"

"Uh-huh, yeah ... actually it is hard. Well, I'm sure his baguette is, anyway."

Yep, this is the kind of puerile humour we shared throughout our time together in York. It's why Suzi and I get on so well.

"OK then Suzi, it's my New Year's resolution to think of a better French stereotype."

"That shouldn't be too difficult. I think my own resolution is to make sure that, by this time next year, I've found Mr Right."

"I'll drink to that ... and perhaps, Suzi, that should apply to both of us. Cheers!"

"OK girls," interrupts Laura. "That's quite enough of such talk for today. Don't think I'm not interested, but I don't want Phil getting any ideas of trading me in for a younger model."

Chapter 7: Cleaning the decks

Saturday 29 August 1992 - Baker Street, London

3:30pm. At the flat. I'm beginning to tidy up.

Hmm-yes, Coogee Beach on New Year's Day was fabulous. The warm sea, the crashing waves, Shane and Zak with their Speedos and six-packs ... mmm-delicious ... and I can just taste the succulent crayfish and that chilled Chardonnay. Oh, which reminds me ... I should get tonight's bottles chilling.

I set the two bottles of white wine and the Prosecco in the fridge, and lay out all tonight's ingredients on the kitchen worktop. The kitchen is a respectable size for a flat: not spacious enough for a breakfast table, but it's about a 4 unit x 3 unit size, if you take a unit to be of average washing machine- or cooker-width. It's fitted with white cupboards and doors, and the units are topped with black granite-look work surfaces. As with every other room in the flat, the kitchen has polished oak floorboards, and the kitchen's design is such that you could close it off with a door to keep noise and smells inside. This one had been left open.

So, our time in Perth was wonderful, and we spent a lovely two days with Laura and Phil when they took us north to see the desert and the Pinnacles rock formations. Shane stayed behind in Perth, which was probably no bad thing for us; although Suzi and I both liked the eye-candy, we had the freedom to talk more openly.

Laura was pretty candid about why her marriage to uncle Jack had fallen apart, and articulated how she'd found a new sense of excitement with Phil. She also talked of different types of bedroom stimulation which, previously, she'd never even imagined existed. And, while Phil was out of earshot in a roadside café, Laura even divulged how different Phil and Jack were as lovers. This was certainly something of an eye-opener for me and Suzi ... I'd never pictured auntie Laura as having such a deliciously dirty imagination.

It was fantastic getting to know Laura in this environment. She was someone with whom I could identify; she was from a similar northern upbringing, but was now following a completely different lifestyle on the far side of the world, and loving every minute of it.

Like most people, Laura did have her share of regrets, and there were things that she was still sad about. She retained positive feelings towards uncle Jack; it's just that they'd wanted different things out of life. It's good that they separated on amicable terms, but it's also possible that they'd have remained together if they'd realised sooner that they were drifting apart.

Having thought about Laura's choices, one of the key messages which hit me was that you only get one shot at life, and if the path you're travelling along isn't bringing happiness, don't be afraid to change it. Don't be put off by the fear of failure ... it's better to try and fail than to live with the regret that you never tried.

Perhaps it was during these days with Laura, that thoughts of straying from James came to the forefront of my mind. It wasn't so much the sight of six-pack succulence in the form of Shane and Zak, as the tales of Laura finding her new love. But I did love James and, before coming out to Perth, I hadn't even looked at anyone else with any intent, let alone considered having a fling. Even if James and I were drifting apart, then I still wouldn't cheat on him ... I just wouldn't. Or would I?

♦ ♦ ♦

As I move from the kitchen through to the lounge to begin tidying up, I start to gather last week's newspapers from the sofa, putting them in a pile to throw them out.

I don't always read a daily newspaper, but, over the last couple of weeks as I've been getting used to living by myself, it has been a good distraction in the evenings ... there's so little worth watching on TV.

And, I still haven't thrown away these ones. (*They are two copies of the Daily Mirror from August 20th and 21st, featuring the Duchess of York and a 'toe-sucking incident' with Texan millionaire, John Bryan.*)

I don't usually go for the *Daily Mirror*; more often I get the *Daily Mail* or *Evening Standard*, but I couldn't resist.

I bet they regret it! Just look at the front-page headlines! -

> "FERGIE'S STOLEN KISSES ... Truth about duchess and the Texan Millionaire."
>
> ... and then this one ...
>
> "OH MY GOD! What John Bryan said when he saw the Mirror photos."

Did you see these pictures? Can you believe it? I don't think that the Queen will be best pleased. I actually feel a bit sorry for her, and I quite like the monarchy ... but really?

But anyway, far more important than that ... is toe-sucking really a thing? Have you tried it? No? Or perhaps you just don't want to tell me, am I right? I've heard of quite a few kinky things, and Laura certainly told me of some new ones ... but toe-sucking? I've never heard of that before, and I'm now really curious.

OK, so changing subject again, as I don't think toe-sucking's on tonight's menu ... although mind you ...

No Megan, get a grip ... remember, BJ's a mate, and it's also not long since he was dumped by Suzi.

Having said that, I bet if I'd offered to suck BJ's toes on that bus from Tennant Creek rather than what I actually proposed, things might have turned out differently ... but now I'm jumping ahead in the story.

I must get the vacuum now and make the place a bit cleaner, or maybe I'll just do a quick sweep with the broom. Ha-ha-yes, that's a good one Megan ... oh, and do please excuse me constantly talking to myself. Yes, it's good though because Broome is the next bit of the story.

Chapter 8: Gin and frolics

Wednesday 8 January 1992 – Broome, Australia

8:30pm. I'm with Suzi, drinking at the poolside bar at Cable Beach Backpackers.

It's been a fantastic start to our trip Down Under. We've had nothing to complain about yet … which, as Suzi might tell you, is unusual for me. I'm not generally grumpy, but I am rather attached to my home comforts. We were so lucky to stay for those few days with Laura and Phil, and the food we had was really awesome. I've already mentioned New Year's Day on Coogee Beach, but we had a handful of other fabulous meals, mostly barbies. It was also mostly seafood … snapper, mussels, prawns, crayfish, crab, lobster … I've tried them all in the last week or so. They were a bit upmarket on the baked potato with tuna I might make back home. But now that Suzi and I are going to be hostelling for the next few weeks, I have a feeling our diet might become a bit more basic again.

We flew to Broome from Perth on Monday, which was way better than the alternative of going by bus. It took about 4 hours to get here, which was a little tedious, but we had some great views over the desert landscape below. It's mind-blowing just how big Australia is … and also how dry; in some parts you can travel many miles without seeing anything green.

This backpacker hostel seems OK; it's quite basic, but certainly better than I'd expected. Suzi and I have a dorm room to ourselves, which makes us a bit more relaxed about leaving our backpacks, although we'll still keep our valuables with us. The place is clean and functional, and the hostel has a pool and also a bar, which means we don't really need to go elsewhere in the evening. That's also just as well, because there hardly seems to be a buzzing nightlife. Although, to be fair, Monday and Tuesday nights in Newcastle aren't terribly lively either.

Refining My Dining

Earlier, Suzi and I had some juicy steaks from the barbie, and I'm waiting for her to bring another beer from the bar. There's a cute guy floating around who we got chatting to last night; he seemed really friendly. His name's Neil, and I think he's totally into me. Suzi caught him checking out my rear view a few times, and he was certainly dishing out the compliments. He's from Cardiff, with curly dark hair, just under 6-foot tall, and a great bum ... I mean, he's probably a good 8 or 9 out of 10 in the tushy department.

Yeah, I know ... and Suzi keeps telling me ... I should remember James. Well, the more I've been thinking about it, with me moving to London and the way things have been lately, the less I think that James and I have a future. Our relationship has changed; things aren't like they were a few years ago ... my god, I'm sounding so old, aren't I? But, over the last few days, I've been considering some of the things Laura said ... that as time moves on, the excitement disappears and you end up wanting different things. And it's true, I don't feel the same way as I once did, and I'm not sure that James does either. So, maybe the move to London is the sign for us both to move on. And OK, hands-up, you've caught me ... after a few drinks last night, when I saw Neil's cute backside, I just wanted to squeeze it. To tell you the truth, it's now nearly 24 hours later, I've had far less to drink than yesterday, and I still can't erase such thoughts from my head.

"Daydreaming again, are we?" *Suzi returns from the bar with two bottles of Tooheys. While I usually prefer wine or maybe a G&T, beer is far more refreshing in this heat.*

"Oh, thanks Suzi ... cheers! And yeah, I guess I was drifting a bit."

"Don't tell me ... Neil again?"

"Well, you have to admit, he is kinda cute?"

"Maybe ... but he's not really my type."

"He doesn't have to be your type; it's me who wants to shag him. Oh blimey! Did I just say that?"

"Uh-huh."

"Well, he has got a nice bum."

"I guess. So, d'you really want to dump James then?"

"Oh Suzi, I don't know. We've drifted apart. But it's not just that, I also want to find myself ... a bit like Laura said ... I've got to discover what makes me tick."

"Uh-huh. You may be right, but I'd take Laura's advice with a pinch of salt, if I were you."

"Yeah, perhaps. ... Oh Suzi, what should I do? What'd you do in my situation?"

"Well, you could shag Neil's brains out, and try to get it out of your system." Suzi raises an eyebrow and smiles. "No, I'm kidding."

I chuckle, but ...

"Ha-ha ... now, that's not such a bad idea. Indeed ... what if ...?"

"Megan! ... I was only kidding."

"But Suzi, why not? Why shouldn't I live a bit? Why shouldn't I say 'screw everything' and light the touchpaper? I'm always thinking about James, or about what Mam would say, or Beth ... or even you. Maybe I should actually think of myself for once." *There, that told her!*

"Well, I'm sorry for having an opinion."

"No Suzi, I didn't mean it like that, and I didn't mean to rant. I'm just saying, perhaps we should forget about home while we're out here, and just let go a bit. I mean, you're young, free and single, and I'm ... well, perhaps only semi-detached."

"Semi-detached huh? Well Megan, all I'm saying is just be sure about it. James seems like a decent bloke, and while he might not have everything on your wish list, I doubt there are many blokes who do. And remember, if you cross that threshold, there's no going back."

"Yeah, I know."

"So just don't rush into anything. And in any case, even if James isn't the guy you're going to marry, there's no need to jump into bed with the first bloke, or the first squeezable bum that comes along. Do a bit of window shopping first."

"Yeah … you're probably right."

♦ ♦ ♦

9:00pm. Suzi and I have had a bit of light discussion about the merits of six-packs and firm buttocks, while surveying the variable standard of eye-candy around the bar. We spot Neil. He's heading our way with a couple of girls: both tall and quite pretty, one dark-haired, the other mousy-blonde.

"Hey ladies!"

"Oh, hi Neil!"

"D'you mind if we join you? And can I get you both another drink? These two lovely ladies are Hannah and Marianne; they're from Holland."

I stand up and kiss-hug the two girls.

"OK Neil, great," I reply, "I'll come and help you with the drinks. Suzi, d'you fancy another Tooheys? Or maybe a change?"

"Tooheys is fine."

I follow Neil towards the bar, while Hannah and Marianne start to get acquainted with Suzi.

"So Neil, what've you been up to today?"

"Hold on a sec …" Neil turns to the barman. "Three bottles of Tooheys and a gin and tonic, and … Megan, what's yours?"

"Oh, another G&T would be good … make it a double!" *Well, he's paying.*

"Cheeky!" quipped Neil.

The barman steps away to attend to the order.

"OK Megan … yeah, today I've been sorting out a Greyhound pass. I'm off to Darwin tomorrow morning … bloody early; the bus leaves at around 6 o'clock."

"Oh, so soon Neil? Just when we were getting to know each other," I tease, as I grab his elbow, seizing the opportunity for some light flirting.

Suzi says that Neil looks like Mark Hughes, the Manchester United forward. Although I don't follow football much, I know who he is. Well, of course I do, he plays for Man U, the same team as Ryan Giggs ... who, incidentally, I now look out for every week on *Match of the Day*. I don't watch the football; I just like seeing blokes in tight shorts. D'you think I'm becoming obsessed? Anyway, I can see that Neil does bear a passing resemblance to a younger version of Hughes, apart from them both being Welsh.

"Well Megan, you can always take the same bus as me ... but anyway, the night is still young."

I'm pretty sure that's a chat up line. Didn't you think so? And he is really cute ... uh-oh Megan, you could be in trouble here. But maybe that's exactly what I need.

"Suzi and I are planning to take the bus on Friday, and we've still got to sort out our bus passes. But we're planning to be in Darwin for a week or so."

"So, there's still plenty of time for ..."

"Here you are mate!" The barman interrupts, placing the drinks in front of us. I let go of Neil's elbow. *Plenty of time for what? What was Neil going to say? Why do people always interrupt when it gets to the critical bit?*

"Oh ... cheers!" says Neil, handing him a couple of banknotes.

The barman gives Neil some change. I pick up the two G&Ts and Neil grabs the bottles.

"Neil, you were saying ...?"

"Oh yeah ... what was I saying?"

"You were saying that there's still plenty of time for ... something. You didn't finish."

"Oh yeah ... there's still plenty of time to finish anything we might start." He winks at me.

OK, this really is a hook-up attempt; no doubt about it, right?

"Uh-huh," I respond, "so, what exactly did you have in mind?"

"I'll tell you later." He winks at me again, and starts to make a move back towards the table.

Damn, how can he leave me hanging like that?

And we're now back at the table. I needed at least a lap around the pool so he could explain what he meant. I suspect I may already know, but … ouch! the frustration of it. *I'll make him pay for that.*

I wait for Neil to sit down first, which he does, next to Suzi and opposite the two Dutch girls. I decide to squeeze in between Suzi and Neil.

"Hey, budge up Suzi."

I think Suzi's a bit annoyed with me, but I'm not treading on her turf … she told me that Neil wasn't her type.

♦ ♦ ♦

10:00pm. Still at the poolside bar, but after another round of drinks.

The last hour has been exciting and frustrating in equal measure. Neil has been paying me lots of attention, while Suzi and the Dutch girls have been talking, mostly about things to do in Australia. There's been lots of eye contact, and I'm pretty sure that Neil wants to make a move, but perhaps he's been inhibited by the presence of the other girls.

I wouldn't be averse to him making such a move; it's been so long since anyone showed any interest in me, and the attention is flattering. I'm feeling more than a little tipsy after the latest double G&T, and I'm in the mood for a bit of fun. Without doubt, Neil's kinda cute, and I'm certainly feeling horny … and … well, let's just say that a bit of snog-n-grope wouldn't be a bad way to end my night out. Forget James: if Neil hits on me, I'm just going to go with the flow.

It must be the combined effect of alcohol and the distance from home, but tonight I don't feel attached to anyone or anywhere ... I'm freewheeling. Maybe I should make a move myself, what d'you think? It doesn't always have to be the bloke, right? But I've got no decent chat-up lines, no slick moves, nor any recent dating experience. So, where do I start?

Thankfully, I don't have to think for long.

Oh, is that Neil's hand on my thigh under the table? Not so subtle Neil but, I have to say, it's about bloody time! Dressed in my cut-off denim shorts, I've had plenty of thigh exposed, and it was overdue some attention. His touch gives me goosebumps as a tingle of anticipation rushes through me ... hmm-yes, things are now looking up.

I place my hand over his, and hold it tight while tilting my head to look into his eyes. He winks and gives me a cheeky smile.

"So Neil, is this what you meant earlier when you said 'starting something'?" I smile.

Suddenly, I'm gripped by a stronger quiver, running head to toe and lingering in my e-zones. His last wink just moved the goalposts and sent my pulse racing ... my hornyometer now registers a significant rise on the dial.

Still smiling, and without breaking eye contact, Neil then moves his hand further up between my thighs, tickling me with his fingertips. He then raises his eyebrows.

"Starting something, Megan? Qui, moi?"

His fingers tell me that's exactly what he's doing.

OK, this is it ... I think Little Miss Horny's coming out to play. I quickly gauge that Suzi and the other girls still have a lot left in their glasses. *That's good, so they don't need any more ... plus Suzi and I do have a room to ourselves.*

I quickly gulp down the rest of my G&T.

"So Neil, d'you wanna get me another drink?"

I don't wait for the answer, but stand up, tugging on his arm. As Neil rises to his feet, I catch Suzi's eye and give her a quick wink.

The return signal is one of disapproval. So be it. Anyway, I don't need Suzi's endorsement to have some fun.

I tug on Neil's hand, and drag him across the terrace towards the bar. The bar is situated close to the pool, but there are also several palm trees and tall shrubs between the tables, allowing different groups to separate. Now a few yards away from our table, I lure Neil up against one of the palm trees, and decide to go for it. I wrap my arms around his neck, and plant a kiss on his lips. *Hmm ... now we'll see whether he likes me.*

It takes less than a second before Neil responds, and our needy lips are locked together. His hand moves to support my back as he pulls me close, pressing our pelvic regions together. I feel a shiver down my spine, and all the way to my core. *Holy fuck, it's a long time since I felt like this.*

Neil continues to engage with his lips, and I soon allow his tongue to explore mine. Unlike James, whose lips and tongue I know well, there's exhilaration in the taste of another man. He's fresh, unexplored, forbidden territory ... and so delicious.

With one hand still supporting my back, his other hand slides down my side to squeeze my butt cheek. *Hmm, nice move soldier.*

We're hidden from view behind the tree, and any of my lingering inhibitions are fast slipping away. I haven't felt a rush like this in a long time ... perhaps never. I'm totally intoxicated ... drunk with a combination of Neil's attention and the kick of that last double G&T. I know that I'm drunk, but so what? I want more ... no ... I *need* more.

We haven't spoken a word in what must be several minutes. As he presses me back against the palm tree, I feel his groin press against mine and, for the first time, I can sense his manhood is awake. Hmm-yes, he feels quite large. Hmm-yes-yes, I want to feel that inside me. *Naughty girl, did I really just think that?* Have I now become Little Miss Slutty? ... Oh, I wonder if that one is included in the *Little Misses and the Mr Men* series of kiddies books. Unlikely, I guess.

As we press against each other, his arousal seems to be strengthening, and I'm getting wetter by the minute. Damn! I have to quench my thirst. I remember the empty dorm room. OK girl, just throw the dice ...

"Neil babe, I need you to fuck me right now."

Bloody hell, did I really just say that? Was it me, did you hear it? Talk about losing my inhibitions.

"What???" Neil steps back in shock.

"Oh sorry, did I just say that? But c'mon Neil, d'you fancy a shag? Why don't we? Suzi and I have a dorm to ourselves, and she won't mind." *D'you think I've made myself clear?*

"Oh, OK then ... d'you really mean it?" Neil's face lights up.

There's zero reluctance on his part as I take his hand and lead him back to the room. Suzi's still at the table, drinking with Hannah and Marianne, and hopefully she'll be gone a good while longer.

We enter the dorm room, and we're both in a hurry as we re-engage our lips and tongues, and begin to struggle with each other's clothing. Thankfully Neil's wearing a polo shirt, which I pull up and over his torso to reveal quite a six-pack. His skin feels a bit sweaty ... well, the humidity is oppressive even so late in the evening, but he also feels deliciously toned ... yum-yum!

"Hey, someone's been working out," I say, before wrestling him onto the bed, and starting to unzip his jeans.

"OW!!! FUCK!!!" he swears, hitting his head on the metal frame of the top bunk. *And I thought my bed at home was tricky.*

"You OK babe? I don't want you knocked out before the first round."

"Yeah ... just about. It's not the easiest of arrangements."

While we've been conversing, Neil has successfully removed my crop-top, and is now working on my bra. Although my senses are somewhat dampened by the alcohol, my spirit certainly isn't.

"Neil, it's a good thing it's so warm ... any more clothes and we'd be here until Christmas." *Do I sound like I'm in a rush?* I finally get his jeans down, and he wriggles his legs out of them.

"Well, things are about to get hotter!" he says, as it's now evident he's succeeded with my bra.

Oh yes ... indeed he has!!!

My nipples feel soooo gooooood under his tongue. Hmm-yes ... that feels like ... well, it feels like ... oh, OK, so how can anyone come up with the right vocabulary when your nipple's stuck in the mouth of a hot stud? It's not that easy, is it, huh? But I have to say, I think my boobs are two of my best features, and it feels awesome to have them so proficiently inspected.

"Hey babe," I say, as my brain suddenly re-engages. "Have you got any protection?"

That's a surprise ... after all that alcohol, my brain still works. I'm on the pill these days, but I still don't want to catch anything, and who knows where Neil has been? Mind you, I bet he thinks the same about me.

"Yeah, don't worry ... I've brought along our friend Mr Durex."

"Well, hurry up Neil and get Mr Durex on; I want you inside."
Fuck, did I really just say that? I'm a desperate old cow tonight, aren't I?

"OK, OK ..." says Neil, sliding down my body. As he moves, he unzips my cut-off denim shorts, and slides them down my legs. "BUGGER! FUCK! WANK!!!" he says, as he smacks his head on the bedframe again.

At this point, I begin to appreciate that performing these sorts of shenanigans is not so easy on such a bunk bed ... and it's terribly squeaky too. Still, at least Mam and Beth aren't listening in next door ... Oh my god! – what would they think if they could see me now?

"Oh my god! ... Ooooohhh-yes ... ooooohhh-mmm ..."

Forget Mammy and Beth ... Neil has suddenly hit the spot. He's pulling aside my knickers with one hand, and exploring with the other. Mmm-yes, nice work babe, is that one finger or two? Who cares? He sure knows where to put them.

Neil works his way delicately around my clit and, unlike the predictability of James, not knowing where Neil's next touch will be, leaves me burning with anticipation.

"Oooooohhh-Neil ... mmm-yes ... ooooohhh."

Oh, yes ... now that's gotta be two fingers. Wow!!!

"Mmm-yesssss ... ooooohhh."

Definitely two digits now, and they're going in-out-in-out-shake-it-all-about ... my god, it's the Hokey Cokey.

This finger-massage has got me totally losing my senses ... you can probably tell. I clutch the bedspread beneath me as, somehow, Neil manages to squeeze into a comfortable position between me and the wall. Well, he may not be comfortable, but who cares?

"Ooooohhh-yes ... keep going babe ... don't stop."

"Are you enjoying this then?" Neil asks as he pauses for a breather.

"Hey babe, don't talk to me ... just keep working."

"At your service ma'am," he says, sliding my knickers down my legs before returning to duty.

I can't remember this feeling ... it's so lush, and it's been such a long time since James gave me anywhere near this indulgence. In fact, I now question whether he ever did so? I also suddenly wonder if I'd be feeling even more right now had I not drunk three bottles of Tooheys and two double G&Ts.

"Ooooohhh-mmm ... yesssss ..." I feel my whole body convulse this time. Uncontrollable pulsing through my core, diffusing up and across my whole body. That must be the real thing ... but how much further does it go? Just checking; I've not had many of these before. But why stop there?

"OK Neil, come on, I want you inside me. Hurry up!" *Oh my, do I sound desperate? Oh, so what? I need it.*

During a short interlude from his digital exercise, I hear the ripping of foil and the packet landing on the floor. Neil now seems to be struggling to put it on.

"OUCH!!! EFFING HELL!!!"

He's just hit his head again.

I giggle before smacking my own head against the wall.

"BLOODY HELL! Maybe we should've put the mattress on the floor."

Neil grabs hold of my breasts, and uses them for balance as he straddles me. The bed creaks loudly again, and shakes as though it might collapse.

His lips re-engage with mine, and this time they taste different … maybe it's the taste of my own excitement from his fingers. Well, I don't know, I haven't licked myself down there … I'm not a bloody contortionist. Anyway, as he kisses me, I now feel his cock pushing against my folds.

I grab hold of his length, before sliding it up and down, rubbing it against my clit.

"Hmm-impressive," I say, as I squeeze him tight and place him ready for entry.

"Megan, are you quite sure?"

"Yeah soldier," I laugh, "you're not a bad size."

"No, not that … I mean, are you sure you want it?"

"Look Neil, quit with the good manners will you, and just fuck me." *Forgive me Lord, for I'm such a dirty bitch.*

Without further ado, I feel a thrust which nearly rips me apart.

"HOLY CRAP, NEIL! You're way bigger than James. Oh my god!"

"Who the fuck is James?"

Shit! Neil has a point; I should perhaps have mentioned him.

"Sorry Neil … keep going … he's just my ex-boyfriend." Well, if not officially ex, then he probably will be after this.

I think the mention of James might have triggered a reaction. Neil has become more deliberate; he's thrusting harder and faster, and OH MY, YES … he's going deeper!

"Ooooohhhh … hmm-yes, oooooooohhh."

A few more thrusts and I'm clenching the bedspread tight as I release and, immediately afterwards, I sense Neil shoot his load …

at least I think he ejaculated, it was quite difficult to feel it through the condom.

Anyway, Neil then falls on top of me. Well, I say falls … these bunkbeds don't exactly allow any great height. We cuddle for a few moments before we swap positions, with him lying beneath me.

After a few minutes, the excess Tooheys from earlier is now making its voice heard inside my bladder.

"Sorry babe … just stay here a minute; I'm bursting for the loo."
"OK … well, hurry back."
"I will."

I jump up, and quickly find my knickers and a t-shirt, and rush out and along the corridor to a washroom. As I step inside, I quickly reflect on what just happened. My god!!! Fuck, that was … indescribable. Let's just say it's something I want to do again.

◆ ◆ ◆

I relieve my bladder and return to the room. Thankfully, I don't pass anyone, and when I get back to the room, I'm pleased to discover that Suzi has yet to return. Neil is still lying on my bed, but he seems to have dozed off.

I suddenly have a naughty thought … and I mean a very naughty one. I've always wanted to do this with James, but he'd never indulge me. OK now, so I'm a bit kinky, but don't be too quick to judge.

Hastily, I take one of the stretchy ties from around my backpack … you know, the type of tie that holds your wet towel or roll-mat to the top. I also collect the one from Suzi's backpack.

Neil hasn't stirred.

I whisper in his ear.

"Shhh-babe, you just shut your eyes and relax."

I give him a quick nibble on his ear, before moving down and using a stretch-tie to bind one of Neil's legs to the bed post. I give Neil a kiss on his torso, and then whisper again.

"Shhh-babe, mmm-yes, just keep relaxing ..."

I gently caress his arms before positioning them above his head, as I try to straddle him without banging my head on the upper-bunk. Next, with the other stretch tie, I secure his wrists to the top end of the bed. He's not bound tight, and I'm sure he could easily escape ... it's just a bit of fun.

I can't believe he still hasn't opened his eyes. Is he really asleep, or just playing along? Anyway, I now have him tied to the bed posts. I slide down Neil's legs and, at this point, he opens his eyes.

"What the fuck?" he says, as he tries to move his arms and wriggle.

"Shhh-Neil ... just relax, and let me play a little." *Did I say that? Another one for the archives.*

I reach for Neil's cock again, and a few strokes brings it quickly back to life. I caress the tip, and rub gently up and down the shaft. I want to feel him inside again for round two, but I decide I'll have a bit more fun first. I continue to stroke him with my hands, while teasing him with my eyes and licking my lips.

I hold his gaze as I watch his eager anticipation. I can tell he wants what's coming next.

He's rock hard now, so I lower my head, letting my tongue connect with his tip, before licking around the end.

FLASH-BANG!

Suddenly the door crashes open and a bright light shines in from the corridor, as Suzi enters the room.

I'm caught in stunned silence as I hear her gasp, and then curse under her breath. She then pauses, looks me in the eye, but says nothing. Instead, Suzi grabs her washbag and leaves the room.

The interruption prevents me from finishing. The moment is gone, and I untie Neil before climbing back into bed beside him. I snuggle up next to him and, within about five minutes, feelings of guilt start to surface.

Suzi returns to the dorm. Without a word, she strips off and gets into her bunk on the opposite side of the room, which isn't very far away ... certainly less than the full swing of a cat.

I know I've annoyed her.

But more than that, what have I just done?

Hell, I've only gone and done what I thought I could never do. I've cheated on my James.

Neil hasn't said anything further since Suzi came back. He seems unconcerned by it all, and has quickly dozed off.

I now lie wide awake, pondering over my actions. I know what I did was wrong, but just a few minutes ago it all felt so right. And it wasn't just the alcohol talking. I really wanted it, and maybe needed it too. How come something so delicious can so rapidly turn into gut-churning guilt?

♦ ♦ ♦

I didn't get much sleep.

It must've been about 4:30am that an alarm goes off on Neil's wrist watch. He climbs over me, finds his discarded clothes, and quietly gets dressed. He kisses my forehead, and whispers that he'll find me again in Darwin. Neil has to go and catch his bus.

Chapter 9: Naughty but nice

Saturday 29 August 1992 - Baker Street, London

4:00pm. At the flat. I've just finished tidying up, and I'm about to prepare tonight's dessert.

So, that was Broome ... and, oh-my-yes, that was Neil. Yeah, that night in Broome was crazy. I bet you think I'm a right-slutty old cow after all that, don't you? Well, Suzi certainly did ... she gave me the silent treatment for several hours the next morning.

Anyhow, before continuing with the story, I must just make a start on the trifle. I'll tell you more in a minute.

Now let's see. I got this recipe from this cookery book that I had in York. I've never tried it, but it looks rather yummy. Mind you, the pictures always do, don't they? OK, let's see ... what does the recipe say?

I check the book.

First ... 100 grams of plain chocolate. I've got Cadburys Bournville. Oh, I do love a bit of Bournville, don't you? Better than sex, maybe? Well, no ... I now know that's not true. Perhaps the chocolate would've given James a run for his money, but I'd have given up more than a bar of Bournville for further horizontal gymnastics with Neil. Well, I guess I shouldn't be too hard on James either, it's just that after a few years the excitement was gone.

OK ... next I need a 500-millilitre pot of custard ... yep, there's no way I was going to make my own.

Then ... 300 millilitres of double cream, for which I'll have to substitute my crème fraiche. I hope that'll still work.

And a chocolate Swiss roll ... well, I've got three large double-chocolate muffins instead. I'll probably only need two.

Then ... 400 grams of tinned cherries and 3 tablespoons of kirsch. Well, I'm going to substitute Baileys ... and probably more like 10 tablespoons. Yeah? Anything wrong with that? You'd do the same, right?

So, I've got everything I need ... and the first step is to start melting the chocolate. It's a pretty simple recipe ... there's not too much cooking-brain required, which is just as well.

I reach into the cupboard, extract a mid-size Pyrex bowl, and a medium saucepan. I fill the kettle, and set it to boil.

♦ ♦ ♦

So, where was I? D'you remember? Oh yes ... Broome.

Well, as I was saying, Suzi really disapproved of me having sex with Neil. I don't know how much of this was about her opinions on cheating as such, versus the fact I was cheating on James. Although Suzi was friendly towards James, I think it was more about the principle. She thought that I'd let my moral standards drop ... and, to be fair, she wasn't wrong.

I do know Suzi felt abandoned with those two Dutch girls, while I was off enjoying myself. We usually went everywhere together. I also think there might've been a touch of jealousy, despite the fact that Suzi had already declared Neil not to be her type.

I guess if the boot had been on the other foot, and if Suzi had been having sex rather than me, then I might've been pretty pissed-off too. Of course, I'd be pleased for her as Suzi's my best mate, but I'd also be jealous, and wouldn't want to pay for a front row seat.

I pour the boiling water into the saucepan, then put the Pyrex bowl on top. I break the chocolate into the bowl and allow it to melt ... well most of it.

Hmm-yum ... I can't resist a chunk or two of Bournville while we go along. I bet you would too, am I right?

Anyway, by the next afternoon, Suzi had emerged from her grumpy mood, and we went to sort out our month-long Greyhound passes which would cut the cost of travel for the next few legs of our journey. And then, during our walk back to the hostel, surprise-surprise, after several hours of blanking me over my antics with Neil, all is forgiven and Suzi suddenly wants to know every last detail. Yes indeed, I now became subject to a full-scale spotlight-in-the-face inquisition ... well OK, the spotlight was a bit of an exaggeration, but the midday sun was rather blinding.

"Was he good? ... How big was he? ... How many e-zones did he hit? ... Did he go down on you? ... Did you climax? ... How many times?" ... and so on.

Yeah, women can be so fickle. Even if we hate the idea, we still want to know everything about it.

In answer to most of Suzi's questions Neil scored pretty heavily, although he was way short of 100 percent. Well, that's not surprising, considering Suzi must've had more than twenty questions, including a few dimensions I hadn't even thought to explore. However, all things considered, despite being an alcohol-induced and rather rapid shag, and not a particularly comfortable one at that ... I have to say my experience in Broome was as sumptuous as this Choco-Baileys trifle.

Ah-now ... but having said that, I know what you're going to ask me. Your question is: "If I likened James to fish and chips, and BJ to scallops and chorizo, what food would Neil be?" I knew you were going to ask ... tell me if I'm wrong?

Well, Neil wouldn't be the Choco-Baileys trifle ... although the naughty treat aspect of it is certainly apt. I think much of my experience was heightened by Neil being a forbidden fruit. As I was still James's girlfriend, I shouldn't have been tempted ... but I guess it might've been anyone at that point in time. With hindsight, I can see I was desperate for a release, and Neil just happened to be there.

But how would I describe Neil?

Perhaps he'd be a burger, or no, better still, a hotdog ... definitely something that's simple, full of meat, and quickly hits the spot. Yes, he'd be the kind of food that you stuff into your mouth without thinking, but not the type of diet you want every day.

Having melted the chocolate, I gently stir in the custard.

After the interrogation Suzi's mood lifted, and her initial stance of disapproval subsided. This was in direct contrast to my own. I started to feel incredibly guilty about cheating on James. Why had I done it? I'd been with him for such a long time, and I knew he deserved much better.

I began to consider what others might think, should they ever find out. I mean, what would Mammy have said? ... She'd have been horrified at my behaviour. Or Dad? ... Well, I guess he'd have been shocked, but probably OK. And what about Beth? ... Well, given Beth's attitude to boyfriends, I suppose she'd have just said "way-aye girl, congratulations." Beth's never taken to James, but she's also got no standards. Having said that, who the hell am I to talk?

I take out the larger Pyrex bowl, and crumble in the muffins to form the trifle base. I then pour in a couple of large slurps of Baileys.

"Oh knackers!" I now wish I'd used the bowls the other way round ... this bigger bowl looks huge.

I grab the tin-opener and start to open the tin of cherries, quickly getting to the point of flipping the lid.

This tin-opener is way better than our one in Newcastle ... our old one is rubbish and every tin takes hours of effort. Whereas this one ... this could break open the chastity belt of Henry VIII's mistress. I don't know why that image sprung to mind, but you know what I mean.

I check that there's no excess water, and then empty the cherries with their syrup into the bowl with the crumbled muffins. Next, I gently pour the chocolatey custard on top. I pour the crème fraiche into the smallest of the Pyrex bowl set, and use a large hand whisk to whip it up a bit. Crème fraiche doesn't really whip up well, but I'm sure it'll do the trick. I hold the whisk up a few times as I check the consistency.

Thinking of whisks, did you ever watch the BBC sitcom 'Allo 'Allo? I know it's a bit un-PC, but I rather like it. If you've not seen it, it's centred around a café in France during the Second World War. There are some great characters, two of which are Yvette and Maria, the waitresses who also supply sexual favours to some of the occupying German soldiers. Anyway, to cut a long story short, one of the sex toys they use is an egg-whisk. I still can't work it out. What would you do with one? Have you ever thought about it? No? Oh, come on, it can't just be me? Oh, OK then ... well perhaps I should ask auntie Laura; if anyone knows, I'm sure she does.

I take a wide spatula and dollop the crème fraiche on top of the custard layer, and carefully spread it around.

"Oh knackers!!!" ... yes, I say that rather a lot, don't I? Well, I now need those chunks of chocolate that I just ate, to grate and sprinkle on top of the trifle. Silly me. Oh well, not to worry ... I might just have to open another bar then. Oooohhh-noooo, except that I haven't got another bar. ... Oh, I know, I've still got a few segments of a Terry's Chocolate Orange ... that'll do. Oh, it's a tough life!

♦ ♦ ♦

Anyway, returning to Broome.

So, Suzi and I had sorted out our bus passes, and the following morning we set off for Darwin, just like Neil had done 24 hours earlier. Rising early to catch a 6:00am bus wasn't so good, but that was preferable to the journey itself, which was close to 30 hours ... yeah, a full day, a full night, and then some. It was about noon when we checked into Paradise Backpackers Hostel in Darwin ... and my god, Darwin was hot and humid.

With so many hours on the road between Broome and Darwin, I spent a vast amount of time alone with my thoughts. Well, not necessarily alone; I did take my Walkman, so I was plugged in to my music. However, when you've only brought 3 cassettes (Madonna's *Immaculate Collection*, *Kick* by INXS, and Queen's *Greatest Hits* ... all quite middle of the road), once you've played them through several times, you want something different. It was only on the next long bus journey that Suzi and I even thought to swap music ... I know, it's a pretty obvious thing to do.

Of course, I chatted with Suzi for a few hours, and I also managed to sleep a bit, but there were still several tedious hours during which I simply gazed out of the window and thought about life.

I began to feel terrible about cheating on James. I loved him ... well, I'm pretty sure I did, even if we were drifting apart. He never deserved this, so why did I do it? I'd managed three years at uni without so much as looking at anyone else, and now I go and shag a total stranger.

And, just so you know, I wouldn't advise my music choices if you want to get your head straight about life. Queen is a good example ... at one moment, I'm thinking about *Love of My Life* and *Crazy Little Thing Called Love*, while a little later it's *Another One Bites the Dust*. Such music did nothing to resolve my guilt, nor indeed to resolve what I should do about it. Would this be, and indeed should it be, the end for me and James?

My sense of shame was one thing but, however much I felt like a betraying bitch for having shagged Neil, I had also rediscovered something long hidden ... the taste of excitement!

James and I had spent several years as friends before the first time we had sex, and I remember our debut shag in my creaky single bed. At least on that occasion, Mam and Beth were both out, and we'd had the house to ourselves. That was when I was fifteen ... just a week before my sixteenth birthday, and James and I had known each other a long time. Anyway, I recall that first time being really exciting, possibly more so because it was still before my birthday, and technically illegal. Yes, I know I was under age, but Mam said as a baby I was ten days overdue, so I took it that those extra days counted. But after that first time, on each occasion afterwards the sense of novelty declined and the excitement somehow drifted away.

With Neil being the only other person that I'd had sex with, there couldn't have been more of a contrast. There was no two-year build up, more like two hours ... I'd only set eyes on him the night before. And there we were, strangers in a hostel bar in Broome, and we couldn't wait to rip each other's clothes off. Now, that's a whole different league of excitement.

During the hours spent gazing out of the bus window over the parched landscape, I deliberated over why James and I had become so stale, and why, lately, we'd been taking each other for granted. But then I thought, even at the start when we were just discovering sex, it was hardly electrifying. James was always gentle, caring and cuddled me a lot, but he was unadventurous, and every time was more of the same. There was hardly ever any foreplay ... although I guess I was just as much at fault for not initiating any myself. Whereas with Neil, well ... wow, his fingers were amazing. You'd have thought, having downed three bottles of beer and two double G&Ts, that I wouldn't feel anything ... but boy, that night was sensational. There's a saying that if you always eat at the same restaurant, you never find a new taste. Well, I had just dined somewhere new, and the experience was delicious.

♦ ♦ ♦

As the bus approached Darwin, my guilty thoughts about James had subsided a little. I knew my relationship with him was never going to be the same again, but I was intent on enjoying my time in Australia, whatever lay ahead.

On arrival in Darwin, I became increasingly eager to find Neil again. While I knew that a one-night stand was unlikely to lead to anything longer-term, it had been such a buzz, and I also felt I wanted to get to know him better. Yes, my mind was all in a jumble, but, despite the guilt, I wasn't dismissing the possibility of a repeat performance if the opportunity came along ... although it did seem rather improbable. It was made all the less likely by the fact that I didn't know which hostel Neil had gone to, but, regardless, I felt the urge to try to locate him.

Suzi and I checked in at Paradise Backpackers, which seemed as good as any of Darwin's hostels mentioned in the Lonely Planet. It was similar to the one in Broome: clean, functional, and featured a pool, a barbecue, and reasonably well-maintained dorms. Unlike in Broome where we had a dorm to ourselves, this time Suzi and I had to share with a couple of German girls, at least for the first night or two.

An hour or so after settling in, during a brief moment when Suzi had gone to the laundry room, I decided to return to reception to enquire whether Neil was staying in the same hostel. I chose to do this without Suzi for obvious reasons; she'd hardly endorsed my short dalliance, so why poke a sleeping bear? That is an expression, am I right? Or is it a sleeping tiger? I think Suzi's more of a tiger.

Anyway, nobody matching Neil's description was staying in Paradise, so to speak. While I was disappointed, in some ways it was also a relief. What would I say to him if we bumped into each other? "Hi Neil, d'you fancy another shag?" Not bloody likely ... at least, not without ten double G&Ts inside me. Well OK, it might have taken only five ... but, what could I have said?

Anyhow, slutty old Megan was lost for words ... you wouldn't think it, would you?

♦ ♦ ♦

On that first night in Darwin, Suzi and I spent most of the time chatting with the other girls in our room, and relaxing in the jacuzzi pool at the hostel. The next day, despite Suzi's protestations, we checked out a couple of nearby hostels to see if we could locate Neil. OK, so I did poke the sleeping tiger but, somehow, I really wanted to find him. Thankfully, although more than a tad irritated, the tiger didn't bite my head off.

Locating Neil would be easier said than done of course as, not only did we not know which hostels to check, but neither did we have any surname to work with. All I could say was that his name was Neil, he came from Cardiff, and he was about six foot tall and looked like Mark Hughes. Oh, and of course, that his rugged-handsomeness made my knees tremble ... but that wasn't so relevant to the hostel staff.

After trying and failing at three of the most likely nearby hostels, I think Suzi was quite pleased when I gave up. Perhaps some things just aren't meant to be.

Anyway, do you believe in fate? What d'you think? I'm not so sure I do; I think life's ups and downs are just the luck of the draw, rather than being predetermined. You simply turn over the cards: some fall your way, while others don't.

Having abandoned our search, Suzi and I spent a couple of hours moseying around Darwin's central district, before retiring to the hostel pool for much of the afternoon. The temperature was well in excess of 30 degrees, and the humidity really sapped our energy.

The poolside area, surrounded by palm trees and vibrant fuchsia-filled borders, was an agreeable place in which to relax and stay out of the direct sun. It also proved a good spot from which to write postcards for family and friends back home. For me that included James ... well, naturally it would.

Suzi and I found a table in a shady spot, from which we could survey the pool, take in an afternoon drink, chat about life, and about our friends from York who we were jointly writing to.

I found it really hard thinking about what to say to James. What could I tell him?

> *Dear James,*
>
> *Missing you lots. Suzi and I had a fabulous time with Laura and Phil in Perth. D'you remember Shane from the wedding? He's now got a six-pack that Arnie Schwarzenegger would drool over.*

> *We're now in Darwin, with the humidity off-the-scale. And talking off-the-scale: I just had the most incredible drunken shag with a Mark Hughes lookalike ....*

... No, I don't think so, do you?

Well, Suzi was amused by it all, and suggested various 'hilarious' alternatives to express my infidelity. I did try to look on the funny side.

Of course, on the postcard I had to pretend that everything was still the same ... which, for James, I suppose it was. I couldn't put pen to paper. All I could manage was 'Dear James,' and then, every time I tried to articulate some coherent thoughts, my act of betrayal entered my mind and forced me to stop.

I decided to go for a dip in the pool, and return to the postcards after clearing my head.

Chapter 10: Nothing to write home about

Sunday 12 January 1992 – Darwin, Australia

Late afternoon, by the pool at Paradise Backpackers Hostel. Suzi and I are writing postcards to send home.

Suzi could see I was still struggling.

"So, what is it that you want to tell him?"

"Oh Suzy, I wish I knew."

"Well, why don't you say something like ... 'Met a guy with fingers from heaven, and a cock to knock your socks off.'"

"Ha-bloody-ha!"

"Or how about ... 'Been swept off my feet in Broome; you'd better brush up your technique.' ... No???"

"Yeah, very droll Suzi. But it's not bloody funny."

"Hey Megan ... come on, you know I'm only teasing. And you're my bestie; I want you to be happy."

"So then, seriously, what should I do?"

Suzi's always been a good sounding board, at least when things were important. When James and I had minor fall-outs during the time I was at uni, Suzi was always saying the right things, making me step back to see the bigger picture.

"OK Megan ... well, the first thing to do is to forget about Neil; put him out of your head, as he's gone. However great his cock might've been, you can forget having it inside you again."

I laugh.

"Suzi, I know you're right, but it isn't going to be easy to rub it from my memory."

"True ... nor so easy for me, having walked in on you. He was definitely packing a punch there ... but regards boyfriends, he's long gone."

"I guess you're right."

"So, your only real question concerns James. Is he THE ONE? Is he THE ONE you can see yourself marrying? Is he THE ONE you can see you'd want kids with? Is he THE ONE you'll feel excited about coming home to after a hard day at work? Is he THE ONE you can talk to about day-to-day stuff, and share your problems? Is James your best friend?"

"Hmm ... well, I used to think he was."

"Look Megan, that's really all you've got to think about. I know your sex life might not be great with him ... but how much does that actually matter?"

I told you Suzi was good at this type of stuff.

"Oh Suzi, I don't know. It's definitely not all about the sex ..."

Suzi raises her eyebrows provocatively.

"Really???"

"Yes, really. You ask, is he my best friend? Well, he used to be ... but I don't think so these days. I can't have the type of conversations that I have with you. And I don't mean about men, I mean about the world ... life ... you know, about stuff that matters. I mean, can you see James and I having a serious discussion about mortgages, health insurance or politics? No, when he looks at a newspaper, he's just interested in the boob-girl on page 3, and the latest Newcastle United match. We just don't share the same interests anymore, and perhaps we never really did."

"Well maybe you have your answer?"

"Oh, I don't know Suzi. I mean, maybe it wouldn't be so bad if I was ten years older, and had seen a bit more of life already. But being out here ... it's a real eye opener. I've hardly been beyond Hadrian's Wall before, let alone to the far side of the world. I've got itchy feet, and I need to discover more about life. And ... well, after talking with Laura, and having sampled some Welsh rarebit, it would seem that I've also acquired itches elsewhere."

"Oh, I do hope Neil didn't give you anything nasty."

"No," I laugh, "at least I don't think so. But no, I mean a bit more exploration in the bedroom department would be quite nice too. I mean, before Neil, I've only ever slept with James. You at least road-tested a few before Matt, didn't you?"

"Well, yeah, a couple ... but they weren't exactly Casanovas, and neither was Matt. I don't think 'Mr Perfect' exists; you just have to find your own 'Mr Better-than-ninety-percent.'"

"Ninety percent? I think I'd settle for eighty."

"Eighty-five."

"OK Suzi, well here goes ...

Dear James,

We had a lovely time in Perth with Laura and Phil. Flew to Broome and took bus to Darwin, and the humidity is extreme. Hostels seem good, and there's a great beer called Tooheys that you should try. Planning to go down to Ayers Rock next. Missing you lots.

Megan XXX"

At least postcards don't really give you much space to write.

Chapter 11: Getting acquainted

Saturday 29 August 1992 - Baker Street, London

4:15pm. At the flat. I've just finished sprinkling grated chocolate onto the trifle.

Right, I should just quickly wash up the bowl and pans. It's always better to do these things as you go along, don't you think? I guess most places these days have a dishwasher, don't they? It's just about the only thing this flat doesn't have ... although to be fair, I'd hardly ever use one.
I begin washing the chocolatey Pyrex mixing bowl.
OK, back to the story ... so, where was I?
Oh yes, Darwin ... and I was writing postcards.
Well, it was mid-afternoon the following day, and Suzi and I had been up to Darwin's central shopping strip to find a post office to buy stamps for our postcards. We were returning to our hostel and, by now, I had reconciled my mind to never crossing paths with Neil again ... but then suddenly, we bumped into him on the street.
Before I had any time to react, or think of anything to say, Neil stepped forward and hugged me. He also hugged Suzi, and then invited us both to join him for a swim and evening barbie, over at the Frogshollow Backpackers where he was staying. This was actually one of the hostels we had previously checked, but evidently the lack of surname and inadequate description had hindered our success. Without any thought, I accepted Neil's invitation before Suzi could conjure up any reason to decline.
So, late afternoon, we both walked over to Frogshollow, just a few streets away from Paradise hostel, to go for a swim. Having bumped into Neil again, my brain was telling me I should run a mile, but my lady parts weren't accepting such a course of action; perhaps

they were hoping for some exercise that wasn't just swimming. Well, there was no perhaps about it ... Neil was evidently still friendly, and I was now tingling in anticipation that 'round 2' might be on the cards.

That afternoon and evening I got to know Neil a little better, and we spent some time mutually-flirting, holding hands, pinching bums and so on. We didn't get the opportunity to repeat our Broome performance, but we had a relaxing time, and to be honest, I didn't feel quite the same urgency and lust as I had done before ... my hormone levels were probably lower, and I'd definitely had less alcohol.

Neil and I talked about life back home, and I told him more about James ... well, after bringing his name up during intercourse, it seemed appropriate to tell Neil a bit more about him. There were noticeable similarities between Neil and James: both were exceedingly handsome (in my eyes), they both loved their football, and they both spent an excessive amount of time preening. It also became apparent to Suzi and I that Neil frequently let his eyes stray towards passing females, especially those in swimsuits displaying peachy cheeks and rather too much cleavage.

♦ ♦ ♦

It was that same evening, as Suzi and I were chatting with Neil at the poolside bar, that we first encountered BJ.

Now, BJ was a shy and unassuming character, and he was poles apart from Neil and James. On first impressions, BJ was definitely not as knicker-wettingly (is that a word?) attractive as Neil, but he was still OK-looking. He was tall, blond and athletic, and had a nice firm butt (yes, of course I noticed) ... but he wasn't tongue-hanging-out gorgeous. Having only just arrived in Australia, BJ also looked exceedingly pale. He hadn't yet picked up any suntan, and was still acclimatising to the time difference, and to the fierce sun and humidity of Darwin.

Suzi got to know BJ better than I did that night, as I spent much of my evening more preoccupied with Neil. She developed a soft spot for BJ almost from the start; Suzi's early impressions were that he was well-mannered, engaging, witty and intelligent, which later proved to be the case. He was also interested in what Suzi had to say, unlike so many blokes that you meet ... you know, those guys that'd stick a dick in your mouth, rather than listen to any words coming out of it.

My memory of that evening is now rather vague. We had a long chat over some great barbecued food; I think it was satay-chicken skewers, but I wouldn't be sure. However, I can recall clearly two things from that night. First, I remember we spent many minutes watching a handful of small lizards, running about on the patio area chasing after crickets or cockroaches. Both Neil and BJ told us that the hostel dorms and shower rooms were full of such critters. I was grateful we'd chosen to stay in Paradise hostel, as I don't think I'd have slept much with cockroaches running about.

The second memory was of our introduction when, after announcing himself as Bruce, he then said that all his friends called him BJ ... I nearly choked on my beer. Despite giving such an outwardly shy and innocent impression, such a nickname naturally brought other images to mind. So what? I bet you had the same vision, didn't you? But anyway, you already know my mind's as dirty as a whore's knickers.

Chapter 12: Slap and tickle

Wednesday 15 January 1992 – Darwin, Australia

9:30pm. Poolside at Paradise Backpackers. Suzi and I are thinking about men.

Today's been rather an enjoyable day, but oh so hot. Suzi and I took a bus out to a nearby crocodile sanctuary. It's one of those places where they keep rogue crocs: you know, the individuals that keep straying into villages or anywhere near human habitation. It's illegal to shoot them these days, so the authorities try to move them to safer places. Anyway, today we saw some massive crocs, maybe three or four metres long, and some really evil-looking buggers.

Suzi and I have been by the poolside since around 5pm. A couple of hours ago we had a bite from the barbie ... crayfish skewers in a sweet chilli marinade; they were delicious. You know, ever since trying that seafood on the beach with Phil and Laura, my appetite for it has sky-rocketed.

And now I'm sitting with Suzi in the jacuzzi pool, waiting for Neil to bring me a drink. We've spent a few hours with Neil over the last couple of evenings; there's been the odd cuddle and kiss, but it hasn't gone any further. I have to say it's been quite frustrating at times ... some moments I've felt like Little Miss Horny again, but there's no real opportunity to misbehave. Neil and I are both staying in shared dorms, and it's not like we could go to a secluded spot outdoors as there are large crocs around. So, other than as a cocktail, sex on the beach will remain just a fantasy.

Although I'm frustrated, I do feel a bit less guilty about James now ... well, at least some of the time. After that discussion with Suzi a couple of days back, I think my mind is concluding that I should start afresh in London. I should make a clean break from James, and return to being free and single again. I don't believe now that James is THE ONE, despite us having been together a long time.

We've drifted in different directions, and I just cannot imagine being happy settling down to a life with him, particularly if it means forsaking all others as long as I live. And, if I do get married, I want to be faithful, else what's the point. No, James is not THE ONE; a clean break is what I need.

Having reached this conclusion, I do feel a bit freer now. But no, before you ask ... this isn't an attempt to justify another shag with Neil. Anyhow, although I say this rather flippantly, actually I'm not so sure I want another bout of naked wrestling with him. I mean, Neil's quite good fun, and he's definitely hot, but we're already beginning to run out of conversation. OK, so you tell me you don't shag a conversation, and it's true ... but, although I ache for the sensations I had in Broome, there's no longer the same electricity.

While Neil and I are still getting along well, the downside to him being here tonight is that he's brought along a mate ... a bloke called Andy, from Romford. And Andy is ... well ...

"Suzi, how would you describe Andy?"

"He's an irritating prick."

Suzi's not one to mince her words. In this case, I think she's right on the money; Andy certainly hasn't made a good first impression. I mean, he's quite good looking ... tall, bronze, nice six-pack, squeezable butt and a bulging package; but he also thinks he's God's gift to women and, quite clearly, he isn't. He has an irritating habit of constantly flicking his quiffy bleached hair, and he's always eyeing up different girls as we try to converse. Added to that, he appears to be the dullest man in Dulltown ... and when I say dull, I mean he's really hard work. I thought I was bad at conversation, but this guy dries up after only one or two words. He says a bit more to Neil, but much of that is just misogynistic bullshit and swearing. In short - he's not our cup of tea.

"An irritating prick huh? So, no holding back then Suzi? What other words would you use?"

"Hmm ... infantile, egotistical, sexist ..."

"So, not your perfect match then?"

"Megan, seriously?" She looks at me, and sticks two fingers down her throat.

"OK Suzi, so I know it's not Andy ... but what type of bloke does float your boat? We've talked enough about me, so, who would you jump on if he appeared in this bar tonight? Another Matt perhaps?" You remember that Matt was Suzi's boyfriend for a couple of years at university; he was OK-looking and friendly enough, but he didn't treat her with sufficient respect. Suzi and I never talk about him much; despite us being best mates, she tends to keep her innermost thoughts close to her chest.

"Oh, I don't know ..."

"OK, well let's start with the looks then?" Everyone begins with looks, don't they? It's only natural ... it doesn't mean I'm shallow.

"Well, OK then. So ... obviously he must be tall and handsome ... and a cute butt too ... and also a big package ..."

"You've started to describe Andy..."

"Eewwww-no-no-no!"

"Well, he's got all of that. And for that matter, so's Neil ... well, except maybe he's not so tall."

"OK Megan ... well, perhaps I'm not so worried about how a guy looks."

"No way girl. I saw you ogling Shane and Zak on the beach ... you're every bit as depraved as me."

"Well maybe you're right ... and I suppose there's got to be a minimum standard. Bottom line, I guess ... they must measure up to being shaggable without use of a blindfold." Suzi giggles. "And perhaps even more shaggable while wearing one."

"Oooohh-kinky ... now you're talking. Girl, I think you need another drink inside you."

"Or perhaps something else," Suzi laughs. "So, are you shooting for a second round with Neil then?"

"Chance would be a fine thing; I can hardly take him back to the dorm. Anyway, I don't know now ... but enough of me, you were describing your ideal bloke."

"Ah-yes, saved by the bell," sighs Suzi, as Neil returns with a couple of beers.

"Tooheys OK again?"

"Great Neil ... thanks," I reply.

"Andy and I are going to shoot some pool; the table is finally free. Come and join us?"

"Maybe in a bit," I respond, remaining seated while Neil disappears off to the pool table. I still want to extract more detail from Suzi.

"So, Suzi ... returning to your ideal bloke?"

"Well, I guess if I found someone else a bit like Matt ... oh, I dunno. Matt did have lots of good points, and I still don't really understand why we broke up."

"But you did ... and from what I remember, he didn't always treat you that well. OK, I'll give you that he was pretty good looking, but he was hardly Mr Considerate."

"Perhaps ..."

"There's no perhaps about it, but anyway, it's now time to move on ... for both of us. A new life in London, a million new blokes out there ... and we should also have some fun while we're travelling."

"I'll drink to that."

"So, still not Andy then?" I joke.

"Megan ... come off it."

"Or, how about Bruce? I can't believe his friends call him BJ ... it's so cruel. I'm sure he could do with a blowjob though; I bet the poor lad's never had one. He seems too ... what's the right word ... sheltered ... middle class ..."

"Oh, come on Megan, you hardly need to be a working-class guy to get a blowjob ... think of all those public-school toffs at uni; there were girls all over them. And anyway, Bruce was just sensitive and reserved. He also made me laugh ... he's quite cute actually."

"Uh-huh? OK ... that's news. So, could he be your type then?"

"Who, Bruce?"

"Yeah."

"Hmm ..."

"OK then Suzi ... marks out of ten? Would you give him one?"

"Oh, you're always so crude," says Suzi, sipping her beer, and pausing for thought. "Having said that ... uh-huh, maybe I would. OK, so he isn't Tom-Cruise-like gorgeous, but he's still quite fetching ... and he looks athletic."

"Uh-huh, yeah ... I'm sure he could go ten rounds horizontally."

"And he does have a cracking bum."

"Oh, you noticed too then?"

"Duh! Obviously. So, how about you then? You'd shag him too, would you Megan?"

"I'm horny enough to shag anyone right now Suzi."

"Oh yeah? Even Andy?"

"OK, there are some exceptions ... and anyway, I think he's got his eyes set on you."

"Oh, fuck off Megan ... no way."

♦ ♦ ♦

11:30pm. Back in our dorm at Paradise Backpackers, I'm waiting for Suzi to return from the washrooms.

It turns out that I was right about Andy; he did have his sights on Suzi and, unfortunately, it was more than just a keen eye.

We eventually joined Neil and Andy to play pool and, at first, it was great because the guys also bought us more drinks. To be fair, we actually had quite a lot of fun. Naturally, I teamed up with Neil and, periodically, I allowed him to fondle my bum as he assisted me with my cueing technique. Of course, it had nothing to do with my cueing, but what did I care?

Flirting with Neil was all in jest. However, when Andy, without being invited, attempted a similar approach with Suzi, it was not such fun, and indeed was totally unacceptable. Needless to say, it didn't go down well with Suzi.

As I was focussed more on Neil, I didn't witness everything that happened between the two of them ... but I did see the final straw, when Andy tried to grope Suzi's boobs, and she smacked him hard around the face. Suzi then stormed off and went back to our dorm. I followed straight after.

If it'd been me, I might've expected it ... as I've been more than a bit flirty since we arrived in Australia. Not so Suzi, I've never really seen her flirty, and there's no way she was giving off any signs to Andy. He just blatantly overstepped the mark, and a smack around the face was the least he deserved. My god, that bloke is such a tosser.

I don't think I've ever seen Suzi so angry. Oh, no actually ... there was one occasion in a nightclub in York a couple of years ago; she decked a guy on the dancefloor for much the same thing. Yeah, don't mess with my girl ... she can take care of herself.

♦ ♦ ♦

11:40pm. Suzi returns from the washrooms.

"Hey babe, I was just remembering the time you punched that bloke in the nightclub ... you've got a great right hand."

"Oh yeah, I'd forgotten about that. What a jerk ... I think he was also called Andy."

"Are you OK babe?"

"Yeah, no harm done ... at least, not to me."

"Good."

There's a pause for a minute or so while Suzi wipes off her make-up, getting ready for bed.

"So, babe, I guess we've established your ideal bloke is probably not an Andy? Perhaps you should move to names beginning with B."

"Yeah, maybe. Hey, I'm sorry if I ruined your fun with Neil."

"Oh, don't worry about it. It wasn't as if I could bring him back here anyway."

"So, d'you think you and Neil will …"

"Nah …" I interrupt.

"You don't know what I was going to say."

"Yeah Suzi, I do. You want to know if Neil's going to be more than just a one-night shag."

"Well, yeah. Is he?"

"Probably not. Don't get me wrong, I like Neil … but he is a bit full of himself, don't you think? It's a shame you can never find the right mix in a guy."

"What, you mean six-inches, six-pack and a six-figure salary?"

"Babe, you're talking like me now … but I was thinking more like eight."

We both laugh.

"No Suzi, like you, I agree it can't be all about the looks. It's got to be someone who really gets you, and makes you laugh. A guy who picks you up when you're down; a bloke that doesn't give you those awkward pauses when you can't think of anything to say. It was like that when I first started with James … but it's not anymore, and I don't think we'll ever get it back."

"It's a shame. And maybe that type of drift is also what happened between me and Matt."

"So, it was not that he only had six inches then?"

"Oh Megan … always so crude. But no, it wasn't … although, I wouldn't have said no to another inch or two."

"Well, it's a shame that Andy's such a moron; he certainly looks quite stacked down there …"

"Yeah … but he's so gross."

"Well, no worries girl … lots more fish in the sea …"

"Yeah ... including sharks ... oh, and there's also crocodiles, jellyfish and sea snakes ..."

"And diving instructors ... don't forget about them. Hey Suzi, have you thought any more about getting out to The Reef when we reach Cairns?"

"Actually no, not much ... at least not in relation to sexy instructors. I did talk about diving with Hannah and Marianne back in Broome, while you were humping Neil. They went on a three-day dive trip out from Cairns. They said it was expensive, but they were so pumped about having done it. Despite the cost, it would be pretty awesome. And, even if we didn't dive, it'd still be great to get out on a yacht for a few days' rest and relaxation."

"And perhaps a little eye-candy?"

"Well, maybe that too. I did see a couple of leaflets in the reception here; we could ask more about it tomorrow ... and I guess we might need to book ahead."

"Good thinking Poirot! I knew I brought you for a reason."

"Well Megan, I'm glad you didn't bring me along to keep you out of trouble ... I've already failed in that regard."

"Perhaps so ... but at least I made sure he wore a condom."

Chapter 13: Sweet potato

Saturday 29 August 1992 - Baker Street, London

4:30pm. At the flat. I've just put the trifle in the fridge, and I'm now continuing with the food prep.

OK now, so the trifle needs to chill for a couple of hours.

Yes, chilling ... that was one of the great things about travelling in Australia; it was such a relaxing place to be. Several of the backpacker hostels had swimming pools, some with jacuzzies, and they also had their own bars and barbecues. It was a great environment in which to unwind ... well, apart from when blokes like Andy turned up. Thankfully, we didn't meet anyone else quite as obnoxious as him. There were a few who ran him close, but he was the worst.

Anyway, you've now been introduced to Bruce ... and although he didn't make much of a first impression with me, Suzi had quickly taken to him. Mind you, back in Darwin, with Andy as a comparison, any other bloke seemed like quite a catch.

Hang on a minute, I just need a quick time check ... BJ should arrive around 7:30 ... so ... yeah, there's still plenty of time.

OK, so next I should get the sweet potatoes going ... I suppose I could get BJ to mash them later, while I fry the scallops. Yeah, if I just peel them now, and then leave them in water. Wow, I'm so impressed with how organised I am today. Suck on that Delia Smith, Megan's on fire!

Oh, hang on though, now that's a thought ... maybe I shouldn't let BJ help too much; he is rather clumsy. If you put him near a coffee machine, he's a total disaster ... three times I think, I've seen him poor coffee all over the floor. And it's not just coffee; I don't think he's great with machines in general. I remember that condom dispenser he broke in Melbourne; we had to pick up dozens of packs from the floor ... I think I've still got one of them somewhere. That being said, BJ really is a sweetie ... he's one of the most caring and considerate people I've ever met.

I open the bag of sweet potatoes, and take out two good size ones, a little larger than my fist. I don't want too much; this is just the starter. I then begin to peel them.

You know, if BJ was a vegetable, he'd be a sweet potato. He's very understated and doesn't stand out from a crowd. And, while BJ mightn't be my first thought of a satisfying feast, there's a subtly different flavour about him. What kind of rubbish am I talking now? Please stop me wittering on ... but anyway, he really is a sweet guy.

So, returning to what I was saying ...

Following that incident with Andy, Suzi and I stayed in Darwin for another two or three nights. We didn't see anything further of Neil or BJ, nor thankfully Andy. We occupied much of our time relaxing by the hostel pool. Then, after Darwin, we took a 24-hour bus ride south to Alice Springs.

We stayed for a night at a hostel in Alice before setting off on a two-day desert tour, which took us to Kings Canyon and Ayers Rock, or Uluru, as it's now known. And my god, it was scorching-hot in the middle of the day; it was a good thing we passed so much of the time in an air-conditioned Landcruiser.

We spent a night under canvas in Yulara, the resort closest to Ayers Rock, so as to be ready to climb The Rock early the next morning. That evening and late into the night, our small group ate an enormous feast of barbecued beef, pork and chicken, as we chilled out with a few beers while gazing up at the stars. It was fabulous, and I've never seen such a star-filled sky.

However, I do remember being a bit disappointed by the sunset. You're meant to be able to watch the colours of The Rock change as the sun goes down but, except for the light fading, neither Suzi nor I could detect any difference.

Chapter 14: Ding-dong!

Wednesday 22 January 1992 – Ayers Rock (Uluru), Australia

6:30am. Suzi and I have just begun the climb up Ayers Rock, and are pleased that we've made it beyond the tricky first part of the ascent.

"Well Suzi, we made it past Chicken Rocks ... so, I guess it's onwards and upwards."

"It's supposed to get easier now," says Suzi, catching her breath.

"It's worth it for the views though, isn't it?"

"And not a cloud in the sky ... I wonder how many miles we can see."

"Well babe, just look at how tiddly those buses are down there; we must be quite high up now."

The initial steepness levels off a little, but then we encounter a series of undulations, some with sheer faces that are hard to scramble up.

"Hey Suzi, gimme a hand, will you? Nobody told us about this part."

"Yeah, you'd have thought it'd be much flatter along the top. I suppose it's the wind that erodes these channels; I guess it can't be water ... it probably never rains here."

Suzi seems to be coping well but, as we arrive at a twenty-foot bank, I'm struggling to make it up.

"Well, DING-DONG!!! Are you a damsel in distress?" I hear a male voice immediately behind me, and turn my head. "May I be of assistance?"

I smile, delighted to see a familiar face that's painted with a cheeky grin.

"Oh, hi BJ! Fancy meeting you here."

"Hi BJ!" calls Suzi from a few yards further ahead. "It's great to see you. It's not so easy-going up here, is it?"

I allow BJ to take my hand, and he helps me up the slope. His palms are a bit sweaty, and so are mine, but it's nice to feel the warmth of his skin. I never used to be touchy-feely with other blokes, partly because of being with James so long ... but today I seem instinctively tactile towards BJ.

For some reason, and don't ask me why because I don't know, I suddenly decide that some theatricals are in order. On reaching the top of the slope, I collapse into BJ's arms.

"Please doctor, will you carry me from here?"

BJ catches me, but is clearly shocked by my actions, and his body trembles under my grasp. I'm unsure as to whether his shaking is a result of the climb, or because he's nervous around me ... perhaps it's a bit of both. BJ steadies me, and puts his left arm around my waist; he's still a little wobbly, but all the same it's nice to have a cuddle. As he holds on to prevent me falling, I squeeze him a bit tighter until, after a few moments, I suddenly feel that BJ's more than just trembling ... he's now got a stiffy.

"Oh BJ! You really are pleased to see me," I whisper. I smile at him, and see a massive blush arrive across his face ... poor bloke.

"You must have that effect on me," he says. "Unless it's just the vertigo."

"Oh Megan, do put him down!" shouts Suzi. I think she's a bit annoyed with my flirting. "I can't take you anywhere; you're so embarrassing."

I steady myself, before releasing BJ and stepping back. It's a good thing he's sporting baggy shorts with his polo shirt, rather than the tight-fitting Lycra that Suzi and I are wearing. While I'm well aware of BJ's excitement, it's not so noticeable to others. *I wonder how big he is though ... mmm-yes, he's certainly carrying a decent package. I know ... my mind's back in the gutter again.*

We continue to scramble over the undulating sandstone, with BJ offering his hand whenever I ask ... which, of course, is far more than I really need. I'm not really flirting ... no, honestly, I'm not. And anyway, I'm sure BJ's not my type, but he does seem really friendly.

We finally reach the official summit of The Rock, which is marked by a metre-high hexagonal granite slab. There's a bronze hexagonal chart mounted on top, engraved with arrows pointing towards different places around Australia, and to the world beyond.

BJ encounters a couple of lads from his tour-group, and introduces them to me and Suzi. I haven't noticed the other blokes from our group anywhere; they quickly disappeared ahead of us at the beginning of the climb.

"It says 15,000 kilometres to London," declares Suzi.

"Yeah, we'd better have fun before going back to start work there," I respond.

"Are you both going to work in London when you get back?" BJ asks. "Me too ... what jobs d'you have?"

Suzi and I tell BJ of our recruitment into the exciting fields of law and finance and discover that, like Suzi, BJ is joining one of the big accountancy firms. The world of work, however, seems so distant, and is far less inspiring than standing at the top of Ayers Rock, gazing out across the desert to the horizon. The views are tremendous: in one direction, the shape of Mount Connor is clearly distinguishable with its massive bulk and flattened top; while looking the opposite way, there's the group of vast red-sandstone rocks known as The Olgas.

"What a fantastic view," I say, placing my arm around BJ's waist, as we gaze across towards The Olgas.

"Too right," he agrees. But BJ's not looking where I am. Instead, he has his eyes focussed on Suzi's bum, totally checking her out, while she's bending over to tie her shoe laces.

"Hey BJ ... filthy mind!" I laugh, as I slap him on the bum. "Just keep your eyes on the wonderful scenery."

"I was ..." he says, smirking. "It's spectacular, isn't it?"

Suzi doesn't notice, and I don't enlighten her. Just in that moment, I realise that I'm a tad jealous of Suzi catching his attention. To be fair though, Suzi does possess a fantastic bum. Mine's not bad either, but Suzi's definitely got the better curves.

◆ ◆ ◆

The descent of The Rock was less tiring than the climb, but just as difficult, and straining on the calves. I spent most of the way down chatting to BJ, while Suzi went more quickly ahead of us. Just as he did on the way up, BJ assisted me when I needed it, and we shared a joke or two.

Although I'd been preoccupied with Neil, and hadn't really noticed him when we first met in Darwin, BJ was definitely growing on me. Suzi's description of 'shy, intelligent and witty,' seemed pretty accurate.

As we arrived back at the car park before re-joining our respective groups, BJ and I discovered that we were both planning to take the same bus from Alice Springs to Tennant Creek the next day. We said our farewells, hugged each other, and then went our separate ways.

◆ ◆ ◆

Wednesday 22 January 1992 – Alice Springs, Australia

9:30am. The Ranges Backpackers Hostel, Alice Springs. Having gone our different ways after climbing Ayers Rock, Suzi and I spent an hour or so walking around The Olgas with our group, before enduring a long afternoon drive to return to Alice Springs. We are now in the pool at our hostel, with a handful of others, but it's far from busy. We're relaxing to the sounds of INXS booming out from the bar. Each of us is sipping from a bottle of Coke ... we're abstaining from alcohol tonight.

"It's great that these hostels have pools," says Suzi. "It's still so warm ... you'd have thought it'd be much cooler in the evening."

"Yeah babe, you would. Hey Suzi, I wonder which hostel BJ's staying in."

"BJ? He made an impression today, didn't he?"

"Uh-huh, yeah, maybe. Why d'you ask?"

"Oh nothing."

"C'mon Suzi, it's never nothing, is it? D'you want to claim him for yourself? Is that it?"

"Ha-ha Megan ... no, not really. But I can tell you like him."

"Well, yeah actually ... he is quite cute ... and ..."

"And what?"

"Oh nothing ..."

"Megan?" Suzi raises her eyebrows; she never lets me get away with only half an answer.

"Well, OK then. Well, you remember me throwing myself at him when we first met above Chicken Rocks this morning?"

"I did notice."

"Well ... when I pressed up against him, he got rather excited."

"What? As in getting a stiffy? ... Megan, you're kidding?"

"I'm not, I swear it."

"Oh, poor BJ. My god Megan, I bet you scared the life out of him."

"Why d'you say that?"

"Well, he's pretty shy ... and I guess he's not dated too many girlfriends."

"Well, that may or may not be true ... but he's packing it where it counts." I chuckle. "Yeah, he felt comparable to James ... but perhaps not quite a Neil size."

"Wow! He truly must've been thrilled to see you."

"Oh, I dunno Suzi, it's not as if guys can actually control when they stand to attention, is it? And besides, it was your peachy backside, not mine, that he was checking out at the summit."

"What d'you mean?"

"Checking out your assets, babe ... your awesome bum. Yeah, when you were bending over to tie your shoes, BJ was totally checking you out. Oh boy, how I wish I had an arse like yours."

"Really? It sounds like his mind's as dirty as yours."

"Oh Suzi, you do say the nicest of things."

Both of us take a quick pause in conversation, while sipping from our Cokes.

"So then Megan ... you say that BJ's going to be on our bus tomorrow?"

Suzi takes another sip of her Coke.

"Yep."

I take a sip of mine.

"OK then Megan ... does this mean it's game on?"

I laugh, and barely prevent a mouthful of Coke going up my nose.

"Suzi, I can't believe you just said that. I've never seen your wicked side before ... I like it."

"I guess you haven't. But, in contrast to you, I never drop my self-respect and just throw myself at anyone."

How dare she say that about me? It was rather catty, don't you think? However, I can't really argue, can I? After all, I did rather throw myself at Neil. It was out of character though, and I never used to do that ... well, why would I, I've been with the same bloke since I was fourteen.

"Hey Suzi, that was a bit below the belt ... but I guess I deserve it. Anyway, changing the subject, how long's the bus ride tomorrow?"

"Oh my god, d'you really want to know? It's a bloody long one. We leave here at 6:00am, and I don't think we arrive in Cairns until late afternoon on Friday ... I don't even want to think about it."

"Yeah, maybe we should've booked our diving trip a day or two later. Still, I guess it's all the sooner that we meet those hot diving instructors."

"Uh-huh ... and I'm sure you'll be testing out your chat-up lines with BJ tomorrow."

"I guess you will too, babe ... you will too."

Chapter 15: Questionable intent

Thursday 23 January 1992 – Alice Springs, Australia

5:45am. The bus station, Alice Springs. I'm with Suzi, waiting to catch the bus to begin our journey across to the Queensland coast.

I don't know why, but I've woken up today with a spring in my step. It's unusual that I'm this bouncy, especially not at this hour ... just ask Suzi.

We are standing next to our backpacks, waiting to board the bus to take us north from Alice to Tennant Creek. I think it's about eight hours to get there, but, after Tennant Creek, we've got a connecting bus for another twenty or so hours over to Townsville on the Queensland Coast. And that's not the end of it, because at Townsville we change for several more hours up to Cairns. The bus ride from Darwin to Alice seemed like a killer, but this journey is on another scale. Suzi and I certainly miscalculated when we booked up our scuba course in Cairns; we should have given ourselves an extra day or two to get there.

We arrived at the bus station a couple of minutes ago. We're also expecting to see BJ, as he told us he'd be taking the same bus. Perhaps he's the reason why I feel so energised this morning. I don't think I fancy BJ, but there is something about him; something different ... and I can't deny I'm a bit excited about seeing him.

"Hi BJ!" Suzi spots him first.

Suzi also claims that she spotted him first in the territorial sense, although I don't think that'll prevent me from flirting with BJ, if I happen to feel like it. I didn't think that Suzi or I were possessive about blokes, but I suppose I've been with James all the time that I've known her and, for more than half of that, she was also with Matt. I guess that being free and single moves the goalposts.

"Hi girls," BJ replies. "I'm so glad we're catching the same bus."

"Hi BJ, my wonderful travel buddy," I say. "I hope you've got lots to talk about; Suzi and I are starting to run out of conversation."

Suzi gets to hug him first, before I take my turn.

"Hey BJ, you're not as pleased to see me today." As I press against him, there's no sign of arousal, but my comment triggers the onset of BJ's blushes.

"What can I say?" he responds. "It's a bit colder at this time in the morning."

I can see Suzi smirk and, at the same time, I think she's a little irritated that I've already started teasing BJ.

♦ ♦ ♦

The bus pulls in on schedule and, assisted by the driver, we begin to load our backpacks into the luggage hold.

"Tennant Creek, onward for Cairns," I say to the driver, as Suzi and I leave our backpacks and climb the steps into the bus.

"Tennant Creek, then for Townsville," says BJ following us.
There are nine or ten other passengers boarding here, but thankfully the bus will be far from crowded.

"Are you not stopping at Townsville?" BJ asks Suzi. "Are you going all the way to Cairns in one go?"

"Yep, all the way," replies Suzi.

"So, how many more hours is that?"

"A few too many," says Suzi. "It's gonna be a long couple of days."

We walk about two thirds of the way towards the back of the bus, before Suzi and I choose seats across the aisle from each other.

"So, why are you travelling to Cairns in one journey?" BJ continues, as he drops his daypack on the seat behind Suzi.

"It's a bit stupid, I know," say Suzi, "... but we've booked ourselves on a five-day diving trip, and we mis-calculated the days a little. So, we're now in a rush to get there."

"Ah-yes! Easy to do when these distances are so vast. I bet it'll be great when you get there. I was hoping to learn to dive when I get to Cairns too, but I haven't really looked into the options. Perhaps you can tell me what you know? We've got a bit of time to kill!"

"Well, that's certainly true," I interject. "Did you enjoy Ayers Rock? What did you do after you left us?"

"I guess much the same as you."

As we settle into our seats waiting for the bus to depart, the three of us chat further, comparing notes about the last couple of days. The trip into the Red Centre had been a tremendous experience, and the desert landscape had been so different from anything I'd ever seen.

As the bus sets off, we settle in our seats but continue conversing, and begin to talk about what we did at university. BJ studied zoology at Oxford, so I guess he must be quite brainy. At York, Suzi studied biology, whereas I did history. Suzi and BJ are also quite sporty: both of them play badminton and tennis, whereas my limit is being a couch potato, and watching the eye-candy on *Match of the Day.* They are also both moving into accountancy jobs when we all start working in London. On the face of it, it would appear that Suzi and BJ are actually quite a good fit.

Anyway, the three of us chat away for the best part of three hours. We talk about so many things, from TV shows to our childhoods, from places we know, to politics and sexism. We also spend several minutes discussing the racism we've encountered in Australia in respect of the indigenous people ... some quite heavy stuff.

♦ ♦ ♦

We stop for a short comfort-break at a roadhouse in the tiny settlement of Barrow Creek, and disembark the bus for several minutes in order to use the toilets, get a quick snack, and stretch our legs. After this we're back on board and on our way again. We resume our seats and, at this point, Suzi decides it's time to switch off, listen to her Walkman, and maybe get some sleep.

"How about you BJ, d'you need a rest from my constant nattering?" I ask, half expecting he'll want some time to himself.

"Not at all," he responds, shuffling over to the window seat, allowing me to squeeze in beside him. I feel a quick surge of adrenalin as I hop across the aisle; I'm really feeling energised.

"Now you're stuck with me," I declare. "OK BJ, let's get on to some more interesting topics."

"Oh ... OK."

I sense a bit of hesitancy in his voice.

"How about your sex life? ... Are you spoken for?" Straight to the point ... *I'm good, aren't I?*

"I usually have to speak for myself," he replies, trying to deflect my question. It won't work.

"No BJ, tell me more; I want to know." And it's true; I'm really keen to find out. "Tell me all about your love life; we've got plenty of time."

He pauses for a moment before replying.

"Well ... OK then ... but only on condition you tell me all your secrets afterwards." I thought that might be a part of it, but hey, that's good ... at least he's interested. "So, Megan, where d'you want me to start?"

"OK BJ ... so, how about your first kiss?" I throw in an easy starter to warm him up.

"Alright then, let me think." BJ hesitates, and turns his head to look out of the window.

"It can't be that hard, can it? Unless you've been with hundreds of girls ... and anyway, they say you always remember the first kiss like it was yesterday."

"No ... no ... I'm just trying to recall." He turns his attention back to me, his blue eyes twinkling as he catches my gaze. "Well, it wasn't yesterday ... and it's been such a long time since I thought of her." BJ pauses, as though composing himself before a performance. "OK ... so ... it was when I was twelve, or was I thirteen? ... It was at this party ... you know, one of those house parties when parents have gone away for the weekend ... at a time when you've just discovered the merits of cheap cider. Anyway, there was this girl ... Sarah ... and despite being only thirteen or so, she already seemed to have quite a reputation. Well ... at this party, I was the one ... or perhaps only one of a few that she pounced on for a snog. Wow! ... I haven't thought about her for years ... but I can still remember the kiss."

"They say you never forget the first," I interrupt. "So, how was it?"

"Hard to describe ... pretty good ... warm, moist ... and alcoholic. She must've been on stronger stuff than cider. ... Mmm-yeah, she was kinda-hot!"

"Then what happened?"

"Well ... it was also the first time anyone had triggered an erection."

"Oh yes ... so it's not just me then," I tease, and glance towards his crotch, just to check. I'm not subtle enough, and he catches my gaze, so I quickly try to deflect with another question. "OK ... so ... who was the next girl?"

Perhaps I'm a bit mean, but I then follow up with a thorough interrogation ... maybe it's useful practice for my legal training. Anyway, I discover that BJ is currently single, and has endured years of frustration, searching for that one special girl who never seems to come along. I don't know if my own situation, being attached for several years without exploring, is better or worse than BJ's. At least I've had more shags, even if they were mostly devoid of climax. Is mediocre sex better than no sex at all? It must be ... surely?

BJ seems so laid-back and easy to talk to. Mind you, I suppose it's relaxing for me, as I'm the one asking all the questions. Perhaps I need to give him a chance. Despite my eagerness to learn more, I pause my questioning, and allow him to surface for air. This gives him the opportunity to change tack.

"OK Megan, now it's your turn. Tell me about you?"

"You don't really want me to tell you, do you BJ? But we were getting on so well."

"Oh, most definitely." BJ's eyes light up, and I can sense he's more relaxed now I've given him power over the questions. "I want to hear every detail. Like you said, we have plenty of time."

"Oh, alright then BJ ... so, where should I begin?"

As I speak, BJ turns his head and, for the first time, we share one of those eye-to-eye moments; you know, the type when you linger for a second or two longer than you should. It's the first time that I'm properly noticing his blue-grey eyes. They aren't piercing like many blue ones; there's a softness, a warmth, a wonderful sparkle ... and they betray that he's full of mischief. He's thinking something naughty about me right now, I just know he is.

"OK," he continues. "How about ... oh yes ... are you currently attached?"

That's actually a good one. Am I, or am I not? I'm stumped by the first question. I used to have an immediate reply of yes ... but, right now, I'm not so sure.

"Well, yes ... sort of ..." I reply.

"What kind of an answer is that? What d'you mean?"

Fair point ... it was a bit of a crap answer, wasn't it?

"Well," I explain, "... back home, I guess I still have a long-term boyfriend ... James. And I suppose we're pretty good together ..."

"And ...?"

"Well, James was my first real love ... like, since we were teenagers ... and before you ask, he was actually my first kiss too. He now works in construction in Newcastle, and wants us to settle down."

"And you ...?"

"Well, I don't know. I think I love him and all, but I feel there's got to be more to life ... you know, it's sort of why I'm out here with Suzi. It sounds corny, but I guess I'm trying to find myself ... I don't know, maybe I'm trying to experience or discover new things ... or maybe just trying to get things out of my system."

"Uh-huh ... and ... so, what was the deal with you and Neil in Darwin then?"

Where did that one come from? Oh fuck! I don't usually blush, but I can start to feel heat in my cheeks.

"What did he tell you BJ?" *Bugger, what did Neil say about me?*

"Hey, not so fast, these are my questions."

"That's cruel BJ." And it was ... so I poke BJ in the ribs before continuing. "Well, OK. So, Neil was a great guy ... I thought he was handsome, friendly, chatty; we just got a bit drunk and a bit friendly, and then one thing led to another."

"This was in Broome, was it?"

"So, Neil did tell you something, didn't he? What did he say?"

"A little," BJ responds. He's not going to tell me.

"OK ... well, yes it was in Broome. Suzi and I were having more than a few drinks at the hostel bar, and Neil joined us. I felt really horny, and ... oh BJ, I can't believe I'm telling you this; I've only known you five minutes."

"True, but you now know all about my first kiss ... so please go on." *Yeah BJ, but a kiss is never an equal trade for a shag, by any measurement.*

"Well ... Suzi reminded me about James back home, but I just needed a good night ... you know?"

"I'm not sure I do know, but do please go on," says BJ, teasing me with his smile. *I'm so going to get him back for this later, but I'm actually finding it quite therapeutic to talk.*

"So, anyway, after snogging a bit, I took Neil back to our dorm. Luckily Suzi and I had a room to ourselves ... although, I'm not sure that other people being there would've stopped me. And then we had the most wonderful fuck. Oh ... lush ... it was so good." I start giggling, realising what I'm saying but, on reflection, that shag with Neil in Broome had been pretty awesome.

My giggles are clearly infectious, and BJ starts laughing too.

"I didn't realise that girls used the word 'fuck'."

"I know, I'm such a potty mouth; Suzi's always telling me."

"So," he continues, "... then what? I want to know all the details."

It's funny, but I thought I'd feel more guarded with this personal stuff, but it's actually quite relaxing to talk about.

"Well ... after shagging, Neil then started to fall asleep ... but I wanted more." I can't stop myself giggling as I talk. "And so, I tied him up to the bed with these straps, and I'm about to give him oral ... and ..." I pause for a minute as I have the image in my head ... "Oh BJ, I still can't believe you get called 'BJ'... I know I have a dirty mind, but BJ? Really?" *I can't imagine the ribbing his friends must give him.* "Sorry," I continue, "where was I? Oh yes ... well ... then Suzi comes back into the room, and I'm sure she was disgusted with me. She doesn't say a word; she just strips off, and goes to bed."

"And ...?"

"And what?... She gets into bed; Neil and I finish off so-to-speak ... and that was it." *Yeah, now I come to think about it ... we'd only just got warmed up.*

"And Suzi ...?" *Wow, BJ certainly wants all the detail.*

"She just got into bed, and tried to pretend we weren't there. And that was it. So, was that what Neil told you?"

"Well, he didn't elaborate quite that much," BJ says with a raised eyebrow. "So then, what happened in Darwin? Neil seemed really keen on you; he was sorry when you left."

"Well, we were getting on fine ... fooling around a bit ... but then I felt really guilty about James. It's terrible, but I keep feeling so horny. That sex was lush ... better than I ever had with James. I just can't get it out of my head ... I want more ... God, why am I telling you this? And ... no, I can't say ... oh, what-the-heck ... well, I'm feeling horny right now just talking about it. It's a good job there are people on the bus BJ, or what I might do with you." *Oh bugger, I didn't mean to say all that. Why don't I ever keep my trap shut?*

I continue ... "And then there was also this guy from Essex; some mate of Neil, and a real idiot. He started trying it on with Suzi in the hostel bar. And Suzi ... well, she's not such a slutty girl like me. She slapped him, and stormed off. I followed, and we haven't seen either of them since."

"Neil seemed a bit sad that you'd gone."

"Ah well ... I liked Neil ... but mainly it was the sex with someone new ... I just can't get it out of my head, you know?" *Oh my god, can you just imagine if I was saying all this to Mammy, or Beth?* I start to giggle again. "I never realised I could have multiple orgasms before. ... Oh fuck! Why am I telling you all this?" *Oh well, I am now ... so why stop?*

BJ continues to smile, his eyes urging me to divulge more.

"Oh, anyway," I continue, "Suzi seems to like you; she gets a bit pissed-off when she sees me starting to flirt. She's not cheating on anyone back home, and has been waiting a long time for the right guy to come along. Suzi's not like me. God, I'm such a slut, aren't I?" *There, I said it.* I breathe out.

BJ allows a pause before he responds.

"Wow! You know, this feels like being on the school bus when I was thirteen, although at least now I'm a bit less nervous talking with girls. Look, I don't think that you're slutty," he smiles, "... although ... well actually, yes I do."

How dare you? I give BJ a playful punch in the ribs, before he responds.

"The last girlfriend I had only went out with me after breaking her wrist. She punched me like that. My ribs are rock-hard, you see."

As he lifts his polo-shirt to demonstrate the firmness of his abs, I can't help noticing that something else might also be a little hard; his cut-off denim shorts are revealing a bulge at the front. My pulse begins to quicken, but he doesn't detect where my eyes have travelled, as he continues ...

"But Megan, you aren't slutty in such a bad way. If you don't know what you want in life ... well ... who am I to say? You and Suzi ... you're both very sexy girls. Now, I'm probably beginning to sound like your dad, aren't I?"

"Blimey BJ! I'd never tell any of this to him; he'd never speak to me again."

We laugh.

We continue talking and discuss how being in Australia, and such a long way from home, feels so liberating. There's nobody around checking up on us all the time ... although, in my case, I guess I still have Suzi.

I rest my head on BJ's shoulder as we chat. It's funny how I feel so relaxed in his company ... and maybe I've also just got a weight off my chest. Talking about James and Neil has been soothing, although I hope I didn't bore BJ too much.

As the hours pass, our conversation dries up, and we doze for a while. I wake up as the bus pulls to a halt. I guess we must have arrived at Tennant Creek, where we have to change buses.

"So, what've you two been talking about?" asks Suzi, peering through the gap between the seats. She's clearly managed to get a few hours of slumber.

"Oh, we were just setting the world to rights," BJ responds, smiling at me.

"Yes, perhaps we were," I agree.

Suzi looks at me quizzically, as if to ask what we've really been talking about. I tap my nose to tell her it's none of her business. She smiles back ... with a distinct hint of annoyance.

♦ ♦ ♦

12:30pm. The roadhouse at Tennant Creek.

The bus sets us down, and we extract our backpacks from the luggage hold, before heading into the main building at the roadhouse. We have at least two hours to kill before boarding our connecting bus towards Townsville.

None of us had seen anything interesting as we came into town (well, I was dozing), but as it's fiercely hot outside, we decide to prop ourselves up in a corner of the roadhouse café. We're a bit disoriented with the time, but it's just after noon, so we decide to get a bite to eat.

BJ sets off towards the back of the building to find the washrooms and, after a couple of minutes, I do likewise. Outside, at the rear of the main building, there's a small yard in which a few young children are trying to feed a group of wallabies. There's also a rather imposing emu ... I'd never realised quite how tall they are.

As I look across the yard, I spot BJ in front of the doors to the washrooms. He's got his back to me. I walk past the wallabies towards him, and find that BJ's standing in front of a condom dispenser, seemingly reading the instructions. I tiptoe up to him and gently give him a smack on the bum ... and he nearly jumps out of his skin.

"Hey BJ! D'you have anyone special in mind?"

"Jeez Megan, you have a great knack of catching me off-guard."

BJ's face was, once again, flushed with embarrassment.

Without another word, I wink at him with a knowing smile, before slipping off into the ladies' toilet.

Was he just looking; or was BJ buying a pack? Maybe he's got his eye on Suzi. Or perhaps even me? I guess it could be ... but what if it is?

I step into a cubicle and sit on the toilet. I can't help it, but thoughts of sex with BJ now race across my mind.

What would I do if he made a move on me? Do I want him to? Hmm ... it wouldn't be the worst thing ever, would it? BJ's quite cute ... oh, and downstairs he is rather well-stacked. Oh my, I'm getting sluttier every day. Calm yourself girl ... he's probably got his sights elsewhere.

I wash and dry my hands, brush my hair, and reapply some lip balm. As I leave the washroom, I meet Suzi coming the other way.

"Hey Suzi, d'you like the animals?"

"Yeah ... but BJ said to keep clear of the emu."

"Oh babe, I've gotta tell you this. I just gave BJ the fright of his life. He was standing over there studying the condom machine, so I crept up behind him and smacked his bum. He must've jumped six feet in the air."

Suzi laughs ... "Oh, you're so cruel. So, did he buy any?"

"I don't know babe, but I think he's got his eye on you."

"More likely you, Megan ... you've just spent the last few hours with him."

"Look, I'll only be a minute. Wait for me; I want to see his reaction when we return inside."

"OK ... I'll be right here with the wallabies."

Suzi's got a bit of a wicked streak; she's just like me. She also wants to see how much BJ blushes the next time he sees us. *Or maybe ... yes maybe, she just wants to prevent me from getting to him first. Yes, perhaps that's her game ... anyway, no matter.*

A few minutes later, Suzi and I return inside. As we approach and smile at BJ, his face flushes again. This time, however, it's almost as though the atmosphere has changed ... it's like we've sussed him out, and he's become all shy and inhibited again.

BJ's got his Lonely Planet guide open, and is looking at the information on Townsville.

"Why don't you come up to Cairns with us?" invites Suzi, before I can say anything. *I wish I'd thought of it first.* I've never really seen Suzi on-the-pull, but I think she might be about to start.

"Well, I'd love to spend more time with you, but you'll be off on a boat for the best part of a week, won't you? If I stop off in Townsville and do Magnetic Island, I'll probably be up in Cairns just as you finish your diving. I'd love to meet up with you then."

"D'you know where you're going to stay?" asks Suzi.

Damn, she's quicker off the mark again. Hang on ... why does that bother me? Am I getting the hots for BJ? Oh dear, perhaps I am.

"Not yet," continues BJ. "The only hostel that I've heard of is called Caravellas, or something like that. Wait, I can look in my Lonely Planet."

"That's where we're going when we get there," continues Suzi, "... Caravellas ... at least for a night, before we catch our boat out to the reef."

"OK, why don't I try to join you there? I'm sure they'll have a noticeboard ... all the hostels seem to, so I can leave you a note when I arrive. I think it'll be about a week from today."

"Good plan," agrees Suzi, "... and we'll leave you a note to let you know where we are. And if there's no board, we'll leave one at reception."

"Great," continues BJ. "I guess we need to get ready for the next bus ... only about 20 hours to go ... and what's it, about another 6 for you to Cairns?"

"Yeah ..." Suzi and I both sigh in harmony.

Chapter 16: The bus from Tennant Creek

Thursday 23 January 1992 – Tennant Creek, Australia

3:00pm. Suzi, BJ and I are about to board the bus for Townsville.

Close to the scheduled departure time of 3:00pm, we board the bus for the long journey via Mount Isa to Townsville. With so many hours ahead of us before we reach the Queensland coast, the time of day seems largely irrelevant.

We take up seats in similar positions to those we had on the previous bus, perhaps a row or two nearer to the front. Once again, it's quite a relief to see plenty of space to stretch out, as this leg of the journey is overnight, and another lengthy one.

As the bus drives out of the centre, leaving Tennant Creek behind us, we all conclude that we didn't miss much by remaining in the café, rather than going for a stroll around the town.

As per the last bus, BJ's picked the seat behind Suzi. He's now got his head pressed against the window, and the two of them are chatting through the small gap.

I know I shouldn't be, but I'm beginning to be a little jealous for the attention. *Come on Megan ... grow up. If BJ likes Suzi, then that's great, isn't it? We're besties, so I'll be happy for her, won't I?*

Fuck, maybe I really do fancy BJ.

I settle in my seat and gaze out of the window, while trying to restrain myself from eavesdropping on their conversation. I find it rather difficult.

Perhaps half an hour after leaving Tennant Creek, there's suddenly a heavy jolt to the other side of the bus, accompanied by a loud thud.

"Oh, poor thing!" exclaims Suzi.

What just happened?

"Don't worry fellas," the driver explains over the PA system. "It was just a kangaroo. No harm done; we get that quite often."

"Heartless bastard," says Suzi. She's clearly upset, and also quite taken aback by the uncaring attitude of the driver.

I seize this opportunity to jump across the aisle, and take the seat next to BJ.

"Bit of a shit, huh?" I say, agreeing with Suzi.

"Yeah," explains Suzi, "I saw them, a couple of them, and one just jumped into the side of the bus. They were quite small, maybe young ones. Perhaps they were trying to cross the road."

The three of us chat for a while about people who have a similar disregard for the wellbeing of wildlife. It's something I feel strongly about: I love animals, and I hate to see them suffer. Well, when I say animals, OK, I don't necessarily mean all of them. Perhaps I'm a bit of a hypocrite as I'm not so keen on creepy crawlies ... but they don't really count, do they?

As our conversation progresses, we chat about the ethics of food choice, and what we've found to be such a meat-intense diet Down Under.

"You couldn't easily be vegetarian in Australia," says BJ, "certainly not from my experience so far. Maybe it's just at the hostels, but every day it's a meat bonanza at the barbie."

"I couldn't be vegetarian anyway," I respond, "I'm rather too fond of my meat." *Shit, that sentence came out a bit wrong.*

Suzi chuckles, evidently amused at my choice of words.

You'll know by now that I'm not a vegetarian; I love eating meat. Nothing beats the taste of a good steak, but I do sometimes struggle with my conscience.

♦ ♦ ♦

5:30pm. The roadhouse, Barkly Homestead.

A couple of hours after departing Tennant Creek, we arrive at a scheduled stop at Barkly Homestead, where we take the chance to get out, stretch our legs, and use the facilities.

As we stand around waiting for the driver to call us back on board, I feel the sudden compulsion to give BJ a hug.

"I'm so glad you're travelling with us," I say, by way of explanation for the cuddle.

I stand in front of him, loosely pressed against his chest with my head resting against his shoulder. A moment later, I feel something pushing into me, slightly lower down.

"Oh, it seems like someone else is happy again too!" I look up, catching BJ returning my smile.

"I'm sorry Megan, it just has a mind of its own."

I might have been unnerved by this but, on the contrary, I begin to feel excited, and even aroused. Regardless of BJ not being my normal type of eye-candy, in this moment I feel the urge to rip his clothes off.

"You're making me horny again," I whisper in his ear. I can feel BJ tense up.

Just then, the driver interrupts, calling us all back to the bus, and we resume our seats ready for the next leg of the journey.

Suzi stretches out and puts her Walkman on, evidently deciding that she wants her own space for a while. I'm not sure whether she just wants some alone time, or whether she's annoyed at me for hugging BJ. *No matter.*

As soon as the bus sets off, I jump back across the aisle to sit next to BJ.

"So, for the next three hours," I ask, "... what are the next three things to talk about? Or would you prefer to have a bit of peace?" *I hope he wants to keep talking.*

"I'm very happy to keep chatting," BJ replies. "What would you like to talk about? Are you into sport?"

"Not half," I giggle, "what would you like to play?" As we lock eyes, I get a vision of us engaged in a specific type of nude horizontal sport ... *hmm-interesting!* "Oh BJ, you really must think me awfully slutty." OK, I was never quite Miss Goody Two Shoes but, in under a month, my mind appears to have transformed into that of a sex-maniac.

"How about cricket?" BJ smiles and tries to keep me in check. "D'you like cricket?"

"It's OK, I guess ... a bit boring though. But Suzi likes it."

"I'm planning to go to a few World Cup games while I'm out here. I'll try to go to the MCG when I get to Melbourne, and then possibly see games in Christchurch, Wellington and Auckland."

"Are you one of the Barmy Army then?" I ask, hoping not to have embarrassed myself with my lack of knowledge.

"Barmy maybe ... probably ... but I'm not really a die-hard England supporter. It's too depressing these days; England haven't won anything big in sport since 1966 ... before I was born."

It was before I was born too; and Dad's always moaning that we never win anything.

"So, do England have a chance this time?"

"An outside chance, perhaps. The Aussies have to be favourites, but maybe ... if Gooch, Hick, Fairbrother, Lewis and others play to their best."

"What about Bottom ... is it Bottom? Is he playing? ... Is it Ian Bottom?" I start to giggle, as BJ looks at me quizzically.

"Oh, you mean Ian Botham? Uh, yeah. He's getting on a bit now but, on his day, he's still pretty good ... and the Aussies still seem to fear him."

"Bottom, bottom ... Oh BJ, why am I now thinking of bottoms?"

And, I am ... yes, and I'm also now trying to control fits of giggling, while all I can think about is wanting to squeeze BJ's rear. They say laughing is an aphrodisiac, and I must've had a triple helping because I can't get the thought of BJ's peachy buttocks out of my mind.

There's a brief pause in my giggles, as BJ continues to natter on about the Cricket World Cup. I don't mind, but I'm not really paying attention; I'm still on a different plane with my dirty and evolving thoughts.

Hmm-now ... how would he react if I kiss him? Oh no, why did I have to think of that? ... I'm now aching to do it. I know that I can't just rip his clothes off and have sex on the bus, but what if we could? How would it feel if BJ was shagging me like Neil did a few days ago? Fuck, I feel so horny ... and I've not had a single G&T.

As BJ talks, I find myself nodding and pretending to listen, but I'm thinking ... calculating.

BJ's not going to make a move as he's too shy. But I think he likes me. So, what happens if I kiss him?

Worst case scenario, let me think ... yes, he draws back, it all gets awkward, then I go back to my seat for the next few hours and, after Townsville, I never see him again.

Best case, probably a snog ... but maybe more. Mmm-yes, I like the idea of more. Oh, you're so wicked Megan ... but what's it going to be? If I wait ... hmm, maybe I lose my chance. He clearly likes Suzi ... and maybe she'll beat me to him. Hmm ... no ... if I'm going to do something, the sooner the better. But ... do I really want to?

BJ finishes his sentence and looks across at me; he's probably waiting for me to respond, but I wasn't paying attention. My pulse suddenly races; I think my hormones are telling me the answer. I look across into BJ's eyes, and then lean over to whisper in his ear.

"BJ, I hope you don't mind, but ..."

I don't finish my sentence but, instead, I gently place a kiss on his cheek. *OK, so no going back now.*

In a split second, BJ turns his face towards me with a look of surprise in his eyes. I don't allow him to speak, but forcibly engage his lips with mine, and cross my fingers for a positive response. And I did ... I actually crossed my fingers.

Although I've taken him by surprise, BJ doesn't retreat. His lips seem keen to connect, so I press more firmly, allowing my tongue to caress his upper lip. I can't believe I'm doing this ... at least, not without five double G&Ts first.

BJ cautiously pulls back to draw breath.

"Wow, there goes my middle-stump again," he says in a quiet giggle.

BJ's eyes are now sparkling and, as they engage with my own, his pupils have become so large that I can further sense his arousal. I can also feel tingles diffusing through my body.

We kiss again.

This time it's long, lingering and passionate, as we explore each other with our tongues. *Hmm-yes, BJ's a good kisser ... uh-huh, yes, delicious.*

We break off again for air.

"So BJ, you do like me a little then ... despite me being so slutty?" I giggle, but I don't allow him to answer, before engaging his lips again. *Hmm-yes, I love his lips.* I usually kiss with my eyes closed, I'm not sure why, but I'm curious as to whether BJ does. I take a peek ... his eyes are shut. I enjoy a moment or two watching his eyelids flicker as he kisses me. Suddenly, a bright yellow light catches his face.

I pull back from the kiss.

"Hey, look at that sunset! Wow, I've never seen a sky so yellow."

Looking out of the window, the sky is a palette of soft yellowy-golds, radiating out from a brilliant white sun, a quarter hidden below the horizon.

BJ turns to look and, a moment later, he puts his arm around me and pulls me in for a cuddle. We hold and caress each other, while we absorb the spectacle as the sun descends behind the scrubby desert.

At this point, Suzi sticks her face through the gap in the seats in front.

"Oh Megan, I can't take you anywhere!"

She immediately turns back, retreating to her thoughts and her Walkman.

For a few moments I feel pangs of guilt. Suzi's annoyed with me; I know she had her eye on BJ. Well, he's a great guy, but he's also fair game. Suzi didn't claim him, did she? Well, now I've discovered he's a great kisser. *And I wonder what else BJ does ... oh, naughty me.*

"I think she's a bit upset with me again," I whisper to BJ. "You know, she's friends with James too, and she doesn't think I should be doing this. I also think she's a bit jealous ... Suzi seems to like you too."

BJ looks as if he's about to say something, but I continue ...

"You know BJ, you're a yummy kisser ... much better than Neil. Oh sorry, I shouldn't talk about him."

I prevent myself from saying any further rubbish by kissing him again.

"Well, I'm sure it's not from having more practice," BJ responds, as he draws breath. "And maybe in Broome you'd had too many drinks to judge."

He might be right about Broome, but BJ shouldn't put himself down; he's got genuine talent in the smooching department.

"No, really BJ ... you're a smooth operator. And who would think it, beneath that shy, sensitive exterior? So, what else are you good at?"

I slip my hand under his shirt to feel his chest. He flinches a little; he's probably not used to this kind of intimacy. I enjoy the softness of his skin, as I caress his belly and run my fingers through the fuzzy curls on his chest. *Oh my god, he's making me so horny, and I bet he can do much more than kiss.*

"Never judge a book by its cover," BJ responds. "Although, to tell the truth Megan, I always seem to do just that. And, if you hadn't jumped on me this time, I'd never have tasted how delicious you really are. I'm always far too reserved ... much too shy."

"Oh BJ, we'll have to fix that, won't we? You make me feel so horny."

There's no alcohol in my blood, and no excuses, but I'm beginning to lose my self-control as my hand strays down to his crotch. I can feel him stiffen further, as I grip BJ's bulge through the denim of his shorts.

"Now, how about a little BJ, for my little BJ?"

Oh my god, what did I just say? Oh fuck, did I actually say it aloud?

"What!?!?" BJ pulls back in surprise.

Oh fuck! Yes, I really did say it.

BJ is shocked, and whispers ... "What, now? But Megan, we're on a public bus."

It seems I'm out of control. I could've taken this opportunity to recoil and pretend I was joking, but no ...

"Oh, you spoilsport," I whisper as, through the denim, I tighten my grip on his erection. BJ winces ... it's either fear or excitement, or most probably both. *What's gotten into me?*

"Perhaps, if we weren't stuck on this bus. But we could get locked up for public indecency." He's right there, I hadn't really considered that.

"But BJ, don't you feel excited? Why don't you live a little?" *Oh my god, I really can't control my lust.*

"I do so want to Megan ... but really we can't. I'm sorry ... we'll have to wait. I don't mean to be boring, but we don't want to do something that we'll both regret." He's right of course, but he's still a spoilsport.

He takes my hand away from his shorts and clutches it to his chest. My brain now re-engages, and I have that 'what have I just done' moment of realisation. All of a sudden, my mind is a complete muddle.

"Oh shit ... James!" My mind suddenly flashes back to Newcastle. *Knackers! What was I thinking of?* "Oh, what should I do? I'm such a dirty slut."

"Well, when I said regret," BJ interrupts, "I meant prison, not James ... but anyway."

Oh knackers! What did I go and do that for? Why the fuck did I offer to give BJ a blowy? He must think I'm a right old slag. Why couldn't I just leave it at kissing, rather than spoiling it? And what about James? He deserves better than that, and much better than me screwing around with Neil. And what about BJ? He's such a lovely bloke, so why am I mucking him about? Fuck, fuck, fuck Megan ... you're such an idiot.

BJ holds me tight; at least he hasn't pulled away. I rest my head back on his chest and close my eyes.

"Well, d'you love him?" BJ asks. "... James?"

"Yes, I guess I love him," I reply. "Oh I don't know BJ ... it's complicated."

BJ allows me to rest on his chest and regain my composure. He doesn't pursue the answers that I don't have for myself. So many thoughts now spin around my head, but central to them all is the disgust at my behaviour. *Why did I have to go there? Why did I lose my self-control, my self-respect?*

I'm so mad with myself as I think about what I'm throwing away. *Do I still love James? Do I still want him? Could I go back and make things work? Fuck, I don't know ... but he doesn't deserve a slutty old slapper like me.*

At some point, I must've fallen asleep, because the next thing I'm aware of is waking up as we approach Townsville. I'm no longer lying against BJ's chest. In fact, he's now sitting beside Suzi in the seat in front, chatting with her about snorkelling. He managed to squeeze out without disturbing me, and I must've been asleep for some time.

We pull in to our scheduled stop in Townsville, and all disembark, before waiting at the side of the bus to retrieve our backpacks.

I suddenly feel a sense of panic. BJ's stopping in Townsville, while Suzi and I are boarding another bus to take us on to Cairns. I don't want to leave things hanging like this with BJ. *There's so much I need to say to him. But how can I? Not in public and, anyway, there's just no time.*

The Cairns bus is waiting, so our goodbyes are short. Suzi hugs BJ first, and then starts off walking towards the other bus.

BJ then turns to me and holds me tight. A moment later, he draws back and plants a big kiss on my lips, and I simply melt.

"Remember this," he says. "There can be more if you like, when I get up to Cairns."

"Yum," I respond, "I look forward to it BJ. Leave a note for me at reception, as soon as you get up."

"I will," he whispers. "Oh, and do have a really great time diving. Oh, and also avoid the sharks ... coz I wannabe the next one to bite you." We both raise a brief smile.

We kiss again for as long as I can hold it before I pull away, pick up my backpack, and then make towards the Cairns bus. The engine is on, signalling it's ready to depart, so I rush to stow my backpack, before re-joining Suzi.

As the bus leaves the depot, I see BJ standing at the side of the road. He spots me, and we both wave. There's a tear in my eye, and my heart is in tatters. Over the next few days, I'll really have to sort out my feelings.

Chapter 17: Walk of shame

Saturday 29 August 1992 - Baker Street, London

4:45pm. At the flat. I'm in the kitchen, peeling the sweet potatoes.

So, now you've got a little more background about BJ. You know, to this day, I still can't believe or excuse my behaviour on that bus. I mean, what was I thinking? Why on earth would I do something like that? Even several months later, I still find it embarrassing to remember, let alone talk about.

OK, so why am I telling you? Well, we're friends now, right? And, I'm telling you because that particular moment when I spewed out those foolish words 'how about a BJ?' was rather important to this story. In fact, it might've been the catalyst which turned my whole life upside down. Well, it was more than just that single act of stupidity; it was the conversation with BJ beforehand which, when combined with this absurd behaviour, precipitated a total rethink of what I wanted in life.

From the moment Suzi and I left BJ in Townsville, the shame I felt about that stupid blowjob proposal affected me deeply. At least my fling with Neil could be explained, if not excused, by virtue of having drunk several beers and two double G&Ts beforehand. My primaeval urges that night were fuelled by the alcohol. But on the bus from Tennant Creek, I'd not had a single drink, and yet I still couldn't keep my self-control. Perhaps years of subconscious frustration with James had been released, and now the floodgates had opened.

Although Suzi knew that something intimate had developed between me and BJ on the bus, she was unaware of the full extent of it. She'd seen BJ with his arm around me, and Suzi'd probably seen one or two kisses, especially the final kiss as we rushed to catch the bus for Cairns. However, this extra bit, the shameful moment … I just couldn't tell her about it, and I usually told Suzi everything.

I mean, I divulged all the gory details about my fling with Neil. But this was different.

The aftermath of that night in Broome was a deep sense of guilt over cheating on James. Somehow though, getting drunk and having a shag with Neil didn't actually seem to cut so deep as what I'd done, or nearly done with BJ. Neil and I had both been drunk, and we'd both wanted a no-strings quickie. But it was so different with BJ; we were both completely sober. BJ and I had spent several hours talking intimately with each other; we'd been developing an attraction that had started to become physically intimate ... but then, out of the blue, I lost control and offered him a blowjob. And on a public bus! It was totally shameful. Not only did James not deserve this extra betrayal, but BJ didn't deserve it either. BJ was a sensitive bloke, and I really liked him ... he never deserved me losing control and behaving like a slag. How could I ever look him in the eye again? And, what made matters worse was that Suzi also liked him.

♦ ♦ ♦

The bus journey from Townsville to Cairns took another five or six hours, during which time Suzi and I hardly talked. I think she was pissed off with me because I'd made a move on BJ, whereas, on my part, I retreated into a shell, disgusted by my behaviour. What on earth had possessed me to behave like that?

I know I may be labouring the point, but BJ was such an awesome guy ... a shy, kind, thoughtful and caring bloke. As such, he deserved a subtle and caring approach ... he's just not a blowjob-in-the-back-of-a-bus type of guy.

Over the space of three weeks, first with Neil in Darwin, and now with BJ on the bus, my personality had totally changed. From being someone who was drifting along, generally content and not overly self-critical, I had turned into a person who, having been tempted by lust, had lost all self-respect and despised herself.

As you know, even before I met Neil, I was doubtful that James and I could make things work when I moved to London. But after this, I was so disgusted with myself, I knew James and I should split regardless, as I no longer deserved him. James had always been kind and, as far as I was aware, he'd never looked at another girl: at least, no more than the odd glance here and there ... but every bloke does that, don't they? It would break his heart if he ever knew what I'd been up to. No, James deserved someone far better than me.

♦ ♦ ♦

I'll pause for a moment, while I quickly check my cookbook. Oh laa-dee-daah, I'm sounding a bit like Mammy now ... "oh, I'd better just go and check the recipe."

Well, I've never attempted to cook scallops before; they're somewhat posher than I'm used to ... but I did want to eat something special tonight. Now that I'm just settling into my new life in London, I guess I have an excuse to celebrate ... and, as I don't know many other people down here yet, I thought I'd invite BJ. He's also just moved to London and, well, as you'll soon see, that bus ride thankfully was not terminal to our friendship.

OK, so the trifle and sweet potatoes are all that I need to prepare before he gets here ... and I've got the wine chilling, so we're all set. The pasta will cook in just a few minutes, as will the seafood. Anyway, talking of seafood now brings me nicely on to the next bit of the journey.

♦ ♦ ♦

So, as I was saying, Suzi and I were heading to Cairns, and we'd booked ourselves on a diving course.

Well, we arrived in Cairns late in the afternoon, and had one night in Caravellas hostel before we began the course. The next morning, the first part of the dive-course was meeting the instructors, and taking an hour-long introductory session in the hostel pool. This was in order to get us accustomed to the scuba gear, and to the experience of breathing underwater.

We met the five members of the boat crew, and also the other people on the trip which comprised a group of four Germans (two couples) and two Dutch girls. Suzi and I were a bit disappointed by the absence of eligible bachelors ... well, Suzi was, as my self-disgust made me want to stay away from guys altogether. However, there was one hot-looking member of the crew, which at least gave Suzi some eye-candy for the next couple of days.

After the session in the pool, we all gathered in reception, ready to be taken off to catch our boat. As Suzi and I waited with the group, we were surprised by the sudden reappearance of Neil. We chatted for a few minutes, and he asked us whether we wanted to meet up again once we returned from our dive-trip. Seeing Neil again had caught me off-guard, and I was pretty stand-offish and non-committal ... 'prickly' was the word that Suzi later used. Inside, my stomach was still churning with shame, and, additionally, I now had PMT ... so perhaps this was the worst time that Neil could have caught me.

As it turned out, that was the last time I set eyes on Neil ... a pity perhaps, as he did give me one of the most fantastic nights of my life. However, even if we had met up again, I don't think anything would've happened. Apart from the alcohol-induced sex, I'd come to realise that we didn't have much in common.

Anyway, having just mentioned PMT, it's also worth me saying that Suzi and I hadn't exactly picked the best possible week for our diving. The trip we'd chosen was a 4-day excursion, which had us sleeping out at sea for three nights. Don't get me wrong, it was an absolutely fabulous experience, but we were a little hampered by our bad tempers. Mind you, a few days later might've been worse. With the distinct possibility of shark encounters, the prospect of having the bleeds while diving wouldn't have filled me with excessive confidence.

Despite our relatively short fuses, Suzi and I both fell in love with diving and snorkelling: the colours and variety of the corals and fish were incredible. And I also got to swim with a turtle ... how cool is that? And the nights out at sea, chatting with the crew, eating freshly caught fish, and gazing up at the clear starry sky ... it was all fabulous. The trip was so good in fact, that we decided to book another one a few days later, to go around the Whitsunday Islands on this tour's sister boat. We got a thirty percent discount, and we both felt it was too good an opportunity to miss. However, this meant that we'd be travelling down the coast beyond Townsville to Bowen, and it also meant we'd miss BJ when he turned up in Cairns.

Chapter 18: Ducking and diving

Tuesday 28 January 1992 – Cairns, Australia

9:00pm. Having returned from our reef trip, Suzi and I are back in Caravellas Hostel. We're sitting at an outside table, listening to Midnight Oil in the hostel bar area. We've taken our clothes to the laundry room, and are waiting for them to finish. I'm a little on edge, as I keep wondering if we'll bump into Neil or BJ.

"You're really jittery tonight. Is it Neil?" asks Suzi.
"Yeah, probably. D'you think he's still around?"
"I doubt it; I think we'd probably have seen him by now."
"Well Suzi, it's not just him, it's also BJ. I don't know which of them I want to see less at this point."
"But why? BJ was a lovely guy. I can understand you getting cold feet about Neil, especially if you don't want to sleep with him again ... but BJ? Why him?"
"Oh Suzi," I sigh. "I know BJ's a wonderful bloke ... and I should've told you."
"Should've told me what?"
"Well, about BJ on the bus."
"I know you snogged him; you can't think I didn't see that. But he's such a sweet guy; you could do far worse than him Megan."
"That's just it ... he really is a decent bloke. And then there's James ... and ..."
"Look Megan, if you don't want to see BJ, well, maybe I wouldn't mind a shot ... even if it is sloppy seconds."
I laugh.
"Yeah babe, I know you like him too ... it's just ..."
"Just what? C'mon, spit it out, will you?"

"It's just I ..." I begin to giggle. I don't quite know how to tell her, nor have much of a sense for what Suzi's reaction will be. However, I've been bottling up my shame these past few days, and I'll explode if I don't tell someone.

"What is it? C'mon Megan, tell me?"

"It's just that I ... well, I ... oh Suzi, please don't think too badly of me ..."

"What?"

"It's just ... well, I tried to give him a blowjob on the bus."

"You did WHAT???" Suzi's jaw drops in surprise.

"Yeah ... I mean, I didn't actually do it. He fought me off, but I did try to persuade him."

"Oh my god Megan!" Suzi now bursts into a fit of giggles.

"Don't laugh babe," I respond, giggling again myself. "It's not funny."

"Oh Megan, it so is ... it's hilarious. And you really are something." Suzi struggles to contain herself. "First you strap Neil to a bunk bed to have your wicked way with him, and now this. Wow, it's no wonder BJ looked confused when chatting with me on the way into Townsville."

"Oh babe, what am I going to do? In the last three weeks I've turned into the world's biggest slag."

We both giggle, and I feel a sense of relief that I no longer have to hold my tongue.

"No you haven't," says Suzi, "... and you're way short of world-leader in the slag stakes. Coming from where we did, if you had been a slag, you'd probably have been pregnant at fifteen, and stuck in a life on benefits ... and I know I'm stereotyping, but you know what I mean."

"I guess."

"I know I probably sound a bit snobby, don't I? And I do know that highly educated people sleep around too. Hey, d'you remember that girl in our hall, the first year we were in York? What did they call her ... oh yes ... 'gurgling-Katie.'"

"What, you mean the Katie who did French?"

"Yeah, that one ... and she did rather more than French."

"I know she had a bit of a reputation ... but never knew where the 'gurgling' nickname came from."

"Oh, c'mon Megan, don't tell me you never knew?"

"No ... but I never hung around with any of that crowd."

"Well," explained Suzi, now giggling again, "... apparently it was because she liked to swill it around before swallowing ... and one heard she'd developed a real appetite for it."

"Eeeeuuww!!!"

"Yeah ... everyone to their own taste. But anyway girl, you've a good way to go yet in the slag-dimension." Suzi rises to her feet. "Don't worry, we'll sort you out; but first though, I think you need another drink. Same again?"

"OK babe, why not?"

I sit by myself for a few minutes, while Suzi goes to the bar to buy another two bottles of Tooheys. I'm not usually such a beer drinker, but it's refreshing when the days are so warm. There aren't many people around, and Suzi's quick to return.

"Here you go ... they'd run out of Tooheys, so I got VB."

"Thanks babe."

Suzi sits down opposite me and we clink bottles.

"So then, my dear Megan, what are you going to do?"

"What? You mean with Neil and BJ?"

"No ... with your bloody nail varnish. Duh!!! Yes, of course with Neil and BJ."

"Maybe I'll just avoid them?"

"Well Megan, the chances are very slim that we'll see either of them again, so I doubt there's anything to worry about. But I really liked BJ, despite his poor taste in women."

I lean over the table and play-punch Suzi.

"Sorry M, I couldn't resist. But BJ did seem like a rarity. He wasn't full of himself, and he really seemed interested, caring ... genuine."

"Yeah, I know ... I liked him too. And then I blew it."

Suzi chuckles.

"I thought you said he didn't let you."

I laugh.

"Oh Suzi ... I'm such a slut, aren't I? My god, what would he think of me?"

"D'you mean God, or BJ?"

"BJ of course ... I know the guy upstairs will send me straight to the inferno."

"Oh, I dunno Megan. I can't say about any god, but BJ still appeared pretty keen on you when we left him in Townsville."

I press my finger to my lips, remembering that kiss.

"Oh babe, he's a great kisser. My god, he made my toes tingle."

"And your lady parts too, I guess?"

"Uh-huh ..." I giggle again. "Oh Suzi, what am I supposed to do?"

"Well, all things considered ... if he's so great at kissing, you could always leave him to me."

"No Suzi, I'm serious ... what should I do?"

"Hey girl, so am I."

Suzi chuckles, and I also burst into another fit of giggles.

"Well Suzi, it'll have to be a threesome then, won't it?"

"That's fine by me ... only, no gurgling!"

It's partly the beer, partly our hormones and, for me, also telling Suzi about my shameful behaviour ... but I haven't laughed so much in ages, and it's been such a release.

"Look Megan, we leave here tomorrow, so we may never see BJ again ... but I hope that we do. And, even if I don't get to taste his luscious lips like you did, he was great fun to spend time with. I think we should still write him a note, don't you? BJ and I talked about some hostels to try in Sydney and Melbourne, so, even if we've missed him here, we might still catch him later. I also agreed that I'd go with him to watch cricket at the MCG."

"Ah-ha babe ... so you were also stalking him?"

"Well yeah, maybe a bit ... but I didn't know then about your ... how shall we put it ... indiscretion."

"Uh-huh."

"You realise Megan, you could've been arrested? Oh my god, just think what could've happened."

"Yeah, I know."

"Imagine the headlines in *The Sun* ... 'Disgrace Down Under' ... or 'British backpackers arrested; your blow-by-blow account.'"

"Okay-okay Suzi, don't rub it in. But, oh my god ... what would Mam and Dad say? Or James?"

"Hey girl, you really need to sort your mind out about James. Is all this Neil and BJ shenanigans just getting stuff out of your system? I mean, d'you really want to let go of James?"

"I know babe, I know ... but I really don't have the answer. It's tearing me apart, but I can't go back to how things were. It'd be unfair on him anyway, but, with me in London and him in Newcastle, how-the-hell would it ever work? And anyway, now I'm not sure I would even want it to. Being out here, tasting something different, and somebody different ... it's been a real eye-opener."

"Well, don't do anything too rash; you've got plenty of time to think about it. C'mon, let's pick up our washing, and then we'll write the note to BJ."

I rise to my feet.

"Yeah Suzi, let's do it. Thanks babe."

"For what?"

"Just for being you."

Chapter 19: Besties

Saturday 29 August 1992 - Baker Street, London

5:00pm. At the flat. I'm in the kitchen, setting all the remaining ingredients out on the side, together with the utensils I need later.

I told you that Suzi was my best mate, didn't I? Well, she'd always pick me up when I fell down, and there'd be no complaints about listening to my rants and meltdowns. And even with BJ, whom we'd both started to get the hots for, Suzi never showed the slightest ill-will towards me.

So, anyhow, Suzi and I wrote a note for BJ ... well, Suzi actually wrote it, and we left it pinned to the hostel noticeboard. We had no idea whether we'd ever lay eyes on BJ again; we thought the chances were slim, as Australia's a large place to go looking for a needle in a haystack.

For me, there was an advantage in not seeing BJ again, as I'd never have to re-live the embarrassment of my behaviour on that bus. However, I did have mixed feelings; BJ was such a genuine bloke and, deep down, I knew that I wanted our paths to cross once more ... and Suzi definitely did.

Over the next week, Suzi and I went out to the Whitsundays for our second diving trip. Although we felt a little restricted for the first day-or-so, due to our cycles, the trip was breathtaking, and perhaps even better than our reef trip from Cairns. There were so many tiny coral islands, and the snorkelling in particular was fabulous; we even got to swim with sharks ... thankfully just small ones. Oh, and there was a bit more eye-candy on this boat too: a couple of German lads, Jurgen and Heinrich, who Suzi and I got quite friendly with. It was no more than a bit of late-night flirting; no cuddles nor snogging ... and, despite the significant influence of alcohol, definitely no further shameful indiscretions.

I walk through from the kitchen to the lounge, and over to the hi-fi system. It's an expensive Bang & Olufsen ... not mine, of course.

What music shall we have tonight? Hmm-yes, what ambience am I trying to create? Is it classical ... a bit of Mozart or Vivaldi perhaps? Or some smooth jazz? Or maybe Madonna? Oh knackers, I don't know ... BJ and I are just friends, aren't we? So, maybe nothing too intimate, nothing overly romantic.

Oh hell, I wish I knew how I feel about BJ right now; but more to the point, I wish I knew whether he feels anything for me. So much has happened since that bus ride ... and it's only a couple of months since Suzi dumped him. When I last saw him, BJ did seem OK. That was when we went for a quick coffee after bumping into each other at Kings Cross Station; but we never talked about Suzi, and BJ had really fallen for her in a big way.

I still find it hard to believe that Suzi got back together with Matt, although I guess he's a lot nearer to Gateshead than London is. If Suzi had stuck with BJ, she'd have ended up with the same geographical challenge that I would've had with James. I must say though, I was genuinely upset when she dumped him ... in spite of a touch of my own jealousy, I could see that Suzi and BJ were great together.

So, as you'll have concluded from what I'm saying about Suzi, we did find BJ again. Well ... duh, that's also pretty obvious if I'm having dinner with him tonight, isn't it? But it doesn't explain why he was with Suzi ... and that's what I'm about to tell you.

I select several CDs for a cosy ambience, and place them on top of the hi-fi. I start to scan the track lists on the back of each CD.

So, to continue the story then ...

Well, after the Whitsundays, Suzi and I continued down the coast. We spent a few days in Brisbane, and a night in a place called Coffs Harbour. The overnight bus also took us through Newcastle before we arrived in Sydney. Suzi and I debated whether we should stop in Newcastle for a day or so, purely to see what the Aussie version of 'our city' was like, but we weren't inspired by anything that the Lonely Planet told us. So, in the end, all we saw of it was a bit of urban sprawl in the darkness of the early morning.

Anyway, when we arrived in Sydney, we were travelling on the bus with a couple of other British girls, Jess and Debs, both from Manchester. Jess and Debs were heading for the Kings Cross area of Sydney … and yes, there's a Kings Cross there as well as in London. Anyhow, the one in Sydney was full of hostels, and was also renowned for plenty of nightlife. This seemed to me like a good choice, and I was persuaded that we should tag along with them. In contrast, Suzi wanted to head towards Glebe Village … she'd previously talked with BJ about staying there.

I was reluctant to go looking for BJ. While I did want to see him, I didn't think I could ever look him in the eye again. By this point, I'd also convinced myself that I didn't want to cheat on James again, and would avoid any further temptation in our remaining time in Australia. I mean, what was the point? A quick fling, and another sack of guilt to place in the pile with the rest of it.

Suzi still wanted to go to Glebe, but grudgingly agreed that we'd stay in Kings Cross. My sweetener, perhaps, was telling her that if we did bump into BJ, I'd step back and let her have first crack. With hindsight, maybe that wasn't so wise. However, I knew that Suzi liked BJ, and I also believed there was almost no chance that we'd ever see him again … so I didn't really give it much thought.

Oh, by the way, Suzi and I really enjoyed Sydney. Have you ever been? It's such an awesome place … well, around the harbour anyway, with the bridge and the Opera House. It's really busy and bursting with activity, but at the same time relaxing. If you've never been, you should definitely go.

♦ ♦ ♦

Still undecided over the music, I leave the few CDs on top of the hi-fi.

So, I'm not really making progress with the music, am I? Maybe I should just let BJ select something? Hey Megan, that's genius ... because if BJ chooses the music, I might be able to gauge his mood a bit better.

And perhaps I should do the same with the videos. I thought that after dinner we might watch a film, so I rented two from Blockbusters a couple of nights ago. One of them's *When Harry Met Sally*, with Meg Ryan and Billy Crystal ... have you seen it yet? I couldn't wait, so I actually put it on last night. I'd heard a lot about it, especially the fake orgasm scene ... oh it's so good. If you haven't seen it, then I definitely recommend it. I also rented *Pretty Woman* with Julia Roberts and Richard Gere, which is fun too ... I've seen it a couple of times. Anyway, let's wait and see; I've no idea what type of films BJ likes. I know that if it were James, we wouldn't get much beyond *Star Wars* or *Robocop* ... certainly nothing romantic.

Anyway, what time is it?

I look at my watch; it's nothing expensive, but an elegant silver bracelet-style Accurist.

There's still a couple of hours before he arrives.

I'd better take a shower and get ready; two hours may seem like a long time ... but it soon disappears.

I walk through from the lounge to my bedroom with its ensuite shower.

I don't usually take two showers in a day. I had one this morning, shaved my legs and pits, and also gave the landing strip a bit of a trim. I hate having to do that, don't you? Is that too much detail? ... Yeah, sorry.

Anyway, morning showers are my normal routine.

So, d'you think I'm making too much of tonight? I know that BJ and I are only friends ... but ... well, who knows?

Watching *When Harry Met Sally* last night got me thinking again about something BJ asked me when we were in Auckland. He asked whether a guy and a girl could ever be just good friends, if one or both were attracted to the other. Can you tell me the answer? I'm not so sure that I know.

I strip to my bra and knickers, discarding my jeans and t-shirt on the bed, before walking through to the ensuite. I check that the shampoo and conditioner are both in the shower cubicle, before walking back over to the sink to rummage amongst the cosmetics and moisturisers on the shelf below the wall-mounted mirror. My eyes are drawn to my silver bullet vibrator ... I pick it up.

Hmm ... have you tried one of these? It's really good. OK, you don't have to say, that's me just being nosy ... but I think all girls should have one. Well anyway, I've not had sex since I was in Australia ... yeah, that's right ... poor deprived old me.

I give the bullet a longing look.

No, there's no time to get carried away now. However, that reminds me of the next bit of the story ... Melbourne. You see, the day that I found this little silver wonder here, I was in one of the shopping arcades in Melbourne.

Suzi and I were staying in a backpacker hostel in the Carlton district. It was the one that Suzi and BJ had talked about staying in ... and yes, I gave way to her this time. Anyhow, when we arrived at the hostel, there was no sign of BJ. On the Sunday, I think, Suzi decided to go off to the Melbourne Cricket Ground ... she actually enjoys watching cricket, but Suzi also seemed pretty convinced that BJ would be going there too. I didn't join Suzi, as I don't understand cricket at all, but, by this time, I'd also accepted that BJ was old news, just as Neil was. They had been interesting, fun, and also embarrassing learning experiences.

So, instead of spending the day at the cricket with Suzi, I entertained myself by browsing in one of Melbourne's big shopping centres. And, as luck would have it, I came across this little silver beauty ... and in the absence of six inches of the real thing, a multi-speed, variable-pulse, stainless-steel piece of magic is just what every girl needs.

Anyway, while I was treating myself to this, Suzi was discovering her own treat at the cricket.

Chapter 20: A new vibe

Sunday 23 February 1992 – Melbourne, Australia

8:30pm. At the Carlton backpacker hostel. I'm in our dorm, stretched out on my bunk, flicking through some sightseeing leaflets while I wait for Suzi to return from the cricket match. Suzi walks in through the door ...

"Hey Megan!"

"Oh, hi! How was the game?"

"Oh, it was awesome. And guess what?"

"What?"

"I found BJ."

"Really?"

"Uh-huh, yes I did. And guess what?" Suzi has a beaming smile on her face.

"What?"

"Well Megan, you were right."

"What d'you mean? Right about what?"

"He's such an amazing kisser ... oh my god!"

In this split second, my heart plummets, and I'm overwhelmed with jealousy. *What-the-fuck happened? Surely not?* Having reconciled that BJ was gone, he now isn't ... but ... *oh fuck!*

"Oh my god Suzi ... you didn't?" *Please, say you're just winding me up?*

"Uh-huh ... yep. Oh, and it was ..." Suzi stops mid-sentence as she sees my expression; I guess anguish is painted across my face. "Oh Megan ... I'm sorry ... are you OK with it?"

I stand up from the bed and give Suzi a giant hug; I need to stop myself bursting into tears. I can't believe I'm suddenly so churned up ... I mean, yes, BJ and I kissed ... and yes, I really like him, but I'm also still messed up about James. Besides, Suzi's my best friend, and I should be pleased for her.

"Oh babe ... don't mind me; I'm just a bit shocked. Perhaps I still thought that ... no, no ... no Suzi, I'm happy for you ... really."

"Oh Megan ... sorry, if I'd known you still wanted to ..."

"No Suzi, just stop. Look, I did agree you could take a shot at BJ if you wanted to ... and ... well," ... I take a deep breath, "... well babe, tell me anyway, how was it?"

"Well, let me leave the gossip until later; BJ's downstairs in the common room. Will you come down?"

"Oh Suzi, I don't know ..."

"There are also three German girls who met BJ in Cairns ... they seem quite friendly. One of them, Brigit, even pounced on him in a bar in Cairns; he told me about her forceful seduction methods on our walk back from the cricket."

"But what about my ..."

"... indiscretion on the bus?"

"Uh-huh."

"Think nothing of it," continues Suzi. "He hasn't said anything ... and I doubt he's likely to; he's evidently seen some other action since then. Look, I understand if you don't want to, but ..."

"No, Suzi ... it's OK. It's better that I bite the bullet and get it over with."

I put my shoes on, then brush my hair while I look in the mirror. Seeing my t-shirt in a crumpled state, I quickly swap it for a freshly laundered white one, with the INXS 'Kick' album cover on the front. It's more of a pyjama-type top than anything seductive, but any romantic engagement is rather off the table right now.

"Do I look OK now babe? ... Oh ... by the way, speaking of biting the bullet ..."

I walk back to the bed and pull a paper bag from my daysack. "I found this little beauty today in one of the malls." I show her the silver vibrator, still tightly contained in its plastic wrapping.

"What is it?"

"Well, maybe you were destined to meet BJ today ... while I was fated for other things. This, my dear, is my BJ substitute ... multi-speed, variable vibe pattern."

"Oh, you didn't?"

"Uh-huh ..." I wink at Suzi.

She giggles, as I return my purchase to the daypack.

"OK, well ... come on then, let's go."

♦ ♦ ♦

Suzi and I leave the dorm, and make our way downstairs to the common room. As we enter, BJ rushes over from the far side, and gives me an enormous hug.

"Hey Megan, it's so great to see you."

"And you too BJ, it really is."

"You're looking well."

"Uh-huh. You too babe; a bit more suntanned than last time."

"Yeah, I guess so."

"Look, Suzi told me that you and her ... well, you know. I'm really so pleased for you both." My stomach churns as I force the words out. "Oh my gosh BJ, Suzi's been cursing me since Cairns for us not sticking around; and I guess she's told you more about the Whitsundays?"

"Yeah, she did, and ... well, no worries Megan, I'd have probably done the same; your trip sounded awesome."

I pull BJ close to whisper in his ear.

"I still think you're hot BJ and, in truth, I am a bit jealous ... but Suzi's my best friend, and she deserves to be happy. So, don't you dare hurt her."

"What are you two whispering about?" interjects Suzi.

"Oh nothing," I respond. "I was just telling BJ how happy I am for you both. You just seem so sickeningly well-suited."

As I speak, I look across to the German girls that had been sitting with BJ. All three are wearing light-coloured, baggy t-shirts, and are clutching their daypacks, as though they've just returned from an excursion.

"So," I ask, "... which one of you girls is Brigit then?"

The tallest of the three, a blond-haired, fairly muscular lass responds, and I notice BJ's face beginning to blush.

"Me. ... Why?"

The other two girls are of a somewhat slighter build, with mousy hair and, on the face of it, they appear a little more reserved.

"Well, it seems both you and I let this boy get away. What a shame ... coz he's quite handsome, and he seems like a good catch. He's all yours now Suzi."

Chapter 21: Three's a crowd

Saturday 29 August 1992 - Baker Street, London

5:45pm. At the flat. I'm stepping out from the ensuite, having taken a shower. I'm wearing a white towelling bath-robe, with a matching white towel wrapped around my hair.

Oh, how d'you like the robe? Shush ... it was one I stole from the Park Towers Hotel in Auckland, and the towel too. D'you think badly of me for it? Yeah? Well, actually, I didn't steal them ... the hotel kindly gave them to me when they discovered it was my birthday.

Anyway, where was I with the story? I'll tell you more about Auckland in a minute, but first I need to take you back to Melbourne.

Yes, so after that cricket match, Suzi and BJ had suddenly become an item. There was nothing I could do about it; I'd simply blown my chance with him ... if you forgive the pun. Don't get me wrong, I was genuinely happy for Suzi, but I suddenly felt so jealous; I was cursing myself for allowing BJ to slip away.

In contrast to my own dampened spirits, Suzi was now on cloud nine, simply radiating joy. In fact, I don't think I'd ever seen her looking so full of beans. She had a spring in her step, the likes of which I'd never seen during our three years in York ... BJ clearly had something that Matt didn't.

However, looking back, BJ really did have something different about him. I still can't put my finger on it, but there's a way in which he can make you feel like a million dollars ... and I'm not talking sex here, because, as you know, I never got to find that out.

Anyway, the day after the cricket, Suzi, BJ and I spent a lovely day at Melbourne Zoo. It's a fabulous place, with some wonderful and rare animals, including a cute koala called Olly, who I got to cuddle. Olly also had a mate called Meg, but she was asleep all the time. Oh, they were both so adorable.

I ended up taking plenty of animal photos that day: rather too many I think, but I was trying to focus on anything other than BJ and Suzi. It was so awkward watching them, as they held hands, caressed, and kissed each other. I ached just to feel BJ's touch, and to taste his lips again ... but, sadly, he was now off limits.

I also found it tough-going over the next couple of days, as I passed the hours with Suzi and BJ. It was clear that they were falling for each other in a big way ... their eyes would lock, caresses would linger, kisses would deepen; they did all of those falling-in-love things that I'd not experienced since being a teenager. I'd forgotten about the joys of courtship, and how new love can be so exhilarating. With James it was just so long ago, and my own brief encounters with both Neil and BJ had been so very different.

The day after visiting the zoo, we went on a trip along the Great Ocean Road, together with the three German girls. It was a fun day out, and the coastal scenery was magnificent. I took tons of pictures again, but ended up taking several photos for Suzi ... of her and BJ, as they posed together. They were a couple in love, and they had such a buzz about them. Despite still being technically 'attached' to James, I couldn't help but feel jealous.

Perhaps years ago, I'd had a similar kind of buzz with James, but it had long since disappeared. As teenagers, we did go through that brief stage of exhilaration, at the point when friendship transitioned to romance. But that new-lovers excitement had evaporated not long afterwards, and our relationship returned to being more like just friends again. OK, so there was a bit of sex too, but it wasn't terribly exciting; it was like we were already in our fifties, with grown up children, a sizeable mortgage, and too exhausted to make much of an effort. I couldn't go back to that; I didn't want to feel that my time had already passed. I wanted to experience new love again, and seeing Suzi and BJ together only served to clarify and reinforce such sentiment.

During those first few weeks in Australia, I had allowed lust to invade my brain and cloud the bigger picture. At least, that had been the case with Neil; I had liked the look of him, and had wanted the physical stuff, but I was never so attracted to him as a person. It has to be said though: that one night in Broome was bloody amazing, even if I do still feel a bit embarrassed by it.

With BJ it had been different though. I'd been getting to know him on that bus journey, and we'd been revealing our innermost thoughts to each other. I was not attracted to BJ physically in the same way as with Neil, and indeed James, but there was just a chemistry, an essence that was so captivating. And then I went and bloody ruined it by surrendering to a sudden surge of lust.

So anyway, there we were in Melbourne, and I just had to watch as BJ fell in love with my best friend ... and all the while, thinking it should've been me.

♦ ♦ ♦

Just three days after Suzi and BJ hooked up at the cricket match, BJ flew off to Christchurch for the next stage of his trip. He was spending a month in New Zealand, hoping to see a few more games in the Cricket World Cup, following which he had plans to travel across Canada.

After Melbourne, Suzi and I planned on another three weeks in Australia, moving on to Adelaide, and then back over to Perth. After that we intended to spend three or four weeks in New Zealand ourselves, before flying to Bangkok to explore a bit of Thailand, prior to returning home.

BJ's intention was to be in Auckland at the same time that Suzi and I arrived, so we agreed to meet him there. Although we didn't discuss it, I guess Suzi thought that after joining BJ in Auckland we might all change plans to spend more time together.

Anyway, BJ departed, and Suzi and I had an extra couple of days around Melbourne, before catching the bus for Adelaide. On the first of those days, we took a tour out to see the penguins on Phillip

Island; they're so adorable ... nearly as cute as koalas. Then, on the other day, we went to see the location-set for Ramsey Street. Having watched *Neighbours* pretty much every day at uni, Suzi and I really enjoyed it; and we even bumped into the actor who plays Harold Bishop ... which, I guess, might mean nothing to some of you.

Well, Suzi and I then spent a week in Adelaide, before flying back across to Perth to spend several more days with Laura and Phil. They were so welcoming, and had offered to take us on a few more trips around the area.

Anyhow, one evening, after having been back in Perth about a week, Suzi came off the phone ... and she looked shell-shocked. She'd called home, and discovered that her dad was now in Queen Elizabeth Hospital in Gateshead, having just suffered a major heart attack.

Our plans were about to change.

Chapter 22: Stay or go?

Wednesday 15 March 1992 – Perth, Australia

10:00am. At Laura and Phil's house in Coogee Beach. Following the previous evening's shocking news of her dad's heart attack, Suzi has just been on the phone to her mother.

"So, how is he?" asks Laura, handing Suzi a mug of hot tea.

"I guess it's much the same as yesterday. I'm still trying to get my head around it."

"How does your mam sound?" I ask.

"Exhausted and upset. I wish I was there to give her some support, even if there mightn't be much I could do."

I put my arm around Suzi, and give her a cuddle.

"Mam still says I should stay out here and continue our trip ... but how can I do that? Shit Megan, why did this have to happen?"

Suzi bursts into tears as I hold her tight. She was in tears for much of last night too, both worrying about her dad and also about whether her mum could cope. Understandably, Suzi's been contemplating whether she should catch the next available flight home.

"Look Suzi, there's no right and wrong answer here; just do what you feel you need to."

"Well, I don't want to ruin things for you. And what about BJ? If I don't turn up in Auckland, I'll probably never see him again. It's not like I can phone him or anything ... and I've no idea where he is."

"I know. Well babe, just take your time, and try to do what's right for you. Don't worry about me ... and whatever you decide, we'll try to find a way through it."

Suzi squeezes my hand.

"But what if he dies? What then, and what about Mammy?" Suzi tries to compose herself.

I wish I could promise that everything would be OK, but I do try to reassure her as I continue to hold her hand.

"I'm sorry," Suzi continues, "I'm going to have to fly home ... I'll never forgive myself if he dies while I'm on the other side of the world."

"Hey babe, don't apologize."

"Well, I've just ruined your plans too."

"Some things are more important, babe, but I'm sure he'll pull through."

Laura comes over and puts her hand on Suzi's shoulder.

"Whatever you decide, just let me know. We can call the airline and try to rearrange flights ... or I could even drive you into Perth; it might be easier to deal with them face to face. Was it STA you booked through?"

"Yes," I respond.

"Well, I'd be happy to drive you to their nearest office, or at least one that's affiliated with them. It may be easier in-person, if you've got a multiple-destination ticket. Look, just finish your tea, and let me know what you decide."

Chapter 23: Casual or slutty?

Saturday 29 August 1992 - Baker Street, London

6:00pm. At the flat. I'm in the bedroom, standing in front of a built-in wardrobe, assessing my clothing options.

Hmm ... what should I wear?

I can't say I've got nothing to wear ... it's too much of a cliché, and besides, I sometimes find I've actually got too much choice. You know, James always said that if I halved the time I took to decide on my clothes, I'd recover five years from my life. Is that fair? Do I really take such a long time? Perhaps I do ... but selecting the right outfit is important, isn't it?

James always used to say - "why does it matter what knickers you have on, if nobody else sees them?" Well, he's a bloke, isn't he? But it really does matter, doesn't it? If I were to wear big baggy briefs like Mammy wears, then I'm going to feel just like her ... all saggy and middle-aged (no offence Mammy). Whereas a skimpy black thong like this one ... *I pull a lacy black thong and bra set from a storage hanger in the wardrobe, and place them on the bed.* ... Well, these make me feel sexy, and more confident. OK, so maybe they're a bit slutty, but it's not like anyone else is going to see them ... chance would be a fine thing. But a girl can always dream.

Oh, OK then, so, I admit it ... maybe I do want BJ to become more than just a good mate. While I love him as a friend, the snog on that bus was positively electric, and the spark between us could've ignited further perhaps, if only he hadn't hooked up with Suzi. And, although the months have passed, this afternoon I've been in the same state of agitated excitement which I felt before boarding the bus in Alice Springs. You know, the butterflies in the stomach and that tingle Down Under ... and you don't get those if your feelings are purely platonic.

Anyhow, all these weeks later, BJ is single again ... at least, I think so. And if he is, I just can't help thinking I should re-explore the beyond-friends territory; after all, we might discover something really special. It's clearly what my libido is telling me ... but, thankfully, my brain is a little more circumspect this time around. Anyway, following this particular train of thought ... yes, maybe I do want BJ to see me in my skimpy thong tonight ... and yes, that's why the clothing choice matters.

♦ ♦ ♦

So, where did we get to? Oh yes, back to Perth.

Well, as I was saying, Suzi had a big decision to make ... whether to fly home or continue our trip. I think if I'd been in the same position, and it'd been my dad who'd had a serious heart attack, I would've flown home immediately too ... and Suzi's much closer to her dad than I am to mine.

In the end, it didn't take Suzi long to reach that decision, and Laura drove us to a travel agent where we tried to rearrange our flights. As fate had it, it was only possible to get one of us on the first available flight back to London ... well, when I say the first available, I mean the first which didn't cost an arm and a leg to rearrange. And any flight that the two of us could've taken together was a day or two later, and also had significant costs involved. Suzi was really torn over what to do ... as indeed was I.

I don't know quite what possessed me to do so, but I encouraged Suzi to take that first available slot and, instead of flying back with her, I suggested that I took our original scheduled flight over to Auckland, to spend a few days there before returning home. I didn't really want to go travelling by myself as I'm not such a confident person, but I could handle a few days in Auckland. It also meant I could still return on the planned route via Bangkok, just without stopping off for any further travel in Thailand.

There were two specific benefits with this course of action. Firstly, for me, there would be no additional cost for changing the flights; and secondly, mainly for Suzi, I could try to find BJ when I arrived in Auckland. We had agreed with BJ on the specific hostel where we'd try to meet, and if I was there for a few days, there was a realistic chance of success. Sure, I guess it would've been possible for us to call the hostel and try to leave a message, but who knew how reliable that would be?

Had I not flown to Auckland, it mightn't have been the end for Suzi and BJ, as we did still have a phone number for BJ's parents back in the UK. However, we'd already stood him up once in Cairns, and we weren't so sure BJ would forgive us a second time. Anyhow, even if these might've been more logical options, Suzi agreed with my suggestion, and I was now heading to Auckland.

After Suzi had departed for home, I spent another night with Laura and Phil in Perth, before flying on to Auckland. I really felt for Suzi over the next few days ... flying home by herself with her head so full of worry can't have been enjoyable. I kept thinking I should've gone with her to give her some moral support, but it hadn't been a practical option. However, knowing Suzi, I guess she probably preferred the time to herself.

♦ ♦ ♦

I peruse my different clothing options in the wardrobe.

OK, so it's definitely the black thong and bra ... but what else? I know ... and it's fitting for this point in the story ... I'll wear my sexy black mini-dress. I love this one ... coz it makes me look so freakin-hot, even if I say so myself. Uh-huh ... well, you can't go wrong with a little black dress, can you?

So, why is it fitting for the story? Well, it means that I'm wearing all black ... and I was flying to New Zealand. The *All Blacks*?

Yeah, you know ... as in the rugby? You don't? Oh, come on, even I know the *All Blacks*, and I know sod all about sport.

Anyhow, when I arrived in Auckland, I wasn't expecting to learn anything new about the *All Blacks,* nor rugby ... nor indeed anything about the game of cricket. However, sometimes in life we make unexpected discoveries.

Chapter 24: Batting for my bestie

Sunday 22 March 1992 – Auckland, New Zealand

8:30pm. At the reception of the Auckland Central YHA hostel. I'm trying to locate BJ.

I'd arrived in Auckland in the early evening, and had taken a shuttle from the airport to the downtown area. I was dropped off close to the central YHA hostel, where I intended to secure a bed for the night, and also track down BJ. I wasn't overjoyed by the prospect of sleeping in another dorm room, but I was stuck anyway when the receptionist announced that their computer system was down. She couldn't allocate me a bed for the night, nor could she check whether BJ was currently staying there.

Before arriving at the hostel, I'd spotted the Park Towers Hotel just along the street, so, with the YHA not immediately an option, I checked my Lonely Planet to see what it said. Park Towers looked like a decent possibility, so I decided to check it out. I figured that if they had rooms at a reasonable price, perhaps I should treat myself for a few days.

I walked along the street, and found that the hotel had plenty of vacancies, and at a pretty good rate for central Auckland ... so I checked in. My room was on the sixth floor, and had an impressive view overlooking the city. It was furnished in tasteful pastel colours, and contained a queen-size bed, a tub-chair, a dressing table, a small TV set, and a clean and functional ensuite bathroom. It might've been significantly more than I'd pay for a hostel bed, but I only had a few days before flying home.

After settling in and taking a quick shower, I walked the few yards along the road, returning to the YHA hostel. I had to find out whether BJ was here, and the sooner the better ... not only did I want to report back to Suzi quickly, but I also felt it would be fun to spend more time with BJ, rather than just exploring Auckland by myself.

♦ ♦ ♦

At around 8:30pm, I'm back at the YHA reception desk, relieved to discover that their computer systems have been restored.

I wait behind a handful of other people queueing at the desk and, while doing so, I flick through a few tourist leaflets on display. On reaching the desk, I ask the receptionist if it's possible to see whether BJ had checked in, explaining the circumstances as to why I wanted to find him. Unlike in Cairns, at least this time I actually know his surname. The receptionist helpfully begins to look for BJ on the system, but before finding anything ...

"Megan!"

I turn towards the voice, and I'm both shocked and delighted to have found the answer.

"BJ ... oh, it's so good to see you."

BJ continues towards me with a beaming smile on his face, but his expression soon changes to a more quizzical look.

"Hi, it's so great to see you." BJ steps in for a massive hug. "Is Suzi with you?"

I hold him in the embrace for a few moments, before stepping back and taking a deep breath.

"Oh BJ ... I'm so sorry, Suzi's not here. It's a long story ... can we go and sit down?"

"What? What's happened? Did you fall out? Is she sick?"

He doesn't hide his stunned disappointment.

"Hey ... just calm down BJ, and let me tell you."

We move out of the reception area, and BJ leads me through a large common room in which a dozen or more people are watching cricket on the TV. We continue towards a quiet spot on the outside terrace, where we find a picnic bench. We sit beside each other, and then I turn to face him.

Now for the bad news.

"Oh babe ... I'm so sorry, Suzi had to go back home. Her dad suffered a heart attack."

BJ is clearly taken aback, trying to process the news.

"Shit! When did that happen? Is he OK?"

"It was only a few days ago, just before we were going to reconfirm our flights out from Perth. So, Suzi re-arranged her flight to go home. I wanted to go with her; I probably should've done ... but Suzi wanted me to come to Auckland to find you. Oh, I really hope she's OK ... perhaps I should've gone with her."

As I regurgitate the story, tears begin to well in my eyes; I can feel BJ's disappointment.

BJ reaches forward and squeezes my hand, before holding me close in a comforting hug.

"And Suzi's dad?" continues BJ. "Do we know whether he's OK?"

"No, Suzi wasn't sure. She only found out when phoning home to tell her parents we were coming here. She spoke to her mum ... it appears that the heart attack was just a couple of days earlier. When they spoke, her dad was alive but still in hospital. Her mum told her to stay out here ... but would you have done so, if it was your mum or dad? No, Suzi had to go ... and I guess she'll probably be arriving home about now. I'll try to phone her tomorrow evening to see how things are."

"Oh boy! Poor old Suzi."

"Yeah," I sigh. "So, babe, I'm afraid it's just you and me." BJ squeezes me a little tighter. His embrace is warm and reassuring; it feels so good ... and I really need it.

"Well, if I couldn't see Suzi tonight, you're a bloody good substitute."

"Thanks babe, and I'm so relieved that I found you here. I didn't really want to come over to Auckland by myself, and I thought I might've missed you ... though Suzi said you'd be here until after the cricket final. She didn't want me to go back with her, because she thought if neither of us turned up, we might never see you again."

"Wow! Well, I'm so glad you did. And you're probably right ... if you hadn't turned up, I wouldn't have known why, and I guess I would've assumed that Suzi didn't like me anymore."

"Well BJ, you don't have to worry about that ... she more than just likes you. And, you know, I'm pretty fond of you too."

I start to overflow with emotion, and tears begin to run down my cheeks. With BJ holding me, it's so comforting and he makes me feel so safe. *I know he's now spoken for, but he could hold me forever.*

He cuddles me in silence for a few moments, and I close my eyes.

"Did you get a room here?" he asks.

I reopen my eyes, and release BJ's grip a little, as I turn to look at him.

"I did pop in briefly over an hour ago to enquire; the shuttle bus dropped me outside. The systems were down, so I checked out a hotel just up the road. I decided to get my own room there, rather than sharing a dorm here ... I feel like I now need to just chill out and sleep."

"I don't blame you. Which hotel?"

"Park Towers, just across Queen Street. It's not too expensive and, anyway, as Suzi and I aren't now going to Thailand, I'll only spend a few days here before going home."

"Oh. Are you going straight back from Auckland?"

"Uh-huh ... yes. I didn't really fancy travelling much further by myself, so I thought I'd just have a few days here, hoping to find you, before heading home. I've rearranged my flight back for Friday evening."

Suddenly a loud cheer comes from the common room.

"Oh BJ, don't let me stop you from watching the cricket; I know that it's England's game."

"Hey Megan, don't worry about that; I'm just so relieved to see you."

"Yeah babe, I know ... but I'm not Suzi, am I? I know you must be gutted. Suzi was certainly missing you a lot; oh my gosh BJ, she just couldn't stop talking about you ... you really don't know how much I've had to put up with over the last month." I laugh. "Yeah, but then Suzi got the news; she was devastated."

"Well, I really can't thank you enough for coming to find me ... I know you didn't have to. I really don't know what to say ... you're an angel."

I laugh-snort ... *I hate it when that happens.*

"An angel? ... Me? ... Babe, you and I both know that ain't true, don't we? But, me coming here ... well, Suzi's my best mate; I'd do almost anything for her. And, I also rather like you too ... in case you didn't know. I couldn't have you disappearing off, thinking that we didn't want to see you again. I know you already kinda got that impression before, when we left Cairns."

"That's true," BJ responds.

"Oh, and I'm so sorry for that too," I continue. "It wasn't that we didn't want to see you, it's just that ... well, things were complicated. But anyway, who knows what might've been different if we hadn't gone off to the Whitsundays?"

"Who knows indeed?" BJ shrugs.

I turn my head again and look into BJ's eyes, which sparkle with the reflection of the lights from the common room.

"You know BJ ... perhaps I missed my chance back then. Suzi's caught herself a wonderful bloke. I really mean that."

And I do mean it. *And perhaps things could've been different, but they aren't.* I smile and tweak BJ on the nose with my index finger.

"I know you do Megan, and you know ..."

"No BJ, don't say any more," I interrupt. "You're together with Suzi now, and I'm really happy for both of you ... although, with you two being on opposite sides of the world, missing each other like

fuck, and with her dad sick, and ... well ... you know what I mean."
Nice and articulate as ever.

"Come here you." BJ hugs me again, and holds me in silence for a few minutes before we're disturbed.

"Hey Bruce! Are you not watching the cricket? ... Oh, sorry, was I interrupting?" A tall bloke appears ... dark hair, mid-twenties, northern European accent.

"Oh, hi Carsten!" says BJ.

"Ah-ha, so, is this Suzi then? I've heard so much about you," says Carsten.

So, what's BJ been saying?

"Oh really? Well, hello," I reply. "And what precisely has Bruce been telling you?"

"Well, he's been missing you for sure. He's been counting down the days, talking about you in his sleep, daydreaming ... all sorts."

"Okay-okay," says BJ, before I can discover more. "Sorry Carsten, this is Megan ... Megan this is Carsten. Megan is Suzi's best friend. Suzi had to return home because her father had a heart attack."

Carsten gasps.

"Oh no! I'm so sorry. And I'm sorry that I interrupted; you must have a lot to catch up on. I must leave you to it."

Carsten then disappears back towards the common room.

"He's my room-mate right now," explains BJ. "I travelled up from Rotorua with him; he's quite a laugh, but he also snores."

"Is Rotorua that smelly volcanic place? Sorry babe, I haven't done my homework about New Zealand, and I guess I won't get to see much of it now."

BJ nods. "You say that you've got until Friday. Well, I fly out Thursday night ... so at least we can have a few days hanging out. Well, that is, if you'd like to."

"Oh, I'd love that BJ ... I really would. We don't need to do much, but it'd be good just to hang out and talk."

"Well, I'd love that too ... and I really am so glad that you're here. I know I'm disappointed at not seeing Suzi ... but ..."

"Yeah, I know."

♦ ♦ ♦

There was a raucous cheer from the common room.

"Look BJ, are you sure you don't want to watch the cricket?"

"No worries, I'm OK." His reply doesn't sound too convincing.

"Are you really sure? Well, look babe, it's getting quite late, and I'm tired." I look at my wristwatch, and realise I haven't adjusted it yet for local time. "What is it, around 9:30? Look, why don't I go back to my hotel, and leave you to watch the cricket? We can meet up again tomorrow morning."

"Well, OK, if that's what you want. Look, how far is your hotel? Park Towers did you say? Why don't I walk back over there with you? It's dark, and I don't know how safe these streets are at night."

There's proof that BJ's a real gent. I know that James would've done the same for me but, these days, I'm not sure how many other blokes would've offered.

"Well, OK then ... if you don't mind."

BJ nips off to grab a jacket and, when he returns, we walk through reception and out onto the street.

"So, you're not at the Sheraton then?" BJ asks, with a smirk on his face.

"No BJ, the Park Towers; you don't think I've got that kind of money, do you?"

"No, of course not," he chuckles.

"So why did you ask then?"

"Oh ... I ... uh, well, I'll tell you later."

"Park Towers is just over there," I explain, pointing in the other direction.

We walk unhurriedly up the road. It's only a hundred yards before we arrive at the hotel entrance.

"So, what time would you like me to come over tomorrow? Which room are you in?" asks BJ.

"Umm ... room 64."

"No kidding! Really?" There's something BJ finds amusing.

"Why? What's up? Tell me BJ?"

BJ doesn't answer, but peers in through the doors to reception.

"Look BJ ... tell me. Please? OK, come for a drink in the bar, and then you can tell me. Please BJ?" *What's he finding so funny?*

"Well, if you put it like that; I could murder a beer."

We walk inside and I retrieve my key from reception, before progressing through to the hotel bar.

"What beer is good here?" I ask BJ. It's quite a warm evening, and I'm drawn more towards beer than to a G&T.

"Steinlager's OK, and they seem to have that on tap."

Taking his recommendation, I order a couple of Steinlagers, charging them to my room, before we settle at a table in front of the TV screen. BJ and I are the only people in the bar.

BJ stares at the screen for a moment, mumbling to himself while he tries to understand the state of play in the cricket.

"How's it going BJ? And please tell me in terms that I can understand?"

"It is ... poised ... that might be the best word for it."

We lift and clink our glasses, before sipping the beer.

"Well BJ ... cheers!"

"Yes indeed, cheers Megan! And, once again, thanks so much for coming to find me. I really don't know what I'd have thought, or what I'd have done if you hadn't turned up."

I remove my jacket and put the room key down next to my beer.

"So, tell me BJ, what was this about the room number, and the Sheraton?"

BJ takes off his jacket and hangs it over the back of his chair. He takes a long sip of Steinlager, looks me in the eye, and smiles; his trademark look of mischief is written across his face.

"It's a bit of an embarrassing story ... well, no, more than just a bit. Are you sure that you want to know?"

I chuckle. *Silly question.*

"Naturally babe, the more embarrassing the better. But you and I share everything, right?"

"Well, OK then," BJ reluctantly concedes. "But I'm not so sure what you'll think. Well, no, actually, I can guess exactly what you'll make of it ... but anyway, don't say I didn't warn you."

I know he's itching to tell me, but he needs to pretend he doesn't want to ... that's one of my games too.

BJ takes a deep breath and another sip of Steinlager, and then begins.

"You see Megan, it was a dream I had. I don't know if you remember back in Melbourne, that you suggested some additional 'rules' relating to the cricket?"

"Remind me BJ. ... Oh, yes, now I remember. What was it, the M-O-T rules?" I lower my voice to a whisper so as to avoid the barman eavesdropping. "Manual for the semi-final, oral for the final, and a total service for the win. Yes, I do recall now." I giggle. "Suzi was really irritated with me, wasn't she?"

"Well, perhaps," BJ continues. "Oh, and before going further, the M-O-T equivalent in New Zealand is 'warrant of fitness,' or W-O-F, which also still works ... wank, oral and fuck. I just thought you'd like to know."

"That's cool." I smile ... he's so on my wavelength.

"Anyway, back to the dream. So, several days ago, I dreamt that England had just won the final. We were all watching it together in a bar somewhere. And, as I was jumping up and down in celebration, you passed Suzi a room key. It was room 64 ... at the Hilton rather than the Sheraton ... and you then said ... well, you said, "I got you two lovebirds a little pressie ... now just go and fuck each other stupid!"''

As he divulges this, I nearly choke on my drink.

"Well, my dear BJ ... you do have some imagination ... and a very, very dirty mind."

"Well, I'm not the only one," BJ grins. "Weren't the M-O-T rules your idea? That's how I remember it."

"Uh-huh ... I suppose that's true ... and actually, I can't deny that 'go and fuck each other stupid' is probably something that I would say. OK, so what happened next?"

"Blimey, you want me to continue? No, Megan ... it really is so sordid."

I know he's going to tell me; he just wants another prod.

"Come on babe, you know me ... the dirtier the better. You can't just stop the story before the juicy bits. Come on ... please? I'll even tell you a naughty dream of mine in return." *Hmm, that was a silly promise ... but no matter.*

"Well, OK. So, we get to room 64 and open the door ... it's a moonlit night, and the light is streaming in, as the curtains are open. There's a massive bed to our right, but we continue towards the window. At this point we're kissing ... and we just can't get enough of each other. We start undressing one another ... our tops first, and then Suzi's bra, and then," ... BJ pauses, "... are you really sure you want to hear it?"

"Yes ... go on." *I always love hearing the dirty bits, don't you?*

"Well, then I get down on one knee, and next I remove her cut-off shorts ... and then it's Suzi's knickers, before, oh yes mmm-hmm ... before I taste between her legs, and ..."

"Oh my god BJ, stop it; you're beginning to make me feel horny now too." *And I'm not kidding ... I'm imagining BJ's tongue running up the inside of my thigh, and my whole body's now tingling at the thought.* "No, actually, don't stop, I really want to hear it ... please continue?"

"No ... but just then ... from between her legs, I look up, and I see the snarling face of a scary girl that I met in Franz Joseph ... and I mean really scary."

"Wow BJ! Were you hoping all this was going to happen for real with Suzi this week? Well, except for the scary bit."

"Well ... yes ... uh-no ... uh-maybe ... well-yes, perhaps. Well, you know, you caught me at that fucking condom machine. Oh Megan, I don't know, but I wouldn't have pressured Suzi into doing anything she didn't want to ... I hope you know that. But ... oh fuck ... that dream ... and, my god, I so didn't want to see that really scary girl, and ... well ... maybe I shouldn't have told you."

"Hey BJ, why not? We're friends, right? And remember, I told you what I did with Neil back in Broome, didn't I? And that was for real, not just in my dreams."

"Well, I suppose so."

"Come on BJ, loosen up! You know you can always talk dirty to me."

We both laugh, and sip our beers.

"Yeah ... and maybe that's part of the problem."

"What d'you mean by that, BJ?"

"Oh ... nothing really ..."

"BJ???" *I'm not having that; he can't just give that type of throwaway comment without explaining.*

"Wait! Wait a minute ... it's another wicket."

BJ looks up at the TV screen. I do too, but apart from knowing it's South Africa against England, and that there are lots of people in multi-coloured pyjama-type kits, I can't really understand much more.

"What's happening?" I ask.

"Well, it's still tight, but maybe, just maybe, England are starting to get on top."

"OK," I respond, half-interested. *Now back to the more crucial topic.* "So, what did you mean just then?"

"Sorry, what?" BJ looks confused. "What was I saying?"

"You said that I was part of the problem; what did you mean?"

"Sorry, did I?"

"Yes ... after I said you can always talk dirty to me, your exact words were: 'Yeah, and maybe that's part of the problem.' So, what did you mean?"

BJ takes another swig of his beer, pausing while he considers how to respond.

"Ah-ha ... I said that, did I?"

"Yes you did, so ... what did you mean?" *I'm not letting him off the hook.*

"Well, I suppose ..."

"Suppose nothing, BJ ... you must have meant something. So, what was it?"

As I press him, BJ suddenly looks uncomfortable, even nervous.

"Well, alright Megan ... but please don't take this the wrong way. Look, Suzi was not the only person I had in my dreams. You know, before we met up again in Melbourne, it was you rather than Suzi that I couldn't stop thinking about. You know ... after that bus journey from Tennant Creek."

"Uh-huh ..."

"Well ... you remember?"

"Yes babe, of course I remember ..." *And that blowjob proposal is something I've regretted ever since.*

"Well, after that ... you know, when I got to Cairns, I would have done anything to re-light that fire. And I kept having these naughty visions of you ... after what you told me about you and Neil, and ..."

Although I want to hear more, I think I'd better stop him.

"Maybe I get the picture now ... and perhaps you'd better stop before you say something you'll regret."

"I think that's best," BJ agrees.

"Look, now that you're together with Suzi, you're off-limits. No ifs, no buts ... and, whatever I may have felt for you before, I have to put that behind me." *And that's not always so easy, is it? When something is off-limits, how often does that make you want it even more?*

Having just imagined BJ's tongue doing wonders downstairs, I certainly had a craving for it.

BJ nods in concession.

"So, Megan, changing the subject ... have you made a decision about James yet? Or shouldn't I ask?"

I wish he hadn't asked; it's still a sore issue.

"Yeah, that's OK, I suppose. I think it's over between us ... it's time that James and I move on. It may be painful, but I need to start afresh in London ... and I just can't see it working for us."

BJ sips his beer again before responding.

"I don't know whether to say 'I'm sorry', or 'good-for-you' ... but I know it might be painful."

"No worries BJ, I'll get over it ... I'm a strong girl. But I know it's the right thing to do. You know, Neil, and then you ... both of you made me realise that my life with James was not all it should've been. And, although you're off-limits now, you did at least help me to realise I should move on."

"Oh, what's happening?" BJ asks rhetorically, while he stares at the TV, trying to understand what's going on. The teams are coming off the pitch due to rain, and it seems that the scores are being re-calculated.

For the next few minutes, BJ is lost to the cricket. I'm also lost in my thoughts ... they're about James, and how I need to begin a new journey without him when I return home.

Chapter 25: Casually accessible?

Saturday 29 August 1992 - Baker Street, London

7:00pm. At the flat. As I wait for BJ to arrive, I walk about the flat, checking my watch every few minutes. I've set the table for dinner: two sets of knives and forks, fruit spoons for dessert, two tulip-shaped wine glasses, and a white 6-inch candle as a centrepiece.

Thinking back, it was probably that first night with BJ in Auckland, and only after hearing myself say it aloud, that I was finally one-hundred-percent convinced I should break up with James. I also discovered a bit more about cricket that night, as BJ tried to explain the bizarre manner by which England had won their semi-final against South Africa.

Anyhow, BJ should be arriving soon ... but I'm now caught in two minds about this black mini-dress. Is it over-the-top? Do I really want drop-dead sexy? Or perhaps more casual and friendly, what d'you think?

It was so much easier in Auckland, when BJ and Suzi were attached, and he was off limits ... but now I'm confused. Should tonight just be a dinner between friends, or should I try to make it more? What do I want out of it? I know I'm itching for a good time in bed, but would I want it to be with BJ? Today's nervous excitement appears to be saying yes, but perhaps that's only hormones talking.

And, even if I did want more, how about BJ? Would he see me as anything more than mates? I know Suzi isn't standing between us now, but I'm not so sure he'll have moved on yet ... and I certainly don't want to risk losing BJ's friendship.

"Knackers!" What shall I do? It's always easier when there's only one option on the menu.

When in Auckland, BJ and I had a wonderful time together as friends. The day after I arrived, we had such a fun time; we had a lovely Italian meal and did some shopping. I even took him around the lingerie section of a department store; it was awesome, and so fun teasing him … he got so embarrassed. But BJ was also really generous; he bought me a couple of blouses for my birthday … oh yes, and when I say generous, I should also tell you about what he did the next morning.

Now, on reflection, I think the sexy black dress might be a bit too much … or too skimpy, more to the point. I don't want to scare him off; seduce him maybe, but definitely not scare him away.

Shit! Did I just say seduce him? Did those words really just creep out? Well, perhaps there's your answer … it seems I might want to re-kindle a little fire between us.

So, that's it then. I'll change into my black crop-top and cut-off denim shorts … easy access, lots on show, but a bit less flashy. And, while I change, I'd better tell you about that next morning.

Chapter 26: Champagne Charlie

Tuesday 24 March 1992 – Auckland, New Zealand

07:30am. In room 64 at the Park Towers Hotel. It's my birthday, and I'm about to get a surprise.

I'm startled by a sudden knock at the door. I'm still in bed, but I've been awake for a while. I wasn't expecting anyone this early; BJ isn't due to come until around 9:00am.

There's a second knock, louder this time. Reluctantly, I get out of bed, throw on my Park Towers standard-issue white dressing gown, and I answer the door.

"Room service ma'am," announces a tall, clean-shaven, uniformed man, holding a breakfast tray.

"Sorry, I didn't order breakfast," I reply, a little confused. "There must be a mistake."

"No mistake ma'am. Here, there's a note with it. And I believe Happy Birthday is in order."

Slightly hesitant, I relieve him of the tray.

"Oh, OK then. Thank you!"

"You're welcome."

I take the tray inside and place it on the bed. There's a plate with smoked salmon and scrambled eggs, two rounds of wholemeal toast, a glass of orange juice, and a quarter bottle of Moet & Chandon.

Never in my life had I been given a Champagne breakfast. And, propped up next to the bottle was a card with the words: '*To my Super-sub, Happy Birthday!*'

♦ ♦ ♦

09:00am. I'm now sitting on the bed next to my breakfast tray, partially dressed, sipping my Bucks Fizz, and chatting to Suzi over the phone. There's a knock on the door.

"Push the door BJ! It's open!"

As expected, BJ pokes his head around the door.

"Come on in BJ ... it's Suzi. Come on over. I won't try it on loudspeaker, as I don't want to press the wrong button and lose her. Here babe, you talk to Suzi while I tidy these things up."

BJ takes hold of the phone and, as I get up from the bed, I give him a quick hug, and kiss him on the cheek.

"Thanks babe ... but you really shouldn't have."

BJ smiles, and blushes, as he begins to speak into the phone.

"Hi Suzi. Hey, it's so good to hear you; how's your dad?"

Having been talking with her for a few minutes before BJ arrived, I knew that Suzi's dad wasn't so good. He was still in hospital after the heart attack, which was now a week ago, but at least he was stable. Suzi actually seemed quite upbeat; it was probably due to the news that I'd found BJ. And, despite her own worries at home, she had also remembered it was my birthday. I told her about the Champagne breakfast, and I think Suzi was a tad jealous. Well, who wouldn't be? These days you don't find too many knights in shining armour.

BJ continues to talk with Suzi for a few minutes, leaving me feeling like a gooseberry, before they start to wrap up.

"I so wish you were here," says BJ. "But it's wonderful to hear your voice again. I promise I'll try to call as much as I can once I'm in Canada. Listen, I don't want to add to Megan's phone bill too much; d'you want another word with her?"

Suzi says something back.

"Yes ... you too ..." BJ says, before suddenly looking rather shocked. "Hey, hold on Suzi, what did you just say?"

Suzi replies ... I know it must be something significant.

"Oh Suzi, you do? That makes me so happy ... because I think I've fallen in love with you too. Wow!"

BJ looks up at me; his face ablaze with joy.

I stick my fingers in my throat pretending to vomit. For a moment I feel insanely jealous; I wish it'd been my words that sparked such elation. I have rarely, if ever, witnessed such euphoria written on somebody's face. I never saw this kind of elation when I first told James that I loved him. But BJ's face is indescribable; I'm just so jealous that his emotions aren't directed towards me.

A few sentences later, BJ passes the phone back to me, and I have a few more words with Suzi before letting her go.

By the time I put the phone down, BJ has moved over to the window, and is gazing out across the rooftops of Auckland. He's all glassy-eyed, in a daze.

"There, you see, BJ? Didn't I tell you that Suzi was still mad about you?"

"Yeah, you did ... Wow!"

It's fabulous to see him on cloud nine, but his own bliss also rips at my heart.

"Oh, and BJ, thanks so much for the breakfast. It was such a wonderful thought ... and there was also a rather dishy young man who brought it to my door." I smile, as I start to lose control of my emotions. "You know, I think you and Suzi have got something really special; I'm so happy for you. You're both such wonderful caring people ... it brings tears to my eyes."

"Hey! Come on ... dry your eyes, and let's go out and celebrate your birthday. Oh, and Happy Birthday, by the way."

I quickly nip into the bathroom, rinse my face, and try to compose myself, before returning to put my shoes on.

"Oh, hang on BJ." A quick thought crosses my mind. I know it will wind him up, and I can't let the opportunity pass. "Just before we go ... what did you mean by the note?"

"Sorry?" BJ looks confused.

I grab the note from the tray, and pass it to BJ.

"I want to know what you mean by 'Super-Sub'? ... Sure, I may be a bit slutty, but even I'm not that kinky."

"Sorry?" BJ looks up, bemused; he doesn't get my joke.

"Super-Sub? I'm not really into dominants and submissives ... you know, bondage and that kind of kinky stuff."

Suddenly the penny drops.

"Oh my god! Sorry ... I actually meant substitute ... you know, instead of Suzi being here. Oh, bloody hell! Did you think I meant 'sub' in that context?"

I start giggling.

"Yes," I tease. *Not really, but it's fun to wind him up.*

"Well, I really did mean substitute, but now that you mention it ... what was it you ended up doing with Neil? No bondage, you say?"

"Oh, BJ ... low blow ... very funny." I stick my tongue out at him. "Anyway, regardless ... breakfast was a wonderful thought. Thank you so much."

"You are most welcome."

I'd decided to dress in the white cotton blouse which BJ had bought for me the previous day, so I perform a little twirl for him.

"OK. So, what d'you think?"

"Yeah ... it really suits you."

"I'm also wearing the crimson undies," I tease, "... but I won't show you."

"Perhaps you'd better not," BJ agrees, "... as I now appear to be spoken for."

"Oh BJ, Suzi's such a lucky girl. But I guess I am too, because it means I've just found myself another bestie. Oh, and who knows? Maybe one day I'll get to be a matron of honour. Oh, shall we go shopping for a hat?"

"Perhaps it's a tad early to be thinking of that."

"No, but it's exciting ... two of my favourite people in the world."

"OK. No hats, but let's head on out into Auckland, shall we? Are you ready?"

"Uh-huh, nearly; I just need to brush my teeth. I think there's a tiny bit of champagne left if you want it, and thanks again babe ... it was really wonderful."

Chapter 27: Just friends

Saturday 29 August 1992 - Baker Street, London

7:15pm. *At the flat. I'm emerging from the bedroom, having changed into a black crop-top and stonewashed blue denim cut-offs.*

So, that was that ... BJ and Suzi had fallen madly in love.

I had to reconcile myself to the fact that BJ and I needed to remain in the 'just-friends-box' ... but, to be honest, I was probably OK with that. I hadn't really fallen for BJ as such: yes, we'd had a fumble on the bus, and yes, I'd really warmed to him as a kind and caring person ... but I'd never felt the depth of feeling that Suzi evidently had towards him.

It helped matters that Suzi and BJ were, and still are, both such awesome people. And the thought of the two of them in love with each other ... well, although I was terribly envious of the love itself, I was truly happy for them.

The next couple of days that BJ and I spent in Auckland were really fabulous; we had such an enjoyable time. We took a boat across Auckland harbour, and BJ told me about some of his wild and sometimes sordid dreams; he made me laugh so much. BJ has an uncannily similar mind to my own ... it's absolutely filthy.

The day before he left Auckland, we watched the cricket final from my hotel room. I was feeling a bit poorly, but he wanted to keep me company, rather than go and watch it by himself in a bar. By the evening, I felt considerably better, so we went out for a night on the town ... drinking and dancing the night away.

Oh, hold on, what's the time?

He should be here any minute, but while I just throw together the side salad, let me tell you a bit about that night ... or at least the morning after.

Chapter 28: So ... did we?

Thursday 26 March 1992 – Auckland, New Zealand

04:30am. In room 64 at the Park Towers Hotel, after emerging from the bathroom. BJ and I came back late after a night on the town; he was in no fit state to make it back to his hostel, so I let him stay over.

BJ appears to have stirred. A few minutes ago, when I got up to go to the bathroom, he seemed dead to the world. Well, I say dead, but there was one part of him which definitely appeared quite lively. As BJ wasn't completely covered by the duvet, I couldn't help but notice the rather stiff pole that was tenting up his boxers ... it was enormously tempting for me to play with. That was in sharp contrast to when we went to bed; he'd never have had any lead in his pencil then. I'd had to help him to undress, he was so drunk. I'd left BJ to sleep in his boxers, whereas I'd just changed into my normal long t-shirt.

"Hey there beautiful," I say, as I see him awake and, seemingly, a little confused. I climb back into bed beside him. "Sorry babe, did I wake you?"

"Oh ... um ... uh ... no ... I just woke up needing the bathroom."

"Well, it's all yours, babe. Quite some night, huh?"

"Uh ... yeah ... quite some night."

As I settle back under the duvet, BJ gets out of bed and walks gingerly over to the bathroom. He closes the door behind him, before switching on the light.

I hear him begin to release the pressure from his bladder. After a few moments I hear the toilet flush, but he waits until it's finished before switching off the light and opening the door. The bedroom is quite well-lit from the residual lighting of Auckland's downtown area, but he's being considerate, and trying his best not to disturb me.

He shuffles back to his side of the bed, and then begins to rifle through his clothes, which I'd folded and left on the tub-chair.

"Babe, what are you looking for? Are you OK?"

"Uh-huh ... yeah, I guess. A headache though."

I'm not surprised, considering the volume of beer and whisky he knocked back last night.

"There's some paracetamol in my washbag, if you want some."

"Thanks ... that'd be great."

"Help yourself babe."

BJ returns to the bathroom, and I hear the rip of foil from a strip of pills, followed by two gulps of water. He then returns to sit on his side of the bed.

"Hey, come back to bed," I whisper, patting the empty space next to me. "You should try to get some sleep."

BJ lies down again, resting his head on the pillow about six inches away from my own. He's now staring up at the ceiling.

"Hey babe, can't you sleep? Try to get some rest ... remember you need to fly out later today." I roll onto my side, facing him, and begin to caress the side of his face. "Just shut your eyes babe, and get some rest."

BJ follows my lead, and closes his eyes again. I enjoy caressing him for a few more moments, before rolling back to my other side to resume my slumber.

♦ ♦ ♦

It's just before 08:00am when I wake again. As I slowly gain awareness, I see BJ's eyes studying me from the other pillow.

"Hi! Good morning," he whispers softly.

"Hi babe." I'm still not fully alert, but soon remember why I've woken up next to BJ.

"How did you sleep?"

"I'm still sleeping," I reply, briefly shutting my eyes again. I open them, and smile towards BJ; he appears a little anxious.

"Hi again," he whispers.

"Some night babe, wasn't it?" And, indeed it was; we had such a laugh, but my god did we get plastered.

"I guess so," says BJ, looking a bit confused.

"What d'you mean, you guess so? We had some fun, didn't we? And you've got some great moves."

He looks at me, seemingly bewildered.

"Great moves?"

"Yeah BJ; you really know how to sweep a girl off her feet."

"Oh, on the dance floor?"

"Well, yeah. Why BJ, what d'you think I meant?" I sit up in bed beside BJ; I'm now a little surprised. *What was he thinking?*

"Well ... uh ..."

"You don't remember last night too well, do you? Well, you certainly did have a lot to drink ... and I mean a lot."

"I can feel it," he says, stroking the top of his head. He's evidently still in a bad way.

"So, tell me BJ, what do you remember?"

"Well ... um ..." he hesitates.

This might be fun.

"OK, well, let's begin with whether you remember coming to bed with me." I look BJ straight in the eye, and lick my lower lip, teasing him. "Can you recall what you said to me? D'you remember what we did BJ; d'you know how naughty we were?" *Yeah, now who's being naughty?*

BJ holds my gaze, but he's like a deer stunned by car headlights.

"Well babe, then let me remind you," I continue, trying to think fast as to how this story is going to go. "Can you recall saying that you loved me? D'you remember coming back here last night? Well, how about when we stood over by the window, or me undressing you? D'you remember any of that?" None of this was a lie ... just a slightly twisted context.

"Oh Megan, I'm so sorry. I really didn't mean to ..."

He looks quite worried now. *I'm so cruel.*

"Didn't mean to what, BJ?"

"You're going to say, did I remember undressing you, and kissing your body and your breasts, and then teasing you with my tongue between your legs ... aren't you? Look, I'm so sorry; I'm such a bad person. I never wanted to mess you about, and, oh fuck, I really didn't want to hurt Suzi."

Wow! That was a bit more than I expected.

I chuckle.

"Oh BJ, what am I going to do with you? You're such a naughty thing ... but I love you. No, I was not going to say all that. I'd have enjoyed it tremendously, if you'd actually behaved like that ... however, all I was going to say was that I undressed you and helped you into bed. Even if you'd wanted to ravish me passionately last night, you were pretty incapable of anything ... you couldn't even untie your shoelaces. No babe, don't worry, you didn't misbehave ... at least not in that way. A few too many drinks and singing in the streets ... that's all really. No damage done."

I lean over and kiss his forehead, a bit by way of apology for winding him up.

"Oh, I must say though," I continue, "... we shouldn't make a habit of this. You're extremely difficult for me to resist, especially when I wake up to discover you've got a stonking erection. I tried ever so hard to restrain myself."

"Oh fuck! I'm so sorry Megan ... really."

"No need to apologize; you're just the sexy bloke I have to resist for the sake of my best friend. It's a pity though!"

BJ rolls onto his back, and lets out a deep sigh of relief.

I feel a bit awful having had fun at his expense ... but it was so worth it.

Chapter 29: Winds of change

Saturday 29 August 1992 - Baker Street, London

7:30pm. I'm now in the kitchen, waiting impatiently for BJ to arrive.

So, did you like that bit of fun I had winding up BJ? You'd have done the same though, wouldn't you?

And don't you think it was a reasonable price to pay for him being drunk? I mean, BJ was completely bladdered; I nearly had to carry him back to the hotel. He was in no fit state to find his way back to the YHA hostel, and I could hardly leave him out on the street, could I? But that morning-after was such a hoot. It was so funny how he couldn't remember anything, and he seemed so convinced that we'd had sex. Even if I had been up for it, BJ was far too inebriated for any such antics. It's got to be said though, when I woke up beside him and saw his morning glory, it was terribly tempting to initiate some real naughtiness. However, I remained impeccably behaved. OK, so there's no need for you to look so surprised!

Anyway, later that day, BJ flew out from New Zealand towards Canada, where he spent the next couple of months. I caught my own flight home from Auckland the following day.

I've only seen BJ once since Auckland, when I bumped into him at Kings Cross Station, just a few weeks ago. We had a quick coffee but didn't have much time to talk. However, I made sure he had my new phone number, and we've chatted a bit since then. But between Auckland and now, so much has changed.

♦ ♦ ♦

A few days after arriving home, I broke up with James. It was the first time we met up after I got back, and I decided to meet him on neutral territory. We met on Quayside for a walk along the river, which meant I could deliver the death blow to our relationship without interruptions from either family. I think he was half expecting it.

There was no point in dragging it out. I don't regret the years we spent together, far from it, but our relationship had become stale, and I think we both needed to move on in different directions. The split was still difficult; we were good friends, and had been together since our early teens. However, from a love-life perspective, there wasn't so much to let go of. I'm still not really sure how James felt about it, but he didn't put up a fight to keep me. Perhaps that just confirmed all I needed to know.

I never told James about Neil, nor BJ, and I was quite glad that I didn't need to tell him. I guess the writing had been on the wall before I went away, and James just seemed to accept that our time together had come to an end. For a few weeks, I felt a bit guilty that I hadn't told him more but, before the end of April, I saw him out in the city centre with his arms around another girl. I can't say that didn't upset me but, in a way, I was pleased he'd been able to move on quickly, and I knew that I needed to do the same.

By the time I met BJ at Kings Cross, it was not only James and I who had split up; Suzi and BJ were no longer an item. Well, they never actually got back together again after Melbourne, despite declaring their love towards each other. Suzi dumped him towards the end of May, as soon as BJ had returned from Canada.

While BJ was away, Suzi got reacquainted with her old boyfriend Matt. I was actually out with them, and a few more of our old uni friends, on the night when it happened. I still can't believe she wanted to get back together with him; he always seemed far too self-centred.

Having said that, I guess I'm hardly the best one to talk about relationships, and about being faithful. But I felt really gutted for BJ. He was so clearly besotted with Suzi, and back in February they had seemed to be such a great match, and with a wonderful future ahead of them.

♦ ♦ ♦

7:45pm. *I'm pacing around the flat. BJ's now 15 minutes late, and my anxiety is increasing.*

BJ should be here by now. I know it's only fifteen minutes, but I do hate it when people are late.

What if he's forgotten? No, I'm sure he wouldn't; he's not the forgetful type.

Or what if he's ill? No, probably not, as I guess he would've called … well, at least if he was home. But what if he's had an accident?

No, stop worrying Megan … it's only fifteen minutes. It's not like agreeing to meet someone in Cairns and disappearing without trace for a month, like I did to BJ. Fifteen minutes is nothing.

Oh, but what if he's never forgiven me for that? And what if he never intended to come tonight?

No, come on Megan … I know that's not true, don't I? I mean, it can't be, can it?

Can it?

No … I mean, as a reader, you know that won't happen, don't you? After all, this book still has several more pages to run. If BJ doesn't turn up, it'll only be a page or two until the end of the story. You know, I'll wait around, get depressed, drink myself stupid and then end up sobbing all night; and neither you nor I will get our happy endings.

No, surely the author won't have done that to us … or would he? Fuck, maybe he would … he's actually a bit of a swine sometimes. Perhaps he's written that BJ is lying in a ditch by the side of the road somewhere, and I'm about to get a call from the police to say they've found his body.

No, that scenario can't happen. That storyline couldn't work, as nobody would call me ... it was only BJ who knew that he was coming here.

Oh, hell ... come on Mr Author, will you just put us out of our misery?

BUZZZZZZZZ!
The downstairs door buzzer sounds.

Well, I guess that's him now; I hope so.

Chapter 30: Buzz

Saturday 29 August 1992 - Baker Street, London

7:50pm. *I walk across to the front door and press the button to answer the intercom.*

"Hello!"
"Hi Megan! It's BJ, sorry I'm late; I got stuck on the Tube."
"Hi babe. I'll buzz you in; come on up."
All of a sudden, I have butterflies in my stomach. I quickly rush to check myself in the full-length mirror in the hallway.
"Don't get flustered Megan," I tell myself, "... remember, we're just mates, not dates."
A few moments later, the doorbell rings, and I open the door. Standing squarely in front of me, there's a broad smile across BJ's face. My heart skips a beat.
"Hey Megan, sorry, there was a bomb alert on the Bakerloo line; I was stuck in the tunnel around Paddington for about half an hour. Hey, it's a great place you've got here."
BJ leans forward, kisses my cheek, and gives me a warm hug.
"Hey babe, it's so good to see you again."
I remain in the hug for a few moments longer than I should.
Mmm-yes, that feels nice. Yeah, nice is the word ... kind of comforting, not electrifying ... a 'friendship' type of a hug. The body contact feels good though ... I've missed the physical touch since I broke with James. Mmm-yes ... he smells good too, and he's shaved not long ago. But more than anything, I feel a sense of relief that he's here ... I was starting to worry.
We step back, and both scan each other up and down, before laughing.
"I must say Megan, you're really looking hot!"
"Thanks babe, you brush up pretty well too," I respond, and I'm right, because he's looking dishier than I remember. Dressed in a light-blue, short-sleeve button-down shirt, light stonewashed

jeans and brogues, BJ looks pretty handsome. He's not film-star gorgeous, but his tall athletic build, blond hair and mischievous blue eyes still make him quite a looker. "Hey, I'll show you the roof terrace in a bit, but come on in first."

BJ steps through the door. He places his daypack down on the floor in the hallway, before unzipping it.

"I didn't know what to bring you, so I hope wine and chocs are OK. It's a New Zealand Sauvignon Blanc, to remember Auckland."

"Oh wonderful, same here," I reply. "I've got a matching bottle in the fridge for later. Let's get this one chilling too, just in case. I also picked up a bottle of Clare Valley Chardonnay; I remember Suzi and I drinking it on the beach on New Year's Day."

"Uh-huh ... sounds good. But Megan, I probably shouldn't drink too much tonight; I've still got to get the Tube back home."

"Oh BJ, just live a little. Stay in the moment, isn't that what you kept telling me? And anyway, you can stay here tonight if you want ... there's plenty of space." *And my bed's large enough for two ... although, perhaps I should cut those thoughts out. Well, who knows?*

"I can see you've got space; this place is fabulous."

BJ starts to look around, and I show him a couple of the bedrooms before leading him to the kitchen, where I put the wine to chill.

"Yeah babe, I've been really lucky with this place. The guy who owns it works for my firm, and he's on secondment to Singapore. They're a lovely couple actually; they intend to pop back for the odd weekend here and there, and have set aside their bedroom for when they come back. But the arrangement means that I'm sort of house-sitting rather than renting, and getting this flat almost free-of-charge."

"Awesome! You've certainly landed on your feet."

"Yep!"

"Having said that, I can't really complain. I found a pretty decent mansion flat which I'm sharing with a couple of great guys: one who's a friend from Oxford. The flat could do with some decorating, but otherwise it's fine. It costs a lot though. I quite like Maida Vale too; it seems a bit more tranquil than most areas I've seen in London."

"Uh-huh?"

"Yeah, it's full of red-brick mansion blocks set in wide tree-lined streets; and we've got four or five pubs within a stone's throw."

"Cool babe; you'll have to invite me over."

"You bet."

"Anyway BJ, let me show you our roof terrace."

♦ ♦ ♦

8:00pm. Up on the roof terrace, which is a small patio area, containing a couple of heavy wooden benches and a few large tubs of crimson-blossoming fuchsia plants.

"I've heard that some of these mansion blocks have lawns and even running tracks on the roofs ... but this one isn't quite that posh," I explain.

"It's still pretty cool to have something like this at your disposal. We've got a lawn out the back, but it's pretty overlooked and doesn't seem to get much sun."

"Uh-huh ... so babe, you can't go out there and sunbathe naked?" I visualise the prospect.

BJ laughs.

"Well, not really, but my room is at the back of the flat, and I'm disappointed that I haven't seen any hot girls out there."

"Naughty!" I say, and give him a smack on the bum.

"You know me, Megan ... and my smutty mind."

"I do indeed babe ... it's why we get along so well."

BJ steps to the edge of the terrace, and tries to look over the side. There's not much you can see, as the fire-escape stairs hamper any views down to the street.

"Hey Megan, d'you remember the first time you smacked me on the bum?"

"Remind me," I reply. I do remember, but I'm trying to tread carefully; I'm uncertain as to whether BJ is still upset after Suzi dumped him.

"At the summit of Ayers Rock, admiring the view." BJ laughs.

"Yeah babe, admiring the view of Suzi's bum ... that's what you were doing."

"Well, if you say so. But apart from Suzi's bum, the views out over the desert were pretty awesome, weren't they?"

"Uh-huh ... they certainly were. It all seems like such a long time ago now, doesn't it? Anyway, changing the subject a bit ... I'm sorry we didn't have longer to chat when I saw you at Kings Cross. I never conveyed how sorry I was about you and Suzi; you two seemed so good together."

BJ sighs.

I can tell he's still sore about it.

"Yeah, I thought we were good too. Well, you know how strongly I felt about her. But I guess some things aren't meant to be. It still hurts, but I can't go back and change what happened. However, at least I feel less guilty now, when it's you who appears in my wicked fantasies." He smiles at me, his eyes gleaming with mischief.

I laugh.

I wonder if he still has those dreams; some were really kinky.

"Oh yes BJ, I remember you telling me in Auckland. So, have you been having more naughty revelations?"

"Oh Megan, that would be telling," he teases. "But there's an old one that's set around here, which I mightn't have mentioned."

"Uh-huh?"

"Yes. Well, d'you know that bar, the one down there on the junction with Marylebone Road, right by the Tube entrance?"

"You mean the large wine bar? What's its name?"

"Yeah, that's the one ... and I can't remember the name either."

"Uh-huh."

"OK, well, this was actually one of the first visions I had about you and Suzi. I imagined meeting the two of you in that bar; you were both dressed in dark figure-hugging business suits."

"Not the normal attire for your dreams?"

"That's true," he chuckles, "... but this was at the top of Ayers Rock, when you told me you'd both be working in London. I guess I was imagining a possible future. But it's so funny that this early vision was on Baker Street ... and now, here you are."

"Yeah, that's weird."

"And disappointingly clean," he adds. "I'll leave my dirty visions until later."

"Well, let's get back to the kitchen ... some wine might help to loosen your tongue."

"OK Megan, but just hang on a minute. Well, you know how it was with me and Suzi ... so, tell me, how was it with you and James? I remember when I was in Vancouver, you told me over the phone that you'd broken up. It was soon after you got back, wasn't it? Sorry, I meant to ask you before now. ... Oh, but only if you want to tell me; sorry Megan, I don't mean to pry."

"Yeah BJ, stop being Mr Nosey!" I pause for a moment, before smiling. "Don't worry babe, I'm more than happy to tell you. So, yes, I'm currently back to being young, free and single. Oh, and before you ask, I've not had any sex for an eternity." I'm trying to sense his reaction, and he smiles when I mention the sex; I'm starting to get the itch to flirt ... and maybe a bit more.

"And James?" asks BJ, rather stopping me in my tracks. With my mind in scheming mode, I'd forgotten the question.

"Oh yeah, James ... well, as I told you, we split up as soon as I got back from Auckland. I felt really bad about it; we'd been together such a long time. But we were suffocating each other, and I needed to move on ... well, probably we both did. And he certainly moved on pretty-damn-quick ... I saw him with a new girl just a couple of weeks later."

"Uh-huh ... and how did you feel about that? Was it hard?"

"Yeah, at first. But in some ways, I think I'd already moved on before coming back from Auckland. I know I've said it before, but seeing you and Suzi together ... well, you just had that young-and-in-love sparkle. It kinda made me jealous ... and I wouldn't have felt that way if I'd been happy with James."

"I suppose not, and I do remember you saying as much when we talked on the bus across to Townsville."

"Yeah well, I guess that sometimes we all have to move on to fresh pastures. Oh, and yes, of course, there was Neil in Broome ... well, he was fresh ... hmm-yeah, I could really do with more sex like that." I giggle, setting BJ off too.

"Well girl, d'you think we should go and open the wine?"

Chapter 31: Now we're cooking!

Saturday 29 August 1992 - Baker Street, London

8:15pm. *BJ and I have returned to the kitchen.*

"OK babe, what would you like to drink?"

As we step back into the kitchen, I flick the light switch on, and BJ surveys my food prep.

"Obviously, we've got lots of wine," I continue, "but there's also beer, and gin, and there's even the odd whisky if you prefer. I remember you like your whisky ... and there's a Glenlivet open."

"Don't you think it's a tad early for whisky? Well, perhaps any time's good, but what are we eating?"

"It's a surprise." I suddenly try to block his view of some of the ingredients that are standing right in front of us. "Oh, sod it ... I'll want you to help me later anyway. So, here goes ... stand back babe, and be impressed."

BJ takes a step back and leans against the fridge.

"OK, well first on the menu ... coz I know you like them ... we've got pan-fried scallops."

"Awesome ..."

"Uh-huh ... yes, scallops with chorizo, on a bed of sweet potato, generously garnished with parsley."

"Wow Megan, I didn't know you could cook."

"You might want to hold your judgement; I've not tried cooking scallops before, so I may need your help."

"No worries, it sounds great."

"And I bought the Marlborough Sauvignon Blanc to accompany it. I found it at the M&S at Marble Arch, and I remembered we had some together in Auckland."

"Excellent ... well, as we've now got two of them, shall we open one while we cook?"

I extract the chilled bottle from the fridge and pass it to BJ, together with a corkscrew. It's nice to have a man around the kitchen ... *Oh, that sounds a bit sexist, doesn't it?*

"Here you go babe. And while you deal with that, I can tell you the rest. So, after the scallops, we're going to have seafood linguine with a green salad ... inspired by that place we found in Parnell Village."

As I talk, I collect the two wine glasses from the table in the lounge.

"Oh yeah, I remember; now that was a good meal."

"It most certainly was. And, you know BJ, it was only out in Australia and New Zealand that I started to enjoy seafood. I never really had much growing up, nor at uni. But we had some fabulous meals with Laura and Phil in Perth, and I guess that's where my cravings must've started."

"You're not pregnant, are you?"

"Effing hell BJ, do I look it?"

"You do have a certain radiance," BJ smirks.

"Hey ... watch it mister!" I pick up a large spatula and playfully poke him in the stomach.

BJ pops the cork, pours the first glass of wine, and passes it to me. He follows with a second for himself.

"Well Megan, thanks for inviting me over. Cheers!"

We clink glasses.

"Here's to a fresh start in London ... for both of us," he says.

"To us," I reply, as I gaze into BJ's eyes and linger a little. I take a sip of wine, and let my tongue trace over my bottom lip, diverting his attention to my mouth. "And to living in the moment." I'm being a bit naughty now, but I can sense there's still a spark between us ... *and why not, now we're both free agents?*

BJ smiles, and averts his eyes.

I can sense that I'm making him feel a little uneasy ... not necessarily in a bad way. Perhaps he's feeling the same butterflies as I am.

A few hours ago, I wasn't sure if I'd want to make a move on him tonight, but now I'm really feeling up for it. If only I was certain our minds were in the same place, I'd probably initiate something, but I don't want to lose him as a friend. I'm also mindful of how I screwed things up for us back in January, when I lost my self-control on that bus. I don't want to overstep the mark again and blow it, so to speak. BJ's so difficult to read sometimes, and he's also quite shy, so, even if he wanted to, I'm sure he'd be reluctant to make the first move. I'll have to feel my way forward carefully.

I press the ignition on the hob ... it's gas rather than electric, which I prefer, as it's much easier to control the temperature. I pick up the saucepan containing the peeled chunks of sweet potato, and set them to boil: fifteen to twenty minutes should do it.

"I'll need you to mash that later," I tell BJ, unsubtly squeezing his bicep. "Oh-yes, nice and firm; seems like you've been working out."

"Appearances can be deceptive ... well, in my case anyway. But you, Megan ... blimey, you look in fabulous shape."

"Oh yeah?"

"Uh-huh, and it's funny, but that was maybe the first thought I ever had about you. D'you remember that day when we first met?"

"What, way back in Darwin?"

"Yeah."

"No babe, I'm afraid not, at least, not very well. But you were with Neil, I do remember that."

"Uh-huh. Well, I remember it like it was yesterday. You and Suzi had just got out of the pool ... mmm-yes, you were in your black swimsuits, I can picture it now." BJ closes his eyes. "And if you don't mind me saying, you looked smokin-hot ... both of you." BJ sips his wine, his eyes still shut. "Mmm-yes ... delicious." He smiles for a few moments, then opens his eyes.

I slap him gently on the arm.

"Hmm-babe ... you're so naughty." *He's started flirting with me now ... that's a good sign.*

"But anyway Megan, you were so into Neil that evening, and I don't think that you or Suzi even noticed me."

"Well, maybe that's true in my case, but it was just a few days after my shenanigans with Neil in Broome."

"Shenanigans??? Don't you mean shagfest? I recall you divulging the details on the bus ride from Alice; your eyes were alight, as though all your Christmases had come at once."

I laugh.

"Well ... why not? After all, it was bloody fantastic ... a bit of an alcohol-induced workout, but, oh-babe, it was still really hot. But my god, I felt so ashamed afterwards; it was the only time I'd ever cheated on James. And BJ ... that night was also the last bloody time I had sex. Knackers BJ! That was nearly eight months ago ... bloody-hell, I must be turning into a nun. I mean, I know that James and I weren't exactly rabbits, and the sex was neither regular nor satisfying ... but ... oh, why-the-hell am I telling you this?"

"Yes, why indeed?" says BJ, with a glint in his eye.

I'm now beginning to sense that BJ might want the same thing as me tonight ... and, just in case I haven't made it sufficiently clear, that means ending my eight-month drought!

The thought that BJ might also want it makes me feel increasingly horny. He's probably bursting for it as much as I am ... especially if he was saving himself for Suzi. However, apart from the sex, where would all this lead? Could BJ and I genuinely become lovers? Or, perhaps we'd never get beyond friends with benefits, if that. Oh, fuck alone knows! Anyhow, that said, I'm still certain of two things: one ... that I don't want to lose BJ as a friend, and two ... that I'm dying for a few special benefits.

But there's another thing I've just realised ... for the first time in years, I don't feel guilty. I'm spending the evening with BJ, and there's nothing to hide; there's no shame, whatever my intentions may be tonight. There's no James nor Suzi to think about, and I don't even have Mammy or Beth listening through the walls ... I'm free!

With such thoughts in my head, I feel a greater spring in my step, as I move around the kitchen preparing the meal.

I take the chorizo and peel away the fragile skin, before placing it on the chopping board to cut into thin slices. As BJ watches me, I'm sure he's trying to think of some quip about how this reminds him of a condom ... me too, but I can't conjure one up.

"Hey babe, shall we put on some music? While I do this, why don't you find something amongst the CDs in the lounge?" *Here's a chance for me to assess his mood.*

"OK ... sure," says BJ, stepping out of the kitchen. "Anything in particular?"

"You choose ... whatever you like."

I continue chopping the chorizo, and tip the pieces into a medium-size frying pan. It's still a bit early to begin frying, so next I turn my attention to fine-chopping some parsley, and lightly scoring the scallops ... I'm told this allows the flavour of the chorizo to penetrate.

"Hey Megan?" BJ calls through from the lounge.

"Uh-huh?"

"What d'you think of Fergie? I see you've got the *Daily Mirror*."

"Oh yeah ... quite a story?"

"Yeah."

"Well, I guess it's her business ... whatever turns her on."

"So, this toe-sucking stuff ... have you ever tried it?"

"Nuh-uh, chance would be a fine thing. No babe, James never really took his mouth lower than my tits."

I hear BJ chuckle at my reply.

He soon returns to the kitchen, with the background sounds of Latin-style jazz now pulsing through from the lounge.

"Are all those CDs yours?" he asks.

"No ... some are, but most belong to Peter and Gill, the owners."

"Ah-ha ... and how about this one? Are you into jazz?"

I begin to shake my hips to the rhythm; it's got a good vibe.

"I've not really heard too much, but this sounds rather ... erm, rather ... oh babe, what's the right word?"

"Jazzy perhaps?" suggests BJ.

"Yeah, that's the one," I agree, continuing to wiggle my butt. I glance at BJ to see whether he's watching. He is. I bend forward over the cooker to prod the bubbling sweet potatoes with a wooden spoon ... and, naturally, I exaggerate my wiggle to tease him further.

"Hey babe, are you admiring the view?"

BJ smiles, and blushes.

"Uh-huh ... yeah, you caught me again."

"So?"

"So? ... So what?" he shrugs.

"So ... how does it compare with the view from Ayers Rock?" *Oh shit, maybe that's poor taste* ... "Oh, sorry babe, I didn't mean to bring up Suzi again."

"Oh, no worries ... think nothing of it. You and Suzi kind of came to me as a pair, so it's difficult not to think of you in that way. However, to answer your question ... hmm-yes, that wonderful view from Ayers Rock ... well, I could stand gazing at it for hours, simply lost in my own dreamland."

I'm now looking at him intently, as he's drawing this out.

"So then, how's the view?"

"Oh, I think the outback is tremendous ... what else can I say?" BJ smiles, his face is flushed as his gaze holds my own. *Things are heating up!*

"Well babe, you can look ... but you can't touch." I smile, and then brush past him through the doorway, pausing briefly before going into the lounge. "No babe ..." I wink, "... at least, not until after we've eaten."

Now, if that wasn't a blatant invitation for later, then, short of taking my top off and thrusting my cleavage in his face, I don't know what else I'll need to do. My intentions are clear ... BJ, it's your move next.

I walk over to the CD player to see what music is playing; this track isn't familiar to me, but I'm enjoying the rhythm. It's 'Mas que nada' from Sergio Mendes ... and I continue wiggling my hips to the beat.

"So babe, d'you like jazz?" I ask, as I return to the kitchen.

"I like this one ... but I've not really heard much. Ronnie Scott and his band played at our college ball a few years ago; I quite enjoyed that. I hear he's got a club somewhere around here."

"Yeah, I think that's The 100 Club ... it's somewhere on Oxford Street. Maybe we should check it out some time."

"Yeah, I'd like that."

"Oh BJ ... talking of The 100 Club ... I remember that phone call you made to Suzi from Vancouver, when you told us about the mile-high-club attempt on your flight."

"Oh yeah ... did I mention it?"

"Uh-huh ... so, tell me, did you really see it? That's so awesome?"

"Well, I didn't actually see them having sex, but yes, it was real. The woman in the next seat seemed to think it was awesome too. Lyn was her name ... I stayed a few days with her on Vancouver Island."

"Oh yeah ... you dark horse BJ."

"Uh-huh ... it wasn't like that though, but I did feel guilty about it ... and, for more reasons than one."

"Oh really?"

"Well, firstly, when we sat together on the plane, I didn't know whether she was flirting a bit. I'm always useless at picking up such signals and, anyway, Lyn was several years older than me. She'd actually been to Hawaii on what should've been her honeymoon, but the guy walked out just before the wedding ... a long story but, anyway, she seemed really friendly, and invited me to stay whenever I arrived in Victoria. Lyn gave me her number, but because of Suzi ... well, I never really intended to call her."

"Uh-huh?"

"Yeah, and actually, I didn't call ... I bumped into her. Yes, when I got over to Victoria, I checked into the YHA hostel. Then, later on, Lyn found me in a pub. She was there having lunch with three of her friends. We got talking, and then she insisted that I came to stay, and that I allow her to show me around Victoria. I felt guilty about accepting, but I also didn't want to be unfriendly."

"So, why did you feel guilty? Well, I guess I can understand it ... during my few years with James, I always felt uneasy about spending time with other guys."

I check on the sweet potato ... it's nearly done, so I now begin to fry the chorizo.

"Well Megan, that wasn't the whole story, but I would have felt guilty spending time with any girl other than Suzi. I even felt guilt when enjoying those few days with you in Auckland ... and not just after I thought we'd slept together. But anyway, Lyn turned out to be quite different from what I expected."

"Uh-huh?"

"Yeah, well, when we talked on the plane, Lyn told me she was a model, and mentioned appearing in a few films. It later transpired that Lyn was involved in 'adult entertainment' ... as indeed were her three friends.'"

"D'you mean porn?"

"Uh-huh."

"Wow!"

"Uh-huh. Anyhow, one day, Lyn took me for lunch to one of these friends' houses. And there was I, poor naïve little me ... and they took me down to show me the basement. I'd never seen anything like it ... it was a sex dungeon, with all sorts of kinky toys and furniture."

"Oh my god BJ! That's amazing ... tell me everything!"

The chorizo is now sizzling, and the sweet potato ready to mash.

"Hey babe, would you drain and mash this for me?"

"Sure," says BJ, taking the pan from the hob, and moving to the sink.

"So, what sort of toys and furniture d'you mean?"

"Well, they certainly made your silver bullet look rather tame. There were whips, tickling sticks, dildos, nipple clamps, plugs ... not to mention wooden stocks and a torture bench."

"Wow babe! So, what did you do?"

"Well, I declined to play with them in that basement. My god Megan, I've never been so shit-scared, but so turned-on, in all my life. After lunch, I ended up in a hot tub with two of them ... well, I kept my boxers on, but they were naked ... and it was so hard to keep my gaze averted from their awesome boobs. I then had to listen to numerous tales of their debauchery ... my god Megan, you wouldn't believe it ..."

"Oh, you poor thing," I laugh.

"Yeah, and I also went skinny-dipping in a forest lake, and sat naked in a sauna with Lyn ... at one minute freezing my bollocks off, and the next trying desperately to prevent an unwanted erection."

BJ starts mashing the sweet potato. I add some chunks of butter, and a sprinkle of black pepper.

"So babe, it sounds like you had some fun."

"Well, fun might be one word. I had lots of frustration and terrible feelings of guilt, if that's what you mean. I didn't do anything, but, at the same time, I still felt I was betraying Suzi."

I place the scallops in with the sizzling chorizo, and then start gently shaking the pan, so as to avoid any of them sticking.

"Ok babe, let's get these served up, and you can tell me more about Canada."

I plate up, arranging first the sweet potato, then scallops and chorizo, with a sprinkle of parsley on top. It looks great, and smells delicious.

Refining My Dining

I refill the kettle to heat the water for the linguine. I pass my glass to BJ, pick up the plates, and then lead BJ through to the small dining table in the lounge.

Chapter 32: Appetizer

Saturday 29 August 1992 - Baker Street, London

8:45pm. BJ and I move through to the lounge/dining room to begin our meal.

The dining table is approximately a 3-by-3-foot square, large enough for four people at-a-pinch, but the perfect size for two. It's on the left-hand side, set against the wall, as you enter from the kitchen. The lounge area opens up to the right; its magnolia-painted walls add a sense of light and space, as they do throughout the flat. There's a double window, and the evening light streams through cream-coloured venetian blinds. It's about half an hour since sunset, but the room is still well-lit.

I set our plates down on the table, and invite BJ to sit down first. He places both our wine glasses, and parks himself in the far seat. Then, before sitting down, I strike a match to light the candle ... a final detail which, despite the warm evening light, still adds that extra touch of intimacy.

Throughout the flat, including in the living room, there are paintings, mainly of colourful objects that are hard to distinguish; the owners evidently love their modern art, but it's not really to my taste. On the feature wall there's a rectangular, gold-framed mirror, mounted above a mantelpiece containing a gas fire. There's also a built-in run of floor-to-ceiling bookshelves containing a library of classics: from Orwell and Shakespeare, to Dickens, Austen, Steinbeck and even Delia Smith (yes, there are some 'classic' cookbooks too). The shelves also house a Bang & Olufsen hi-fi system, and a large collection of CDs, and there's a 30-inch TV and video combo in the corner. A pair of comfy red sofas are pushed together in an L-shape, and are decorated with four golden velvety cushions, which I hope we might snuggle up with later.

BJ tops up our glasses with the Sauvignon Blanc, and prepares for a toast.

"To old friends, and to new beginnings," says BJ.

We chink glasses.

"Not so old babe ... but anyway, please tuck in."

With surgical precision, BJ cuts one of his scallops in half, and brings the first piece to his lips. My eyes fix on his, hoping he likes it.

BJ catches me watching, and the scallop pauses at his lips. A mischievous smile appears, as his eyes hold mine and linger; the flickering candle now reflects in his devilish gaze. Without breaking eye-contact, he delicately plucks the scallop from the fork, and sucks it into his mouth. My god, food can be so arousing ... I imagine my nipple in place of the fork, and feel a tingle in my breast as my pulse begins to race. *Snap out of it Megan!*

He chews for a moment before swallowing, but his face doesn't give away any clues.

"So babe, how was it?"

His tongue reappears and traces across his upper lip. I want to dive across the table and bite him.

"Mmm-hmm," he says, "... good ... really good."

BJ drops his gaze, as he returns to his plate for some chorizo and sweet potato.

On this cue, I begin to attack my own first scallop.

"So BJ, tell me more about Canada. Were there any other people as 'interesting' as Lyn?"

BJ hums with satisfaction, as he finishes his mouthful before responding.

"Well, I guess Lyn would probably win the prize, but I did have another couple of narrow escapes ... or perhaps, in view of Suzi dumping me, I should now call them missed opportunities."

"Oh BJ, I still can't believe what Suzi did ... sorry babe. Oh, hang on, I won't be a sec ... but let me just get the linguine cooking."

I stand up and pop back to the kitchen, pour hot water into the saucepan of pasta, set the hob to a medium flame, and return to the table. It's only a short distance, but BJ holds my gaze all the way.

"OK babe, tell me about those others; I'm all ears again."

BJ smiles as he looks me up and down.

"There's a bit more to you than that," he says. "For starters, you just showed me a tremendous view of 'the outback'."

"Naughty!" I smile, delighted by the comment. "But do tell me more about Canada, and your near misses."

"OK then ... if you really want to know."

I teasingly threaten him with my fork.

"Yes BJ ... tell me."

"Well, when I arrived in Vancouver, I met this girl from Chicago. We were both staying at a really dismal hostel ... mould on the walls, pungent smell of marijuana, that kind of place. Anyway, both of us abandoned the hostel and got rooms instead at the nearby YMCA. Anyway, this girl Frankie ... she looked like a young Aretha Franklin, and apparently was also named after her. Anyhow, one night we went out for a bar meal together, and of course, all the time I was thinking of Suzi, and feeling guilty."

As I listen to BJ's story, my mind wanders as I savour another scallop. There's something immensely sensual about devouring scallops ... it's a bit like eating Godiva chocolates, they simply melt on your tongue. But now I'm imagining another Godiva, Lady Godiva ... only it's me, and I'm riding naked through Regent's Park ... and BJ's running after me. I fall off the horse. BJ catches me. We roll around in the grass ... *Hmm-yes, I like the idea of us rolling around.*

He continues. "Well, after we eat, Frankie then squeezes my hand, and drags me across to the dance floor. She doesn't let go of me until we begin dancing, and until Frankie's got both her hands interlocked with my own. Then, as she starts to do a twirl to the music, she releases my hands, but leaves me holding a pair of lacy black knickers ..."

"Oh my god BJ, you really are a dark horse."

Hmm-yes ... rolling around in the grass ...

"It wasn't me Megan, I swear."

"So, what happened next?"

"Well, we danced a bit ... and I tried to tell Frankie about Suzi."

"And then?"

"Well, Frankie didn't seem to care, and maybe was frustrated that I didn't start groping her on the dance floor." BJ takes in another mouthful of scallop. "Mmm-yes, these really are delicious." He closes his eyes, savouring the taste.

"And, then what?"

"Well, nothing happened. Oh, except that when we got back to the YMCA, she wanted to wrap her thighs around my face ... and all the rest of it."

"Wow BJ ... and who'd have thought it of a shy boy like you?"

"But Megan, it wasn't me ... really it wasn't. And naturally I declined the offer ... but fuck, I still felt guilty about it."

"What, you mean guilty for turning down Frankie?" I couldn't resist it.

"Ha-bloody-ha ... no. I mean guilty for even spending time with her."

"Yeah, sorry, I know what you mean ... but I haven't forgotten that you declined one of my offers too." I smile, before slowly licking my top lip, aware that he's watching me intently. I'm teasing, but BJ must realise I want him tonight.

"Uh-huh ... yeah, I remember it only too well. I still can't believe you would've actually done it. Come on, there's no way you would've gone through with it ... surely not, not on the bus?"

"Oh babe, who knows?" *If you play your cards right BJ, maybe I'll offer again tonight.*

There's a long pause as we smile at each other.

"Are you done?" I ask, looking at his empty plate. "Let me clear these away."

"That was really delicious, thanks Megan ... you can cook for me anytime."

I collect the plates and return to the kitchen.

"D'you need a hand," he shouts.

"No, don't worry babe, I won't be a minute." I return to the table with the salad. "Just relax, and get ready to tell me your next story."

I drain the linguine, pouring the water into the pan containing prawns and mussels, and I allow them to rest for a minute or two while I proceed. I then get the tomato, garlic and herbs cooking in the same frying pan I used for the starter ... well, there's no point creating more mess than is necessary. Next, I drain the seafood and add it to the tomatoes and garlic. I add some finely chopped slices of smoked salmon and, after a few stirs, it's ready to serve. I plate up, add a sprinkle of black pepper and a sprig of fresh parsley, and then return to the table.

"I tried to copy that seafood linguine we had in Auckland, but my culinary skills still have a way to go."

"Well, it looks wonderful."

BJ tops up our wine.

"Help yourself to salad BJ, and tell me more about Canada."

Chapter 33: Dish of the day

Saturday 29 August 1992 - Baker Street, London

9:15pm. *BJ and I are beginning to eat our main course.*

As BJ begins telling me about a rather brazen landlady from Prince Rupert, I start to realise that linguine mightn't have been the best food choice for tonight. After only a few mouthfuls, I'd already got several splatter-marks on my top, and BJ was having even more problems than me ... partly, I guess, because he was also trying to talk at the same time.

Or, hang on, perhaps the linguine wasn't such a bad choice after all ... hmm-yes, I have a cunning idea.

After BJ describes meeting this landlady's daughter several weeks later in Montreal, BJ suddenly slops rather a large quantity of garlicky-tomato sauce down his shirt.

"Oh bugger! Oh, I'm such a clot," says BJ.

My opportunity?

"No worries babe, it's a warm evening, why not take your shirt off? I can put it in the washer dryer; it'll be done in an hour or two."

"Don't worry, it's OK."

Although he doesn't take the bait, I see this as my chance to spice things up, so I'm not taking no for an answer. I spring to my feet, step beside BJ, and start to tug at his shirt.

"C'mon babe, let's get this off you and all cleaned up."

Thankfully, BJ doesn't offer any resistance ... so, I see my chance. I begin to undo his shirt buttons and, after a couple, I slow down and test the water by caressing his chest. *Oh, naughty me! I just hope I'm not going too fast.*

"Hmm-babe, nice and hairy ... all man!"

He allows me to continue; his gaze is now fixed on mine. My heart skips a couple of beats; I suddenly realise this might be the point of no return.

"Megan?"

"Uh-huh."

"D'you remember in Auckland, when I asked you whether we could ever be 'just good friends'?"

I'm thinking of the exact same moment, as I undo the last button. As I do so, he struggles to his feet, and allows me to release him from the shirt. All this time, although merely a few seconds, our eyes have been locked together.

Without any words, BJ places his right index finger to my lips, and gently traces the outline.

I emit a quiet moan, as I feel my entire body shiver.

His finger moves to my cheek, where it lingers with delicate caresses. Instinctively, I close my eyes. BJ allows me a moment to absorb the intimacy of his touch, before the next thing I feel is the connection between our lips ... tender, soft, soothing ... and I'm now tingling with anticipation. It lasts just a moment, before his lips are gone and I open my eyes.

"I'm not so sure we were ever meant to be friends," he says. "D'you remember our first kiss?"

"Remind me," I say, seizing the initiative, and locking our lips together again.

BJ places his hands around my bare midriff; he draws me closer as I run my hands up his chest. Oh, I've so missed this type of intimacy ... but tonight feels strangely different. Tonight, I've drunk less than two glasses of wine, and tonight, more importantly, I've not invited guilt to the party. It's just BJ and me now ... nobody else, and no other distractions. I'm both sober and free, simply savouring BJ's kiss, his touch, his closeness ... his arousal.

I surface for air, and press myself even closer as my tummy feels the stiffening in his trousers. By the way, don't you just love it when you're making somebody horny?

"Hey babe, d'you think he's pleased to see me again?"

BJ laughs.

"Hey girl, you got me again. But, you know, I haven't forgotten the thrill of holding you in my arms that first time, on Ayers Rock."

"Me neither babe; I think that's when you first started to grow on me." *OK, so that pun got lost, but never mind.*

"Although, back then, just like when we first kissed on the bus ... well, I felt a bit uncomfortable ... coz I knew you were into Neil."

"Uh-huh, well babe, don't talk to me about guilt; I've had my fair share of it. But yeah, when I kissed you back then, I couldn't get James out of my mind ... well, unless perhaps it was Neil."

We laugh.

After the initial burst of electricity, my body and mind have both reverted to a more relaxed state. Being intimate with BJ seems to feel natural ... and now that I know he's not going to run away, there's not quite the same sense of urgency. It was as though that first kiss broke the ice, and now we can take our time. Yes, of course, I'm still eager to rip his clothes off, and hope he'll do the same with me ... but it feels like we should just take it slow, and really savour every moment. I take his hands, and extract myself from our embrace.

"I'll be right back BJ, let me just get your shirt in the washer."

I gently release BJ to resume his seat and continue eating, while I take the shirt through to the kitchen.

I place the shirt in the washer, find the detergent, and pour some into the appropriate slot. I stand back from the machine, and check the dials.

"I think you'd better wait a minute," says BJ, putting one arm around my waist. He then spins me around, and plants his right hand on my left boob. A big grin stretches across his face. As BJ removes his hand, a large tomatoey handprint is left behind. "I thought you might also want to wash your top."

"Oh, you cheeky so and so ..."

Before I get more words out, we are pressed together, body-to-body, lips-to-lips, and BJ's tongue is now making some moves. Oh my god, I hadn't dared dream this might happen tonight. OK, so I know that's a lie ... but you know what I mean?

BJ's hands begin to move under my top, and I feel the warmth of his caress as he slowly pulls it higher. The feel of skin-against-skin is driving me wild; I've forgotten how sensual this can be. It was so different with James, as, after years of familiarity, we no longer really cherished each other ... and with Neil, I'd been way too drunk to feel it. But this evening, each touch is so freshly delivered, and every single stroke trips my senses.

Momentarily, we disengage to allow the crop-top over my head.

"There ... now we're both properly dressed for dinner," he declares.

I laugh.

"Well babe, I must applaud you for that devious, but most excellent move."

He winks.

"I'm learning."

I throw my top into the washing machine.

"Perhaps I won't switch it on quite yet, but you don't need to waste any more of your dinner just to make a point."

"OK, I'll behave ... well, at least until dessert." He kisses me again, and then, hand-in-hand, with me now topless but for my bra, I lead him back to the table.

"C'mon babe, let's finish the pasta. And I've already invited you to stay over, so we can take our time."

"We wouldn't wish it to get cold now, would we? But then again, I wouldn't want you to get cold either."

"Well babe, you shouldn't have robbed me of my top then; you'll have to warm me up again in a few minutes."

"You bet!"

We both sit down and hold hands across the table. BJ then extracts his right hand, and lifts his glass.

"Here's to living in the moment."

I raise my glass.

"To the moment BJ ... Cheers!"

We both take a sip ...

"Oh look babe, speaking of moments ... in a few moments the wine bottle will be empty. Shall we open another?"

"You wouldn't be trying to get me drunk now, would you? ... Like you did in Auckland."

"What? You can't possibly blame me for that; you hardly needed any persuading."

"Well Megan, it is conceivable that I may want to remember tonight, but yes, let's open the other bottle ... I'll go."

BJ gets up, and fetches the other bottle of Sauvignon Blanc from the fridge.

"So babe, how much d'you actually recall from that night in Auckland? If I remember rightly, you were more than a little confused in the morning."

As BJ returns with the bottle, he sneaks up behind me and kisses my neck, sending shivers down my spine. An involuntary groan escapes from my lips.

"I recall getting exceedingly drunk, and I also remember my feelings being muddled up. I was gutted that England lost the final, elated that Suzi said she loved me, and guilt-ridden that I ... well ..." BJ pauses to pour the wine as he continues. "... well, guilt-ridden that I still had the hots for some weird girl called Megan."

BJ grins before sitting down and helping himself to another mouthful of prawns. I also take another bite, before continuing.

"D'you remember waking up in the morning, worried that we'd had sex?"

BJ smiles, as he sucks in a trailing strand of linguine.

"Uh-huh, yeah, I still think about it."

"Well babe, so do I."

By now, I've eaten as much of the linguine as I want, and BJ's also nearly finished his. So, I stand up, move behind him, and place my hands on his shoulders, beginning to massage them as he takes another bite.

"I was relieved we hadn't done it back then," he says, mumbling with his mouthful. "I don't think I could've resisted, if you'd made a move ... but equally, I'm not a bastard, and I'd never have wanted to hurt Suzi ... I still wouldn't."

"Yeah, I know babe ... me too. You know, tonight's the first night in I don't know how long when I've actually felt relaxed about being with a bloke. When I first kissed you in Australia, I felt ashamed because of James ... but I also felt guilty about leading you on. And then with Neil ... oh my god, did I feel guilt-ridden about that one. But then again, throughout uni, and more so afterwards, I also felt uncomfortable when James and I spent much time together. I kept questioning myself: was James the man I really wanted, or was I just settling for him?"

I take another sip of wine, then continue ... "Oh BJ, I honestly don't know how much mileage we might have together, but, for the first time in years, I actually feel free. I don't feel ashamed about being myself, or just letting go."

"Wow!!! That guilt-trip thing is a real bugger, isn't it?"

"It fucking is, babe." I giggle, realising I've let out another expletive. "Oh, sorry about my mouth ... you know how it is."

BJ puts down his knife and fork, and twists in his chair to look at me, while I continue to massage his neck and shoulders.

"Hmm-yes, your mouth ... do I know how it is? Perhaps I need some reminding?"

He pulls me in for another kiss.

I feel so relaxed tonight; the flickering candlelight and the choice of music has created the perfect ambience. The room has become significantly darker over the last thirty minutes, and the music is now Café Brazil's version of *The Girl from Ipanema*. The mood is seductive.

"C'mon babe, shall we move to the sofa?"

I tug his hand, before leading him over.

"Oh, now look who's the smooth operator? Miss Turner, are you trying to seduce me?"

"Who, me babe? What could possibly make you think that?"

I don't wait for BJ to reply or resist; instead, I shove him onto the sofa and straddle him. He's now exactly where I want him. A moment later, I force my lips back to his, and run my hands up his hairy chest.

"Hmm, Miss Turner," he gasps, "... you are really something."

"Uh-huh, I hope you mean something good." I can hardly get my words out, as I'm mid-flow, engaging tongue to tongue.

"Oh yeah ... really good," replies BJ, catching his breath, before re-joining our game of tonsil hockey. A few moments later, unexpectedly, BJ pulls back.

"Oh, just hang on a mo! Miss Turner, please may I ask you a question?"

Shit! BJ suddenly looks quite stern.

"What's up babe? Yeah ... sure, go ahead."

"Well Miss Turner, you told me earlier that I had to wait ... so ... well ... I have to ask ... is now an appropriate time to touch your bum?" BJ doesn't wait for my response.

"Oh babe, I thought you'd never ask."

As we wrestle on the sofa, BJ rolls me over, pinning me on my back. He kisses my neck, and my body tingles with every touch.

"Mmm-yes, now what was for dessert? You taste delicious."

Before I can even consider an answer, BJ's kisses migrate down my chest and nuzzle at my bra. At the same time, he's successfully unhooked it at the back, so he gently strips it away. His kisses return their attention to my boobs, and, a moment or two later, I close my eyes, after watching my left nipple disappear into his mouth.

Oh yessssss!!! ... Now things are getting steamy.

Chapter 34: Sweet!

Saturday 29 August 1992 - Baker Street, London

9:45pm, *or something like that ... fuck, who keeps track of time in this sort of state? I'm with BJ on the sofa, and we're just starting to get frisky.*

"Oh, fuck Megan, when you taste like this, who-the-hell needs chocolate-trifle?"

I open my eyes and instantly catch BJ's gaze. His eyes are just inches away from mine. In the last few moments, he's become even more mischievous, whereas me ... well, I'm fast heading to another planet. After BJ's slick move with my crop-top, and deft manoeuvre with my bra, a few moments ago I surrendered another piece of clothing ... my cut-off denim shorts now lie on the far side of the room. I've also just experienced heaven between my legs, and mind-blowing tremors right through my body. Sometime in his life, BJ has learnt some amazing tricks with his hands.

BJ suddenly pauses.

"Oh, I'm sorry ... I didn't mean to criticise your trifle; I'm sure it's yummy."

"Oh, shut up babe ... finger food's all I want right now. Please babe, just keep going."

I can hardly speak; I'm panting. My whole body's going numb as I'm approaching a climax. Well, numb might not be quite the correct description, as I'm quivering in places I never even knew existed ... but hell, I bet you'd also fail to get the right words in this situation?

As shuddering pulses race through my core, BJ cuts off my oxygen with further mouth-on-mouth action. All the while, his fingers remain playing sweet music down below. *Hmm-yes, I can tell he's studied anatomy ... he damned-well knows how to find my sweet spot.*

My body buckles, and I gasp for air. Momentarily, the intensity is overwhelming. BJ allows the pace of his fingers to slow, and seconds later, a flood of tension suddenly releases. BJ smiles with satisfaction; he knows he's just brought me to that place of dreams. I squeeze him tight, unable to speak for a few moments while my body relaxes and I regain a little composure.

"My god babe, where-the-hell did you learn that? And before you ask ... yes, I want a shed-load more of it."

BJ laughs.

"Well sweetie, the benefit of you abandoning me in Cairns was that I went on a cinema date in Brisbane."

"Oh yeah, what film was it? *Emmanuelle* or *Debbie Does Dallas?*"

"Well, *JFK* actually ... but there was this girl called Jeannie, and, well, she rather took advantage of me."

"Well, fuck me!!!"

"Uh-huh, well..."

Oh shit! I can see BJ's a little shocked by my choice of phrase.

"Oh no, sorry babe, forgive my mouth ... I meant to say please tell me more."

"Uh ..."

Oh shit! He now looks more surprised.

"Oh no babe, I'm sorry, I mean ... that wasn't to say that I don't want you to fuck me, because I do ... but ... oh, I'm sorry, I'm gibbering again, aren't I? Ok ... look babe, let me start again." I pause and take a deep breath. "Ok ... so ... please BJ, would you tell me all about Jeannie, and about how this goddess taught you such wicked ways with your fingers?"

My incoherent babbling has resulted in an interlude, and to the removal of BJ's hand from my knickers.

I hope it won't be for too long.

♦ ♦ ♦

During the intermission, BJ tells me about his date at the cinema in Brisbane. Interestingly, BJ had been with Neil ... yes, the very same Neil who gave me such guilty pleasure in Broome. Anyhow, unlike me, this Jeannie had turned down Neil's advances, in favour of asking out BJ instead. Anyway, to cut a long story short, Jeannie, the dirty cow, had enticed BJ into pleasuring her throughout the film. Maybe a dirty cow, but you've got to hand it to her ... nice going girl!

While BJ's been telling the tale, we've lost a little momentum ...

"So babe, d'you fancy a bit of Choco-Baileys trifle? Let me just clear the dishes."

Still enfolding me, and still holding my gaze, BJ smiles. I can't tell if he's disappointed about the break in action, but I get the sense he might actually be a little relieved.

He contemplates for a few moments, before suggesting ...

"OK, well, let's re-set. I'd love to try some of your dessert; a bit of extra fuel to keep me going. But first, excuse me, I must just go to the bathroom."

BJ breaks off, and takes the dirty plates into the kitchen, before making his way into the ensuite attached to my bedroom. At this point, I'm now standing beside the dining table, naked but for my knickers, and I'm hesitant about what to do next.

I notice that the Latin Jazz CD is on its penultimate track, so I decide to change it. It's from a double CD set and, as the first one worked wonders tonight, I swap in the second to stick with the same mood.

I'm starting to get goosebumps. I don't think it's the temperature, because it's a warm evening ... it's more probably because I'm now suddenly feeling exposed.

My lack of clothing reminds me that I haven't turned the washer-dryer on, so I step into the kitchen and set the machine to run. Next, I take the trifle from the fridge, grab a couple of bowls and spoons, and return to the table.

BJ's still in the bathroom, so I head back to the kitchen and survey the dirty dishes. If there's one thing I hate, it's seeing a pile of washing up that I know I'll need to do later. So, without thinking, I put on the white cooking apron, and begin to run hot water into the sink.

The next moment, without my hearing him, BJ re-emerges behind me. I suddenly feel him kissing my neck and, at the same time, he runs his hands over my butt cheeks. I still have my knickers on, but thongs leave rather little to the imagination.

I feel his warm breath on my ear, as he whispers ...

"Hey lady, I love your new dress ... oh yes, white apron, butt-naked; you're the stuff of boyhood fantasies."

"Mmm-hmm ... and I love your touch."

"Here sweetie, let me do the washing up ... you've done all the cooking."

Mmm-yes, I like this ... a modern man, very considerate. There are lots of good points to this guy, besides his exquisite fingers. But I already knew that, didn't I?

"Thanks babe. Look, there's not much to do; I'll wash and you dry, then we'll get through it quicker. Many a hand makes light work ... and I'm enjoying your hands precisely where they are." Indeed so ... soft caresses to the butt-cheeks are so underrated, don't you think?

I hadn't anticipated BJ and I doing the washing up this evening, but, actually, the experience is rather arousing.

♦ ♦ ♦

10:15pm? *Time flies when you're having fun. We're still in the kitchen, having just finished the washing up.*

"You know Megan, my view now really does surpass that one from the top of Ayers Rock."

I turn around from the sink, to see a wicked grin. BJ's totally checking out my butt. He steps forward, closing the gap between us, and again places his hands on my cheeks.

"Yep, it's hands-down a better view," he adds.

"Hmm ..." I reply, now turning to look at his chest, "... not such a bad view either."

"What, you mean the non-existent six-pack? Did you know that 'abs' actually stands for absent? There's not much here, is there? A four-pack at most ... or maybe a keg?"

I laugh.

"Well babe, I think you're just fine as you are. So, would you like some trifle now?"

"I'm not sure, how about you?"

I run my hands up his chest.

"Babe, d'you know what I would like?" I kiss him firmly on the lips again, almost losing my balance in the process ... it's hard on tip-toe, when the guy is over 6 foot tall.

"No, sweetie, what would that be?"

I'm sure he can guess.

"Let's leave the trifle for later. BJ, why don't you come to the bedroom and make love to me."

Was that last bit a question or a demand? I don't know, but, surprisingly, I didn't just use the F-word; maybe I'm transforming into 'refined Megan' now that I'm a Londoner. But my god, I'm horny as hell, and I'm getting impatient for him to enter my nether regions.

BJ doesn't reply, so I take him by the hand and guide him through to the bedroom. He's tentative, perhaps even nervous. I discard my apron and we stop beside the foot of the bed.

I pull him close, keeping my eyes fixed on his, and begin to unbutton his jeans. BJ's definitely hesitant ... far more so than earlier.

"Babe, are you OK?" I'm now kneeling, as I release his jeans to the floor, allowing him to discard them. "Tell me to stop if I'm going too fast; just talk to me."

"It's not that ... it's just ..."

Although I'm eager to get to his arousal, I stop at his jeans, leaving his boxers in place. I look into his eyes, inviting him to speak.

"It's just that I think the world of you Megan, and I don't want to disappoint you."

I stand up again, and place my finger against his lips.

"Shhh-babe, there's no rush, and there's certainly nothing to worry about."

I sit him down on the bed, and stand over him, caressing his head as he nuzzles into my tummy.

"No rush babe," I reassure him, "... we've got all the time in the world."

I can sense him relax as he moves his head up, nuzzling a bit higher, now with his face between my boobs. I've not remarked on them before, but I do have awesomely-comforting tits ... I just thought I'd mention it.

I can feel my nipples hardening again, as BJ surprises me by gently removing my knickers; I was expecting more of a warm-up, based on his recent hesitancy. BJ begins to kiss me, first on the breasts, and then slowly down my stomach. His kisses are soft, soothing, hypnotizing ... a sensual intoxication that forces my eyes to close. His fingers gently caress my butt, and stray up and down my inner thigh.

"Mmm, that feels good babe."

I still have my eyes shut, but I sense BJ easing himself down from the bed to sit on the floor.

Oh my ... I think he's going down there. Phew, I'm so glad I tidied up the garden earlier; I know it shouldn't matter, but 'make it neat before they eat'... isn't that what they say? Probably not, I just made it up. I'm not thinking clearly, but at least he won't get a mouthful of hair.

I'm soon proved correct when, suddenly, I feel a wave of hot breath warming my pussy. I now stand over him, with BJ's head between my thighs.

After a few moments savouring this heat, I then feel the delicate touch of his lips as BJ kisses me, taking his time, while seemingly circling his target. It's totally electric; my skin's prickling, and my whole body's now tingling with anticipation. BJ's arousing me in ways I never expected, and in ways that I never experienced with James, nor indeed with Neil. BJ's already given me one incredible climax with his fingers, but now I'm just fizzing at the prospect of discovering what his tongue can do.

And then I feel it ...

I clutch his head between both hands, feeling the need to steady myself. BJ's own hands are clasping my butt-cheeks, so I'm in no danger of falling ... only of falling apart beneath the tender strokes of his glorious tongue.

He licks my folds, and circles my clit ... and, oh my god, the feeling is unreal. I'm sorry girls, whatever you say about toys, I still don't believe there's anything better than a real tongue. Not that I'm an expert, quite the opposite actually, because nobody's ever given me such delicious treats before. James tried a bit in the early days, but this brings fine dining to another level.

After applying his tongue to amazing effect on the outside, BJ tries to push it in, but then immediately retreats. I briefly open my eyes, and lose my balance a little, as he lifts my left leg before resting it over his right shoulder. He looks up, catching my gaze, and licks his lips.

BJ says nothing, but returns his tongue to duty, this time pressing deep inside. My eyes close again as my body quivers; his tongue now circling, licking, teasing, pushing, flicking. He pauses again for a moment, allowing me to re-group. I open my eyes.

"Hey sweetie, am I hitting the right spot?"

"Oh babe, you're hitting spots I never even knew about."

"Just tell me what you like. You told me in Auckland that you like a good tongue ... and I aim to please."

"Wow, did I? Well, I don't have much experience ... but you're doing just fine."

BJ seems overly concerned about pleasing me. In a way, it demonstrates he cares, but it'd also be great if he was more self-assured. Having said that, James was extremely confident, but he was also lousy. Anyhow, BJ's confidence can build with more practice ... and, based on tonight, I'd happily be his guinea pig.

Following this brief interlude, BJ's tongue resumes action. After a few gentle, deliberate strokes, he raises the pace for a few moments before slowing again. Next, BJ tries different directional and pressure variations, and probing inside to different depths. Each time, I sense that he's carefully monitoring my body's reaction; it's like he's testing and responding to every signal I'm giving off. It does feel a little strange being part of an experiment, but BJ's so attentive ... and, I have to admit, it also feels bloody fantastic.

"Yes-babe, just like that ... mmm-yeah, that's so good." *I must keep encouraging him.*

BJ continues, learning as he goes, and he appears to be raising his game. My pulse increases further as his fingers return to the scene, and I'm soon teetering on the brink of another climax.

He pauses for a moment, and looks up. I open my eyes, curious about the interruption. His eyes have such a mischievous look.

"So madam, what else d'you desire from the taster menu?"

As he speaks, I feel another pulse shuddering through my core, courtesy of his perfectly placed fingers.

"Oh babe, d'you mean there's more?"

"Oh yes madam ..." BJ then explodes with laughter. "I'm sorry sweetie, I've just got the words 'finger-licking great' stuck in my head."

I snort with laughter.

"What??? Kenfucky-bloody-fried-chicken?"

He giggles at my response, and immediately I'm in stitches over this inane humour.

BJ goes down again and, a moment later, I feel his tongue repeatedly probing a place that no self-pleasuring can reach. My fingers grip his hair, not that he's got much, as I hold tight to the head between my thighs.

But I now can't stop giggling.

The giggles are making my upper half tremble while, in parallel, BJ's tongue induces shudders down below ...

"Oh-yes, yes-babe, oh-yes ..."

... My god, it's an overwhelming combination. I can't believe the incredible sensations; one moment he's got me whimpering, squeezing his head till it bursts ...

"Oh-yes babe, that's it, yes, keep going babe ..."

... Then the next, I'm floating away on marshmallow clouds.

"Oh-yes, yes, that's-it-babe, yes-babe, yes, yes-there-babe, yes, so-good-babe, yes, so-good, yes, yes-babe, yes, oh-yes, yes, mmm-so-good, yes, that's-it-babe, yes, keep-going-babe, keep-going, yes, yes, yes-babe, yes, yes, yes-babe, yes, yes, yes, fuck-yes, yes, yes-yes-yes-OH-FUCK-YES!!!!!"

That was me releasing again ... in case you couldn't guess.

♦ ♦ ♦

Wow!!! Unbelievable. That's two orgasms he's given me already, and I still haven't seen his cock.

Moments after this second climax, the music stops, and we look at each other.

"My god babe," I pant, "... where and when did you learn to do that?"

"Why, did you enjoy it?" BJ grins, before burying his head against my tummy.

"Could you not tell? And babe, don't tell me you learnt those tricks in a cinema."

"Well, I'm either a good student or a natural; I've not exactly been practicing."

BJ smirks; he's the cat that got the cream.

"Fuck BJ, your tongue is incredible. My god, if your cock matches that ... well, bloody-hell babe, don't keep me waiting."

"Hey ... slowly girl, there's plenty of time."

How can BJ remain so calm and measured? I'm the exact opposite; I'm buzzing, I'm now all flustered, and I'm itching like crazy to feel him inside me.

BJ gets to his feet, still clutching my hand.

We lock eyes and smile.

He caresses my cheek, and places some wayward strands of hair back behind my ear.

Suddenly, he looks a little hesitant again.

"Hey babe, are you OK? We don't have to go any further; was I misreading things? ... It wouldn't be the first time ... but ..."

"Well ..."

"Well, what babe? ... Is something wrong?"

"No Megan, nothing's wrong at all ... in fact everything is perfect. It's so perfect, I simply want to savour every moment."

"Oh babe, that's so sweet."

I plant a long sensual kiss on his lips.

As I release him to breathe, he breaks off.

"Wait a minute Megan ... that's not all. I'm sorry, but I must confess I'm nervous about the next bit. I've had so little practice. My fingers and tongue ... well, that's one thing, as my brain can control them. But when it comes to the little soldier, it does rather have a will of its own ... well, you already know that."

I seize both his hands, and bring them to my lips to capture his gaze.

"Hey babe, just try to relax ... and yeah, of course we can take a break, if you'd rather we slow things down. Y'know, to be honest,

I'm a bit nervous too. Although you might think otherwise, I'm hardly well practised in sex either. Sure, I was with James for several years but, when we did sleep together, it was like 'wham-bam-thank-you-mam' ... it wasn't so great."

BJ smiles as I continue.

"And babe, don't feel anxious about pleasing me, or about how you measure up. I'm not thinking of James when I'm with you, and anyway, he rarely brought me much satisfaction, let alone a climax. But you ... well, you've already shaken my world ... twice actually, and ... well, that's without your soldier even leaving the barracks."

BJ smiles. He stands in front of me, gently holding one hand while stroking my cheek with the other; our eyes fixed together as he listens to my reassurance.

"And babe, the only other time, with Neil ... I admit it was really hot, but I was too drunk to know what I was doing. It was also bloody funny ... he kept smashing his head on the top bunk."

BJ chuckles.

We're now standing eye-to-eye, skin-to-skin, holding each other close.

"Well sweetie, at least you've had a few workouts ... whereas I've had next to nothing. Maybe I already told you, I can't remember, but for me it was only the odd fumble back at uni ... and, well, that now seems longer ago than the Cretaceous Period."

"Well babe," I giggle, "I bet you're a Triceratops. He was the big horny one, wasn't he?"

BJ smiles.

"Yeah, he had three of them ... but I'm not quite that well-endowed."

"Oh really? Well babe, I believe your boxers tell me a different story." As I speak, I gently squeeze his erection through the cotton material. "And remember babe, this isn't the first time we've met."

BJ pulls me close, and kisses me on the lips.

Next, he breaks away, retrieves his jeans from the floor, and then fishes around in his wallet. He retrieves a condom, and then returns to face me, his right hand held to his forehead in salute.

"Here Sir! Soldier reporting for duty!"

I tell you ... this guy is nuts.

♦ ♦ ♦

As BJ holds the condom packet, it looks strangely familiar.

"Hey babe, is that one from the pub in Melbourne?"

"Uh-huh."

"Oh, that was so funny; I remember your face when the machine broke and the packets flew everywhere."

"Megan ... you really take pleasure from my embarrassment, don't you? Well, that's a blessing, considering the performance you're about to receive."

"Oh babe, why are you so hard on yourself?"

As I spoke, I hadn't realised my double-entendre ... but BJ noticed, and set us both giggling.

"OK my dear," he says, as he throws the wrapped condom towards the pillow for later. "You may not witness a great performance, but at least the date stamp hasn't expired."

"Oh, come here," I say, pulling us both onto the bed. I begin to caress his face, as I look into his eyes. "Look babe, don't worry about your performance; opening night nerves are common in so many things ... but at least we don't have an audience."

"We could open the blinds," he suggests, jumping up and walking over to the window. He takes a quick peek. There are flats opposite, and several windows overlooking us ... perfect if you're an exhibitionist.

I'm uncertain about his delaying tactics, but BJ still seems anxious. He returns to the bed and, this time, he grabs one of my feet, my left one ... and he begins to give it a massage.

"This reminds me," he says, "d'you think there's anything to this toe-sucking business?"

At this point, he raises my foot to his lips ... I can't believe it. Next thing I know, BJ begins to suck my toes, starting with the pinky-toe, and working his way along to the big one.

"My god babe, will you cut it out?! I want your cock inside me, not a fucking pedicure." *OK, so, was that a bit harsh?*

BJ, slightly shocked by my reaction, releases my foot and resumes his place next to me on the bed.

I'm getting impatient, so I decide to take things into my own hands, so-to-speak. I reach across and put my right hand into his boxers, and begin to stroke his cock.

"There now, I think he's pleased to see me again," I say, as I move my hand gently from tip to root, and back again, before setting the motion to 'repeat cycle'.

As my rubbing progresses, BJ appears to be relaxing again, and his eyes tell me he's enjoying it. He caresses my thighs and butt, as I continue to work my magic. Once he seems sustainably hard, I then decide to remove his boxers ... it feels like the right time. Thankfully he doesn't bolt for the door, but he still seems a little on edge.

Sensing his lingering hesitancy, I quickly contemplate two possible courses of action. Option one, we slow down, maybe we even call it a night. The other option is that I step in and take the plunge; just dive straight in and see what happens. Reading the situation as anxiety as opposed to reluctance, I consider option two as the preferred choice ... *yeah, you know I'm right.*

So, I continue rubbing the shaft and teasing the tip; I also throw a pinch of ball-squeezing into the mix for a little added flavour. Before long, I've brought him to what I gauge as full-hardness. I think he's relaxing more now that I've seized the initiative, and his dreamy expression tells me he's relishing it.

I grab the condom from the pillow and break open the wrapper, before bringing it to the tip of BJ's helmet.

"Oh yum, ribbed for my pleasure," I notice, as I squeeze the bulb to free the air, then roll it over the end and down the shaft. At least I've had a little practice at this, but I also remember this stuff from biology classes at school ... it was with bananas in those days. It wasn't proper sex-ed back then; it was more about how to avoid pregnancy and STDs.

Anyway, now that I've thought about it, I know BJ's clean, so maybe we could actually ditch the condom? No, now that I've started, the ritual is actually quite arousing; BJ's eyes were glued to mine as I rolled on the latex and, moment by moment, I could sense his excitement building.

"OK babe, soldier in uniform, ready for action." I try to mimic his voice as much as I can.

"At your service captain," BJ salutes.

As I'm taking the lead, I push BJ onto his back and straddle him; clearly, me on top is the easiest opening gambit. With my left hand on BJ's shoulder to steady me, my right hand holds his shaft, and rubs it against my entrance.

"Soldier, are you ready for your first mission?" I'm desperate to feel him inside.

BJ licks his lips, his eyes full of lust ...

"All ready to go in, captain."

I know it's a bit silly, all of this military play. Perhaps it's a bit like trying to spoon-feed a baby, when you pretend the spoon is a steam train. But hey, it seems to be working.

I ease myself down, and feel his length press deep inside ... and yeah, it's pretty deep; he's certainly no chipolata. I carefully begin to glide up and down, as BJ's eyes lock on to mine. This is predator-prey stuff, like a leopard meeting the eyes of a gazelle just before the kill. I'm not sure which one of us is the gazelle ... *oh, OK yeah, so, quite obviously I'm the leopard.*

The intensity is irresistible, and there's a type of connection that I've not experienced before. With Neil there was passion, but you can't maintain focus with twenty-times the driving limit of alcohol in your veins. And with James, well, in later years, there was all the intensity of a wet lettuce.

"You OK babe?"

"More than OK," BJ responds, now beginning to meet me thrust for thrust, as I continue to glide up and down. *Oh yes, soft and slow ... it's really good.*

We continue at a modest pace for what must be several minutes, while we savour the lust in each other's eyes. I then suddenly sense that I might be losing him ... his erection is beginning to soften.

I increase the pace, and his rod stiffens sufficiently that, after a couple of minutes riding like a cowgirl on a mission, I'm lost in my third 'big O' of the night ... an almighty quiver and shattering release, before I collapse exhausted to BJ's chest.

A few moments of silence follow as he holds me tight, gently caressing my hair. BJ breaks the silence first.

"So, how was it?"

"Mmm-babe, that was amazing ..."

I sense that it wasn't quite so wonderful for him; and I hadn't felt him release. "So, how about you?"

"Uh-huh, yes, it's wonderful to feel you so close. But I think the soldier needs better training; he wasn't up to finishing the job ... I think it's the uniform, it dumbs down the sensation."

"Oh babe, I'm sorry. I think we'll need to change that, won't we?"

♦ ♦ ♦

After a short period of holding, caressing, and recuperating from my last high, I move my hand to remove his condom, discarding it to the floor. Apart from the external lubrication, it's dry, and it's clear that BJ didn't climax. He's given me so much tonight, it's now my turn to feel that I've let him down, that I've not given my all. Guilt has just turned up, and it's trying to ruin the party. Somehow, I knew it would; it always does ... only, at least this time, I can think of an immediate remedy.

So, the next bit, I decide to do purely for his pleasure; BJ also needs a release ... and he deserves it. Well, OK, who am I trying to kid? Of course, it's not just for him ... I mean, why stop with three 'big O's when there's still a chance of four? Should I just stop now and call it a night? Hell no!

"Babe, d'you remember the bus from Tennant Creek?"

"Uh-huh ... why?"

"Well, we still had some unfinished business, didn't we?"

"Did we?"

"Yes, I believe we did."

OK, so you may not believe me, but I've never performed fully-blown oral before ... and please excuse the pun. Years ago, I did have a quick try with James, but we were interrupted and, after that, he never seemed interested in trying again. I was also interrupted before getting there with Neil. It's entirely possible that I'm rubbish at it, but now seems like the perfect time for another try.

I move up from BJ's chest to be eye-to-eye again, and, at the same time, reach with my left hand to grab his manhood. I run my tongue across my top lip, and smile.

"How about a little BJ ... for my little BJ?"

He laughs.

"Oh Megan, you really know how to say the right things. I'm sure-as-hell not gonna stop you this time."

Chapter 35: Unfinished business

Saturday 29 August 1992 - Baker Street, London

11:30pm? ... Lost all sense of time now. We're in bed, and I've just rudely interrupted your sex scene.

OK, well, I'm sure that you didn't want me to continue in such a graphic manner.

Oh, so I was wrong, was I? Really? So, d'you enjoy this kind of stuff then? But, isn't it becoming just a tad gratuitous? Well, OK then, if you're quite sure ... I suppose that you know best. Anyway, you can always skip this chapter if you've had enough.

So, where did we get to?

Oh yes ... the unfinished business from that bus ride. So, do I think I'd have actually followed through with my sordid proposition, had BJ not stopped me? I honestly don't know. I felt so bloody horny then, but maybe I'd have found some self-restraint from somewhere, who knows?

OK, sorry, I know that you've heard this bus journey bit before. I also know that if you're still reading this part, it's perhaps only because you want more of the sex, am I right? Well, OK ... and, to be fair, as we left the last chapter, I wanted more too.

So, anyhow, as we left off ... I was just about to try a new taste of Down Under. Well, after removing BJ's condom, I'd begun to work with my hands, bringing the limping soldier back to life. It doesn't take too long before I sense a renewed spring in its step. Yeah, I know cocks don't have legs, but you know what I mean.

♦ ♦ ♦

Continuing on ...

While I'm doing my handiwork, BJ's left hand is tenderly stroking my hair. His caresses then continue their way down my back; his touch is so delicate, and yet still quite firm.

His soldier is also pretty firm again now. I give BJ a cheeky grin, teasing him once more with my eyes, while still maintaining my left-hand grip around his cock. I lick my lips, and I can feel him flinch in anticipation. I then break eye contact, and lower my head to take my first lick of the tip.

Hang on, this position won't do ... we need the full effect, including eye contact. I move around to reposition myself between his legs.

I begin again, and once more lick the tip of his cock. It still has a residue from the condom lubricant, a metallic-sort of taste, and not terribly pleasant. Why don't they make lubricants with fruity flavours, or even chocolate? Oh yeah, you're right, they do ... congratulations, you certainly know your stuff.

It's so funny, I remember BJ breaking that vending machine in Melbourne, and the packets flying everywhere. I suggested he got a pack of the ribbed ones; oh-yes, ribbed for my pleasure, a great choice me-thinks ... although back then, they had been intended for Suzi. Oh boy, how she missed out. Anyhow, ribbed for a girl's pleasure, but not so much for BJ's, if it prevented him from feeling anything.

I continue to move my tongue around the head, and then work my way down the shaft, and even lick his balls. Now that's something I never thought I'd hear myself say ... but there, I did it.

I trace my tongue up-and-down a few more times, before engulfing the head in my mouth, and starting the 'shake-n-vac-slide-n-suck' combination. Hey, maybe I'm not too bad at this after all. I look up at BJ, who now has his eyes shut; a look of relaxed enjoyment across his face. Actually, I might be quite proficient ... perhaps I'll give myself a B-plus.

I continue my pursuit of an elusive A-grade, by taking him further into my mouth, until it's so deep I'm almost gagging. As I continue to suck, I glide up-and-down along the length, all the time watching for his reactions. Intermittently I break off, giving my mouth a time-out, and substituting my hands while I continue to monitor his facial expressions.

"I think you're enjoying this," I say, watching his eyes open.

"What makes you think that?" he smiles.

I return to action with my mouth. Despite the initial taste of lubricant chemicals that have long since dissipated, I'm surprised how much I'm enjoying it. Seeing such ecstasy in BJ's eyes is giving me goosebumps ... but besides, giving him head just feels so empowering. I thought that I might find it degrading, but simply knowing he's completely at my mercy ... my god, it's such a buzz. *With just one bite* ... but no, I'm completely into him right now, after all, why would I ruin the night for someone who's just given me three climaxes?

And, perhaps a fourth one is still on the cards. I sense his excitement rise. Keeping my hands working, I come up for air.

"Babe, perhaps I should've told you before ... I'm on the pill, so we should be safe. Shall we try you back inside?"

"Oh, fuck yes!" replies BJ.

I think that was endorsing my suggestion, don't you? It's certainly the right side of consent.

I crawl up his body again, straddling him, before repositioning his erection ready for entry. As I take him inside, this time I can sense that he feels more relaxed.

I start riding him and, as my own pleasure begins to build, I can tell that BJ's enjoying it more. He's really getting my juices flowing, and I can hardly believe that he's soon hitting the spot once again ... Blimey!!! We're nearly at number four.

BJ matches my motion, first slowly and steadily, but soon his thrusts become stronger ... and then, suddenly but deftly, and without dis-engaging, he flips me over into missionary.

Clever boy!

He resumes his thrusting, but this time it's stronger and deeper. *Mmm-yes, wowza!* This is the first time that his real beast has come out to play.

BJ clasps my butt-cheeks as he penetrates, thrusting harder, deeper, faster ... ever building his momentum. I'm fizzing up, like he's shaking a coke bottle, the pressure rising steeply with every thrust.

"Oh-my-god-babe ..."

Deeper, faster, harder, he continues ...

"Oh-my-god, harder-babe-harder ..."

Fizzing, bubbling, hissing, until ...

"Oh-my-god-babe, oh-my, oh-my, oh-yes, oh-yes-babe, OH-YES-OH-MY-GOD!!! ..."

I let go.

And when I say let go, this was like a bullseye, a jackpot, a three-for-one-special-offer orgasm ... a totally mind-fucking release.

My limbs are shaking, and I've lost all control, as I feel BJ shoot inside me with the biggest thrust since the Apollo launch. OK, so that was a bit of an exaggeration, but just in the last few minutes, I've been coming (excuse the pun) to realise what I've been missing these last 22 years. Well, OK, maybe just the last five years or so, as I know that underage sex is wrong ... but, why-oh-why did I have to wait so long for a fuck like this?

After finally releasing, BJ collapses on top of me and rests for a while. We are both totally spent.

After a few minutes, we reposition so we're side-by-side, just holding each other. No words, just a few soft, exhausted caresses ... before we fall asleep.

Chapter 36: A new morning

Sunday 30 August 1992 - Baker Street, London

02:27am *(I checked the alarm clock) ... In bed.*

I fidget, and open my eyes. I'm lying on my side, and I can feel a lovely warm body pressing against me, all the way from my shoulders down to my bottom. I'm lying on a wet patch, but it's warm, and I don't care.

We can't have been asleep for long.

I lie motionless for a few moments, gaining consciousness and savouring the realisation that last night wasn't a dream ... yes, there really is a naked man in my bed. Well, not just any naked man; it's somebody that I've become fond of, a guy who really connects with me and cares about how I feel.

So, this naked man ... am I in love with him?

I don't know ... perhaps.

Maybe I am in love with BJ, whatever 'in love' actually means ... oh, hang-on, didn't Prince Charles say that about Diana? Well, Charlie's probably right ... love is such a big word. I thought that I loved James ... well, I know I did, but now I know he wasn't my ONE AND ONLY. So, what about BJ? Well, it wasn't exactly love at first sight ... but, right now, I wouldn't kick him out of bed for anything in the world. Except toast ... I could really murder a slice of buttered toast.

After a few minutes pass, and my toast craving dissipates, I realise that I'm bursting for a pee. While BJ had sensibly taken a bathroom break before our romp last night, I hadn't done so. A few hours later, and I could now feel the effects of several glasses of Sauvignon Blanc, not to mention the bladder-stress associated with high-octane humping.

Leaving BJ's body warmth, I carefully slip out of bed and walk into the ensuite. After shutting the door, I flick the light switch, and adjust my eyes to the brightness. After relieving my bladder, I look into the mirror and smile at the dirty, bedraggled, slutty image smiling back.

"You little minx," I whisper, with immense satisfaction.

I wash my face and give my genitals a quick wipe. I brush my teeth and return to bed, gradually sliding in again beside BJ, and gently pulling up the duvet which had all but fallen to the floor.

"Hey sweetie," says BJ, without opening his eyes.

"Hey babe," I respond, kissing him on the forehead.

He pulls me close, and opens one eye.

I smile.

"Did you get some sleep?"

"A little," he responds.

I lean in, and place a soft kiss on his lips.

Moments later the kiss is full on, but of low intensity, and delicate. The urgency we felt last night has disappeared, leaving us now with all the time in the world.

Over the next few minutes, or maybe even an hour, we are locked in an affectionate embrace, and we make love again, slowly and tenderly. We remain mostly in the 'side-by-side clasping position' or similar ... yeah, why don't you look it up in the Kama Sutra? I feel a soothing sense of peace as I'm intertwined with BJ's body. We don't climax again, but it's so deeply connecting, and we both fall into a doze, with him still inside me.

♦ ♦ ♦

I wake up properly again around 7:00am, and, leaving BJ sleeping, I take a shower. I know that 7 o'clock is a tad early for a Sunday morning, but I feel the need to freshen up. I'm also feeling a little achy, and have considerable soreness in my nether regions ... I think certain parts of me overindulged last night. Well, no gain without pain, I suppose ... but, oh my god, those gains were so worth it.

After a few minutes under the warm spray, I step out, dry myself off, and put on my white towelling bathrobe.

I emerge from the bathroom, and look towards BJ. He's still sleeping and mostly submerged under the duvet. There's a beam of sunlight streaming through the blinds, striking the pillow and just starting to catch his face. I watch him for a few minutes, and soon his eyes begin to twitch with the light. BJ looks so cute as he begins to wake, gradually emerging from his dreamworld. I wonder what fantasies he had last night.

I suddenly remember that BJ's shirt is in the washer-dryer, so I amble through to the kitchen and check. Both his shirt and my top are suitably clean and dry ... a tad creased, but OK to wear.

I take the laundry back to the bedroom, and place it at the end of the bed. BJ still hasn't woken up, although he's now fidgeting rather more. I contemplate what to do. I'm now wide awake, but it's still early ... and way too early to be active on a Sunday morning.

I then remember the chocolate trifle. I walk through to the dining table and check on the dessert we failed to eat last night. It's a shame that we didn't try it, but I've no complaints about the dessert I was treated to instead. The trifle still appears in reasonable shape, and the crème fraiche on the top looks OK, so I place it back in the fridge to chill.

I return to the bedroom, and BJ still has his eyes shut. He looks so peaceful, so adorable; I just want to cuddle him.

Hell, why not?

I remove my bathrobe and climb back into bed. BJ stirs a bit as I begin to snuggle up to him, spooning him from behind, and feeling his warm back and buttocks against my front.

He suddenly jumps.

"Fuck Megan, your feet are bloody freezing." He laughs, as he turns over, and pulls me into a cuddle.

"Good morning beautiful," I reply.

"Hey sweetie," he says, stroking my cheek. "What time is it?"

"Half-seven-or-so."

"Uh-huh ... so still some time to sleep."

"Sure babe, if there's nothing you need to do today."

"Not that I can think of ... except perhaps a few more kisses."

His eyes are closed, but he puckers his lips, inviting me to kiss him.

I respond with a gentle kiss on the lips, and a smile immediately appears. He pulls me tight, and we cuddle.

"How-you feeling?" he asks.

"I'm good," I respond. "Well, I'm a bit sore this morning ... some night huh?"

"Oh-yes, it was some night."

We cuddle a bit more, and BJ re-engages his lips with mine, softly and delicately.

"Is there anything you need to do today?" he asks.

"A little bit," I reply. "I've got some studying to do before work tomorrow ... an hour tops, but I can do that tonight."

"So, can we spend the day together?"

"Sure babe, if you haven't had enough of me."

"Are you kidding? I've got a new craving, an insatiable appetite."

He pulls me closer, and his soft kisses now deepen in intensity. I can also feel his arousal pressing into my thigh.

"Hey babe, I'd like to ... but I'm too sore this morning. Last night was intense."

BJ looks at me, and I can see the disappointment written on his face ... but maybe that's a good thing ... at least he's itching for more.

"No worries sweetie." He cuddles me again, this time with my head against his chest. "But just so you know, I thought last night was awesome, and if making love is on the menu again ... well, just let me know."

"Babe, it was awesome for me too ... and I really want to do it again right now, but I'd probably split."

♦ ♦ ♦

We spend another hour or so, snuggled up together in a state of semi-consciousness, with Capital FM playing quietly on the radio alarm clock.

At around 10:00am, BJ's bursting for a pee, so he gets up to use the bathroom and take a shower. I get dressed, and head to the kitchen to make some coffee and toast.

I walk around the flat, drawing back the blinds. The weather outside looks fine; it's a beautiful bank holiday weekend.

Hey, it's a bank holiday, so no work tomorrow ... which also means no study today ... woohoo!

I know that I should've realised this before, but a few details disappeared from my mind with the intensity of the last 24 hours. So, perhaps today we could go for a long walk in Regent's Park, or venture up to Camden Market, or Primrose Hill?

BJ finishes in the bathroom, and joins me in the kitchen. He sniffs the air.

"Mmm-yes, expensive coffee. And last night, the wine and scallops ... Girl, you're really moving up in the world."

BJ picks up the cafetiere, and fills two mugs with coffee.

"Well babe, I don't know about moving up, but maybe I've started refining my dining."

BJ takes a sip.

"Colombian?"

"No, Costa Rican. Oh, and BJ ... congratulations, you never spilled a drop this time."

"Well, perhaps I'm becoming more proficient with my hands."

"Not half," I snigger, and close the distance between us to put my arm around his waist. "Oh, and by the way, I just realised it's a bank holiday, so you could stay over again tonight if you like. No pressure ... but if you want to?"

BJ kisses me.

"Well sweetie, I suppose we do still have that trifle to eat."

I'll take that as a yes.

THE END

Epilogue: A new Megan

Saturday 5 September 1992 - Baker Street, London

10:00am. I'm alone in the flat, preparing my breakfast.

So, last weekend went well, didn't it?

In fact, I think much of the last week went swimmingly. The job has begun well, the people on the course seem nice enough, and so far it's been quite interesting ... although I can see it's going to be hard work. I've just about kept up with the homework in the evenings, but I can see it becoming more difficult, depending on how things go with BJ. Don't get me wrong, I'm not getting cold feet at all, but I think that juggling the evening study around our 'extra-curricular activities' might prove quite challenging for both of us.

Well, who knows what the future holds, or whether BJ and I will last the course? I guess, at the beginning of any journey, you never know exactly when and where you'll end up. And BJ and I are both only at the start ... adapting to life in a new city, with new jobs and a new relationship. We've both agreed not to talk about the future right now, and to take days as they come, and try to live in the moment. We know that we'll soon start thinking about the weeks and months ahead ... but there's no rush.

Anyway, getting back to last weekend, BJ and I spent a wonderful Sunday, and also part of Monday together ... and yes, before you ask, we did sleep together again on Sunday night ... and yes, before you ask, it was also deliciously X-rated.

But BJ also came over on Wednesday night, and that was ... hmm-yes, really exhausting. I'd already had quite a long day of study beforehand, so, by 8:30pm, I was already quite tired by the time he arrived. We got a *Domino's* pizza delivery to pep up our energy levels, but, oh my god, we needed them. I felt shattered in the morning ... so much so that my energy's only just returning.

Yeah, Wednesday night was truly amazing. After having spent Monday and Tuesday apart, by Wednesday our hormones must've gone crazy ... we just couldn't get enough of each other. Oh boy, I'm so glad I'm not sharing this flat because, apart from respecting Peter and Gills out-of-bounds bedroom, BJ and I must've had sex in every room in the flat. My god, I could never have done that in Newcastle! For us to have a free run of the lounge, two bedrooms, the kitchen and a shower, all without worrying about other people bursting in or eavesdropping ... wow, it's really liberating.

I remember thinking before moving here, that I might get a bit lonely living by myself, but it really has some advantages. I'm sure you recall me telling you about how quiet I was in bed with James, for fear of Mammy or Beth hearing us. Well, maybe I shouldn't tell you this, but I was hardly very quiet on Wednesday night ... no sirrie, and the neighbours must've heard us. In particular, early on, when we'd got about half way through our pizza ... we were just talking about how we'd enjoyed the weekend, when we discovered that neither of us had ever tried doggystyle. So, that was it ... moments later, we were both half naked, and BJ was taking me over the dining table. Oh my god, the screams I let out with that orgasm ... they'd have shaken the roof off Madame Tussauds.

Anyhow, I've not seen BJ since leaving for work on Thursday, but I can't wait for tonight, although I suspect we might need to be a bit more reserved. I'm going over to his place in Maida Vale ... and he shares the flat with a couple of other blokes. I bet it's a typical bachelor pad, but it'll be interesting to see. BJ says it's rather downmarket compared to this place, and I don't doubt it; I've been so lucky with this one.

You know, when I moved down here from Newcastle, I felt some apprehension about living on my own with no family around, and without Suzi or any other friends close by. And, to be honest, during the first few days, I did feel a bit lost. However, my experiences over the last year have left me more secure about myself, and more confident I can adapt to whatever life throws my way. And life does seem to have a way of surprising you, doesn't it? After all, I hadn't anticipated meeting up with BJ again. When Suzi dumped him back in May, I didn't think he'd want to stay in touch, and indeed he never phoned me for a chat. But then, in July, we had that chance meeting at Kings Cross ... and I'm so glad that we did.

If there's one thing I've learnt over the last year, it's just how much of a role luck plays in our lives. You can never tell what awaits you around the next corner ... but you'll also never find out, unless you go and take a look.

I realise that I need to keep trying new things to get the most out of life; in corporate-speak, they call it 'growth'. I mean, I'd hardly tasted seafood before going to Australia, and now I'm so addicted, I even bought crayfish-tail salad all last week for my lunch. I hadn't really thought about it before, but I think it's the delicate, almost hidden flavours, which give me such pleasure.

And, it's not only the food, but my taste in men is also changing. With James and then Neil, I was attracted to their good looks and bullish confidence; I seemed to have that sort of search image in my head. When I first met BJ in Darwin, I didn't even notice him, but now I'm discovering it's the quieter types that you need to watch.

And naturally, my thoughts dwell rather a lot on sex at the moment, and why wouldn't they, given what I'm discovering with BJ. It's not that we've done anything too kinky, at least not yet ... but who knows? I actually quite like the idea of a bit of roleplay, or some handcuffs, or ... no, my mind's now wandering again to visions of that basement BJ told me about. That might be pushing things rather too far ... but BJ did offer to wear a Manchester United shirt, in case I missed my fantasy dose of Ryan Giggs.

The last few months have also given me a fresh perspective about guilt and shame. Perhaps the most embarrassing thing I've ever done was on that bus across the outback, when I offered to give BJ a blowjob. We might've been locked up, and I felt so ashamed about it for weeks ... but, if things had been different, perhaps BJ wouldn't be in my life today. And also, if I hadn't cheated on James, maybe we'd still be stuck in a relationship that had lost its way, rather than both of us embarking on exciting new adventures.

I spoke to Mammy and Beth last night, and told them how the job was going, and I also phoned Suzi on Thursday. I haven't told any of them yet about BJ. I will do soon, but BJ and I have only been dating each other for a few days, and, anyway, they can all wait. I'm sure that Mammy and Beth will be happy for me, and I think they'll both take to BJ; Beth especially, as she'll love his dirty mind. No doubt Beth will still tell me to hold out for a stockbroker with a penthouse in Chelsea ... although she might take a different view, if I ever reveal BJ's talent with his tongue and fingers.

However, I'm not so sure about how Suzi will take the news. I know things are still tough for her, with her dad's health still being a problem; but she does seem pretty upbeat about how things are going with Matt. Anyhow, dumping BJ was Suzi's choice, and in any case, I can claim to have kissed him first. I actually think Suzi will be happy for me, but if not, well, it's really none of her business.

Anyway, later today, I'm off to Maida Vale, and there's a spring in my step. I'm looking forward to the days and months ahead with genuine optimism ... and, at this moment in time, that's a pretty wonderful place to begin the next chapter of my life.

With thanks

I wish to thank all the people who provided the inspiration for writing this book. Firstly, to the two girls I met long ago who, without knowing it, provided the ideas for the characters of Megan and Suzi. To all those who read and enjoyed the *Shy Backpacker* series, and particularly some of my author friends on Instagram who encourage me to keep going. A special thanks to Sheila for your continued encouragement and support with editing and proofing ... and lastly, of course, to my wife and daughter who help me to keep focussed on the things in life that really matter.

Final note from the author

Thank you so much for choosing to read this book ... I really hope you enjoyed it. And, if you did, please would you consider leaving a positive review on Amazon. As an independent author, it's a challenge to become noticed and to build readership, and every single review, however brief, can really help.

As an author, it's also wonderful to receive positive feedback, as it is our reader's enjoyment that provides the fuel which helps to keep us going.

Lastly, if you did enjoy *Refining My Dining*, then you might also enjoy reading about BJ's own journey in the *Diary of a Shy Backpacker* series. Why not give it a try, and also come and find me (@brucespydar) on Instagram?

Diary of a Shy Backpacker

What people have said ...

i. Awakening Down Under
"A saucy, fun, entertaining read which perfectly captures the backpacking experience."
"Break out the beers and barbies because this Down Under adventure is hilarious."
"I felt like I was there ..."
"Hit right in the feels."
"No worries, this one is a winner!"

ii. Eye on the Prize
"It just keeps getting better."
"Oh BJ! I think I'm a little in love with you..."
"Colourful characters, beautiful landscapes and of course ... throbbing loins."
"BJ is back and wittier than ever!"
"What have you done, Bruce?"

iii. No Looking Back
"I absolutely loved the third part of this trilogy."
"Seriously BJ, not once did you sniff those panties! WHAT is that all about?"
"Great job author Spydar for providing us with another laugh inducing adventure."
"Muffins, cougars and dirty thoughts, oh my!"
"Best one yet."

Thank you to all my readers, and a special thanks to all those who help by providing reviews on Amazon and Goodreads.

Printed in Great Britain
by Amazon